MONKEY GOES TO MOUNTAIN

A P JOSHIPURA

Copy right @ AKHILESH JOSHIPURA 2007

**Abner Haugen Library
Zumbro Lutheran Church
624 Third Ave SW
Rochester, MN 55902**

CONTENTS

Chapter 1 : This is Zanzibar

Chapter 2 : Time for Change

Chapter 3 : Work Begins

Chapter 4 : Tancell Oye

Chapter 5 : Success at last

Chapter 6 : First attempt

Chapter 7 : When it rains.....

Chapter 8 : Technical man

Chapter 9 : First Love

Chapter 10 : The Lion sleeps tonight

Chapter 11 : Missing you

Chapter 12 : Serengeti Adventure

Chapter 13: Second Attempt

Chapter 14: Lead, kindly light...the night is dark

Chapter 15: Swinging in concrete jungle

Chapter 16: Africa calling

Chapter 17: Rolling stones

Chapter 18: Monkey runs away to Jungle

Chapter 19: Jaambazi!

Chapter 20: Voodoo thunder

Chapter 21: Passion Flowers Bloom

Chapter 22: Up above the world so high.......

Mungu ibariki Afrika na watu wake, watoto wake.

Chapter 1: This is Zanzibar

Zanzibar. The Persians called it the Coast of the Blacks. The Arabs called it FairLand. Some call it SpiceIsland, some StoneTown. About four thousand years ago, Africans arrived on the island. During the seventh century, Arabs and Persians arrived here. Then came the Portuguese, the British, the Indians and many others. It was a place notorious for the slave trade. The island also boasts of slave traders like Tipu Tip who had one official wife and two children and over thirty mistresses and their children.

The Omanese ruled it for a century and left their legacy behind. About 97% of Zanzibar's population follows Islam. Like Ireland in Britain, the Kurds in Iraq, the Chechens in Russia, the Pakhtoons in Pakistan, and Kashmir in India, Zanzibar is a boil on the forehead. The local Arabs want independence or the Omanese rule the way it was before the British took over. As a result, the mainland pampers Zanzibar a lot, granting subsidized power, a loose localised legal framework and poor customs controls and so on.

It was 6.30 in the morning. Zuly had boarded a boat to Zanzibar. He had many missions there. One was that his UK client had arranged for a payment of $100,000 for buying beetle nuts and seashells from him. This would have to be collected from a local Zanzibari Arab trader. The Arab used to import bathroom tiles and other hardware from Zuly's client and had not paid for a long time. So this exchange was most convenient for the UK company. The Arab trader had an account in a local bank in which money transfers were risky and as slow as getting it in a dhow.

Zuly had to withdraw 110 million local shillings with the maximum denomination of 10,000 and deposit it into his bank account. The Arab needed Zuly's contacts to increase his imports, and Zuly had just got a contract to build a new parliament building for the legislative assembly of Zanzibar through the Arab.

So he had to make an investment before being paid from the treasury. This was how all three businessmen had each other's tails in their hands.

Zuly's other mission was to meet a minister and buy old buildings made by the British. Zuly would offer the minister a stake in converting the buildings, the lush green campus, and internal roads into a five-star hotel. He also wanted to erect the cellular towers at two prime high elevation locations.

Zuly was excited. For the first time, he was embarking on ventures that were his own creation and not inherited from his ancestors. It would boost his image in his Jamaat (community) as an achiever.

It would take about an hour and a half to reach the island. The boat was comfortable and could accommodate about 250 people and their luggage. People would carry unfinished meat from their hoot or a bucket of fish, if given as a gift. The only problem with travelling by boat was that many people would feel nauseated. So the travellers would be served with black tea, soft drinks and light snacks and after 45 minutes, they would be given thin, black plastic sick bags.

Zuly was lost in his own world. The more he thought about his progress, the better he felt. After a long time, he had no telephones to disturb him. He had a faint smile on his face. He noticed that a small African boy sitting next to him was watching him intently. Zuly felt a little awkward that the boy had caught him daydreaming.
He gave him a big smile and said, "Hu Jambo!"
"Shikamo-o," the boy replied.
"Maarhaba!"
Zuly patted the child's cheek. The boy's mother gave him a faint smile. Zuly's 'feel good' excitement was so high that he not only liked the boy, but the mother also.
"Toto janja saana (boy is very smart)!" Zuly said.
They exchanged smiles again. He bought toffees and groundnuts for the boy and passed them to the mother also. He thought, poor Africans! They deserve our love.

Zuly played with the boy for a while. Then he got up to look at the sea. He ordered a tin of Coke and a packet of potato chips, stood on the deck at the rear to watch the choppy waves. He found everything exciting and adventurous. After his little snack, he returned to his seat. The monotonous drone of the engines and the boat's lulling movement made everyone sleepy. Zuly slept, a man walked past them with a bunch of sick bags. The mother did not ask for it.

Suddenly, Zuly woke up. The boy had vomited in his lap. Zuly was wet right up to his shoes. He could not move for a few moments, he did not know how to move the boy away and get up to clean himself. Some people looked at them and smiled as the boy had made the 'Muhindi' dirty.

Zuly's 'feel – good' excitement vanished instantaneously. He was disgusted and looked scornfully at the mother. He told himself that it was a lousy way to begin the day; it was not a good omen.

He was received at the port by the Arab, Ali Nasoro. After exchanging pleasantries, they went to his home, which was also his office. He was served black tea in a pint-sized tea cup with a slice of jaggery and some nut cake. He was also offered jelly-like cashew nut haluwa, originally an Indian delicacy. Zuly wanted to avoid eating anything as he used to suffer from a common gastrointestinal disorder known as a nervous colon syndrome.

But Ali would not hear of it. "This is our Zanzibar specialty. You must try it, Bwana," he insisted.

They talked about Dar and Zanzibar.

Zuly asked, "Ahaan, so when do we go to the bank?"

"Don't worry Bwana Zuly, I have told my people to gather money."

"What? I asked you, you said money is there!"

"Money is there, you will get it before I go for Suali (prayer)."

It had started raining. Zuly thought of getting started on the other missions on his mind. He decided to go to the Registrar of Lands office in Ali's car. Zuly expected a warm welcome because he would be piggybacking on a minister's reference to get his work done. But he was disappointed when, after a bit of introduction, a desk clerk told him that the boss was out.

"Unfortunately, government has not given him vehicle. It is raining. Maybe he has no umbrella. You just wait. He will come, surely."

Zuly waited for a while. He also had work with the Ministry of Revenue. Running under trees and extended roofs to dodge the rain water, Zuly reached the car and jumped in. The driver took some time to locate the office; the revenue officer was out of town. His assistants gave Zuly a list of documents required for submission. Zuly went back to the Registrar's office.

He asked the clerk "Is your boss in?"

"Yes, he was, but has gone out."

"Why?"

"In Zanzibar, we call it mini lunch."

Fuming privately, he asked the driver to take him to a nearby hotel. The rains had stopped. He sat under an almond tree facing the sea in a nicely laid out hotel. Zuly did not know how he could kill time. A waiter stood by him. Zuly looked at him for some time. His stomach was full of chips, coke, tea, nuts, jaggery, haluwa and two bottles of water. Zuly was thoroughly confused.

'Some drink, Saar!'

He decided to skip lunch as it would take long and ordered coffee and sandwiches. He was not in a mood to appreciate the ocean that lay in front of him.

The sea was calm and many dhows were anchored near the shore. Most of them had motor engines. One such dhow was approaching the sparsely populated north–eastern cost. It stood a little away from the coast. A small raft approached it. A bundle of fishnet, some empty jerry cans and a few sacks full of long Sangara fish were delivered to the raft. They waved and parted. The raft slowly went along the coast and anchored next to a beach resort. The dhow was emptied and the fisherman lay down on the heap of net.

After about an hour, two men and a lady dressed for a swim came out from the resort. They strolled on the beach and passed by the fisherman a couple of times.

The fisherman asked, "Unataka (do you want) Sangara?"

The trio approached him. One man asked, "Sangara of Zanzibar or Dar?

"Dar."

"Is it in a bag or loose?

The fisherman's eyes gleamed. He looked around for a while carefully. So did the others.

Then, he opened the net and pulled out a sack. The lady picked it up. One man pretended to be interested in the other sack. He opened it, pulled out one fish and talked for a while to the others. They looked around again. There was no one there except for a white couple swimming some distance away.

The man bent down and seemed to be pushing the fish back into sack. Immediately, the fisherman got up to help out.

The man straightened up and tried to tuck in his vest properly. He dropped a bundle of notes near the fisherman's leg.

The fisherman thanked him and turned back to put the other things back on the raft. The trio slowly walked into the hotel as if they had gone to the beach for a swim and were returning with a bag of clothes.

They went to their room and opened the sack. There was a pistol and a machine gun inside. One man checked to see if it was loaded. The lady looked scared. The men smiled and raised their thumbs. They were Jambaazi (bandits) planning to loot a bank.

Zuly went back to the government office. The registrar was back after his mini lunch. "It can be done. You have come with a big minister's reference. He is the ultimate authority. But tomorrow he should not be questioned in the assembly. I may lose my job and you, your property. We have to make a good case. I can do it. But, you know Bwana this is Zanzibar. Everybody wants Takrima (favour or bribe)."

"Sawa. How fast?"

He asked for some documents. Zuly was prepared. He went through them. "See me after two hours."

"You mean by one?"

"Oh, I go for prayers and then lunch. Others will also go. Come on Monday."

"I have to go back?"

"These buildings are standing for more than a hundred years. You cannot stand for two days!"

He laughed. Zuly gave up.

He rushed to Ali for his money.

"Karibu Bwana Zuly! Be happy. We have money now. This is Zanzibar. You have to be patient. Now my son is coming with you to withdraw money."

"No Ali, you must come."

"I can't make it to Suali (prayers) if I come with you."

"Please, saidia Bwana (help). If some signature is required or any problem arises, then again it will be tomorrow. I will get stuck. It is not a small sum. Tafadali (please)."

"Inshah Allah, I can attend both. I will hand over money at my bank. Then you go with my driver to your bank. I go to mosque."

"No, no, Ali. You come and give money to your son. Let him keep the money till we reach my bank."

"Why?"

"I do not want to take a risk on the way."

Ali was angry, "Look here, Bwana. Our deal was that I pay you, not where and how."

Zuly had no choice.

They went to the local bank. Ali walked straight to the officer and after exchanging the usual greetings, he introduced Zuly to the officer. Zuly produced proof of his identity and was given a token.

"Sawa Bwana, mi na kwenda (I am going)," said Ali.

Zuly was tense, "No, no. Wait and help me to count the notes. Wait till I get the money."

They waited for a while. Zuly was summoned by the officer twice for more signatures. The bank was very small; all staff members seemed to know that a lot of money was being withdrawn. Everybody was looking at him every now and then. Zuly was nervous. He looked around.

There were only two or three customers chatting casually with the staff who were working. Zuly felt an uncomfortable sensation grip his stomach. Half an hour had gone by. Zuly went to the cashier, "How long will it take?"

"Just wait."

After a while, the cashier pulled out some bundles, piled them up on the counter and called Zuly. Just as Zuly approached the counter, the power went off.

"Now machine cannot work."

"You do not have a generator?"

Cashier smiled, "No."

Zuly's stomach started to ache now. He wiped the sweat off his forehead and broke wind.

"I do not mind waiting, but give me sealed bundles."

"It will take a long time. Talk to my officer."

Ali was trying to humour the cashier and keep him in good spirits till Zuly's transactions were done. He explained what had to be done. The cashier called another staff member and gave her a few instructions.

"Okay, just wait."

Another half hour went by. The lady appeared with a tray full of bundles, all tied with sisal ropes. She almost dropped it on the cashier's counter and said, "Ah! Kazi (work) Jamaani (people). So many bundles!"

Zuly wanted her to shut her mouth. Again he looked around wishing nobody had heard her remarks. He could not do anything about the pain in his stomach and his uncontrollable urge to break wind. *Coke and cake could sit easily in the stomach since one was effervescent and the other was porous. But, impermeable haluwa and jaggery could not get along with them. His bowels were adjusting to this cultural collision and were trying to push all quarrelsome elements out.*

Zuly was now also worried that the bank would close for the day. He picked up all the bundles, one by one. He checked the denominations by flipping the notes while Ali helped him.

"Sign here," the cashier said.

"'Yeah, but wait. How are we going to carry this?" Zuly looked at Ali in desperation.

Ali went out and got some thick plastic bags and packed the money. Ali decided to accompany Zuly since he looked rather scared. When they came out of the building, a few beggars came close.

A man came said softly, "Mzee." Zuly skipped a heartbeat. The man pulled out a smuggled watch, "Very cheap."

Zuly got into the car with the bags and checked if Ali had also put the bags with him safely. The car moved slowly through the narrow streets.

A few minutes later, a police constable waved them down. The driver slowed down. Ali shouted, "Do not stop, just go."

The driver hesitated. The police constable seemed to be in a great hurry. He banged his baton on the car bonnet and shouted while wildly gesticulating.

Ali got out of the car and started shouting, "These people are from the mainland! Wewe (you) ofisaa. You do not know me?"

"Wewe Mharabu (arab). Get out of the way, Waziri Mkuu (prime minister) is passing."

"But why are you banging my car?"

Zuly's heart started pounding. Any police involvement would open up Pandora's Box. The manner in which he was transferring money was dubious. In Tanzania, it is the police and not tax authorities who can start a commercial investigation.

They would first allege that Zuly was a robber and would accuse him of charges one could not even dream of. Then, depending upon the amount of money in question and how urgently the 'accused' wanted it, they would demand a part of it.

The driver could hear the sirens and see the flashing lights of the escort cars. He immediately tried to squeeze the vehicle into the side of the narrow street, but couldn't. Zuly's bowels had been sending distress signals to his stubborn mind. But this time, it was his mind that was sending distress signals to the bowels. Zuly jumped out of the car and ran to Ali. He was almost in tears.

He pleaded with Ali, "Bwana, leave it now."

He folded his hands in prayer in front of the constable, profusely apologising for Ali's behaviour and pulled him away.

The escort car passed by. It slowed down. The constable saluted senior officers inside the car. The rear window rolled down and an officer waved Ali's car further away. Ali defiantly got into his car.

Ali, Zuly and the driver looked into the car. A senior officer shouted, "Wewe Mharabu!"

Ali smiled and waved at him. A few Land rovers followed by two black Mercs passed by. They were followed by the Field Force unit, a special armed force, the men in brown uniforms wielding guns in the open armoured car. Everybody was out to have a look at the convoy.

Some waved. Some cheered and clapped. There were policemen every few metres coordinating via radio sets to clear the traffic.

They reached Zuly's bank. The security guard was bargaining with a food vendor. His gun was resting on the wall. Zuly went into the building and heaved a sigh of relief. But the frequent spasms in his stomach made him move with some urgency.
"Now relax Bwana Zuly, you are inside your bank. Let me go for Suali."
"Just wait Bwana Ali, It won't take much time."
There were five people in the queue. Zuly was impatient. His forehead was cool but drenched with sweat.

When Nature calls, it gives you a buzz the first time. If you ignore it, the pressure subsides temporarily. It rings an alarm the second time with greater pressure.
It numbs you for a second and challenges you to ignore it again. It subsides again if you still command it to do so. But it comes back within a shorter time. As it's calls are turned back, Nature becomes more and more impatient. It waits for lesser and lesser time and finally bangs open the stretchable door ignoring your command completely.

When Zuly took his place in the queue, he got the first call. He started planning for an emergency. The queue shortened and now only two men stood between Zuly and the teller.
Zuly was shifting his weight from one leg to another, looking around him and trying to distract his attention from his bowels and the money. The customer at the teller

counter was chatting with the teller about their mutual friends. They were talking for quite some time. It was a well-known and expected nuisance for the locals, but for Zuly it was physically unbearable. It would be quite insulting if they were asked not to talk while working. He also knew that his transaction would raise questions, so it was better not to anger the teller. Zuly wished desperately that the teller would get back to work.

Nature's second alarm call had Zuly dancing, trying to suppress the pressure in his intestines. Zuly asked Ali to stand in the queue and went looking for the toilet. He got the key and almost ran into it, fumbled with the key, and shut the door with a bang. His pants fell down. He collapsed on the seat, taking off his briefs quickly. The briefs rolled down tightly and looked like a spectacle frame without glasses. There was thunder and showers. Zuly felt very relieved, like a mother in the maternity ward. He had forgotten about his money.

After a few moments, he realised it was risky to leave such a huge amount with Ali who might run away with it. He might be busy chatting with someone and a crook would walk away with a few bundles.

He shortened his act against the wishes of his bowels. It took some time to uncoil his brief and dress up. He rushed to the teller counter. Ali was still standing there; there was only one man ahead of Ali now. The Arab had understood what Zuly's problem was.

He laughed at him and said, "Do not worry Bwana Zuly, this is Zanzibar."

The torture inside the grave is known only by the corpse. (Adhabu ya kaburi aijua maiti.)

Soon, it was Zuly's turn. Ali and Zuly piled the bundles of notes on the teller's counter.

The teller exclaimed, "Ah, Kazi (work)!"

A lady drove straight to the entrance of the bank. Two men got off quickly. One man pulled out a machine gun from under the car seat while the other pointed his gun at the security guard and then shot at the glass doors.

The security guard ran away and so did all the other people passing by. Shopkeepers ducked under the counters of their shops and taxi drivers abandoned their vehicles and ran away.

Everyone inside the bank heard the shots. Zuly looked at the main entrance. He turned back and the teller had disappeared. She had taken cover under the table, as had all the other tellers in the bank.

Zuly pushed all his money off the counter and letting it all fall down.

He whispered to the teller, "save my money, Dada (sister)."

The bundles showered on her.

He ran towards the toilet, he still had the key. Ali was trying to get behind a water dispenser. The dispenser had not been moved for months; a thick curtain of cobwebs greeted him. Several cockroaches that had taken refuge under the dispenser ran around.

The robbers sprayed bullets on the furniture and on the wall.

"Maneja (manager) come out. We want money not people's lives."

The manager was trembling, he shook while walking to the safe and opening the door. One man guarded the main entrance, and the other one with the pistol held out huge sacks. He ordered the manager and two other employees to fill it up cash.

The word of the robbery had spread. Most of the policemen were generally unarmed. Those who had arms were not issued bullets. Those who had bullets had no vehicle to rush to the spot. Radio calls buzzed through the whole of Zanzibar. The Field Force unit accompanying the prime minister was summoned. The prime minister was attending a conference on the Millennium Development Goals.

A Kiswahili proverb says – Jogoo hulia "uta wangu u kule". The rooster crows "my bow is just over there" (when hawk preys on chickens).

A police commander fired two rounds in the air while his officers cautiously approached the main entrance.

He shouted through the loudspeaker, "Come out, we will not do anything, or else it will be bad."

The man inside shouted at the manager, "Enough, tie this rope. Remaining, next time. Fasta fasta (be fast)."

The man guarding the entrance sprayed bullets through the window and the main door.

The FFU men ducked and dived for cover. The commander dived too while firing in air, but the bullet struck an old man who was standing on a balcony facing the bank. He cried out and fell like a huge tree. A woman started yelling from the balcony, "Shoot the Jambaazi, not an old man."

The bandits got together and asked, "Choo wapi? (Where is the toilet)?"

They tried opening the door but Zuly was inside. He was not sure if he should open it. The robbers finally kicked the door open, caught Zuly by his neck and threw him out. The other bandit used the butt of the machine gun like a hammer and broke the wall around the window. The other man threatened the manager, "Go out and tell them we are coming out."

"But they will shoot me by mistake."

"I will shoot you without mistake."

The commander looked at the balcony and the fallen old man. He looked at his assistant. "It must be their bullet," said the assistant quickly. The other members got distracted. They were caught between the machine gun and verbal fire.

The commander shouted, "Ignore her. Attack them. Move in."

The manager ran like a cockroach across the floor, stopping every now and then and shouting, "Halo, simame (stop), mi maneja hapo. Stop firing, stop firing, they are coming out."

The commander said, "Wait. Be ready."

Then he crawled near one of his shooters and whispered, "Shoot them as soon they come out."

He shouted on the loudspeaker, "Sawa, Jamaani, simame faya (fire)."

The police heard something like a window break and moments went by. The guards surrounding the building were called to position themselves in front of the entrance. The 150-year-old lime and mortar wall of the toilet gave way. The window frame fell off. It was at the back of the building.

One of the bandits peeped out of the window first. It was safe. He jumped out of the window and started walking as if nothing had happened.

He came to the main road and waved at their car. Two bags of cash came out next. The second bandit fell over them. Their lady partner drove up to them. They escaped with the money.

The manager was too scared to declare the escape of the bandits as he could not see what was happening inside the toilet. People around the bank saw the bandits get away and shouted from windows and waved to the policemen indicating that the bandits had escaped.

Kiswahili slang is very mild. So the commander uttered a few from his own kabila (sect). He stormed into the bank and then left to chase the car. A few policemen were left behind to take down eyewitness accounts.

The bank manager told them the whole story. Zuly stood near the counter. His intestines were chafed like strips of asparagus.

Ali came out from behind the dispenser, dusting cobwebs off his clothes. Some spiders walked on his long beard, marvelling at the the black oily fiber with a faint smell of chickens.

Zuly spoke to the teller, "Mama, please check if my money is safe."

"I can see your bundles down here, but not counted," she said.

The police officer asked them to go into the waiting lounge. Nobody was allowed to go out. After the commander returned, their statements were recorded.

The cash on the counter was counted and sealed along with the teller's statement. Pictures of the toilet and the damaged walls and entrance were taken. The commander was too angry to speak, but the manager told Ali not to worry about the money and come the next day.

Zuly went to a hotel and Ali for his prayers. Both thanked God for saving their lives. Zuly spoke to his family and asked them not to worry. By 8 pm he felt better, and so did his stomach. He had turned philosophical about life and his mundane existence.

He was prepared to even forget about the money and, of course, Zanzibar, and go home.

Ali called him up and suggested they go out for dinner.

Ali introduced Zuly to an Asian man. "Bwana Zuly, meet him, Mistaa Popo. Though his real name I do not know, but whole Zanzibar knows him as Popo."

Popo in Kiswahili means 'a bat'. Zuly smiled.

"My real name is Popatlal Kanodia. You can call me PK."

They went for dinner at a wayside joint known for mishkaki, roasted fried chicken or beef crumbs pierced on skewers.

"This Bwana Popo knows everybody in Zanzibar. He can solve any problem. He is a doktaa (doctor). Yes, you have to tell all your problems to him without hiding. Una jua (you know), *Mficha uchi hazai, (without being nude, you can't give birth to a child.*"

A doctor in the Tanzanian sense is a person who solves problems. An advocate or some other professional can escape from problems by giving excuses, but a doctor has to solve the medical problem of a patient otherwise he will die. The status of doctor is extended to car mechanics and company directors, provided they solve problems.

Popo was told about the adventure in the bank. Zuly and Ali needed his help in getting the money deposited safely in Zuly's account.

"No problem. The police chief of Zanzibar knows me."

He spoke to the hotel owner and dialled the police chief's residence.

"Hujambo, Chifu (chief), Popo hapa sorry to distaab you at this time…," he narrated Zuly's plight briefly. "He is just like my brother." This was a much-heard phrase. It meant that his commission and the benefactor's Takrima were assured.

Doktaa Popo declared with a broad smile, "You can sleep peacefully tonight. You will get your money tomorrow."

Popo knew the amount involved so his smile would not fade away very quickly. Zuly talked about his hotel project and cell tower project.

Popo started his harangue on who he was. He had the only license to play the games Lotto and Housie in hotels. His art of calling the numbers had made him very popular. Popo held the contract for running the government's ramshackle amusement park. It had a merry-go-round, a giant wheel and a toy train running on a small diesel engine. His only credentials were that he could get cheap fundi (mechanics) from India to repair the aging equipment and of course, would regularly give a cut to the people who mattered. He was an office bearer of a political party in power. He was good at arranging deals on property and licensing. He was a moneychanger and inland tour operator too. He was a man for every need.

"How long are you here for?"

"I want to leave tomorrow, if I get my money."

"Okay, but tomorrow is Friday. We'll go to the registrar's office first. Let him start working. We finish the bank then and go to meet the IG of police. Then again work for your hotel plot. Friday is generally half day here. People go for prayers, then lunch and then, you know these people from the government. They do not come back."

"Do they work half-day on Saturday?"

"No, no. Saturday and Sunday are official holidays. But I will try. Early next week, if the minister signs the land transfer agreement, you will be the owner of all their office buildings," Popo smiled.

He added, "But to get the buildings in your hand, you have to give them some people to pack their files and furniture, give them transport and chakula (food). Luckily, the new building is ready and it is in the city centre, but we have to check that there is water in the toilets; all plug points, lights and fan have electricity and so on. Otherwise, they will take one year to shift."

"But why me?"

Ali started laughing, "You want their 150-year-old offices in such a good area for almost nothing and you do not want to spend?"

Popo went with Zuly to the registrar's office in the morning. Zuly waited on a wooden bench while Popo disappeared inside. The benches were located at the entrance in such a way that everybody had to pass by them, and would have to salimia (greet) persons sitting on the benches and shake hands even with strangers. Zuly was tired of shaking hands and acknowledging everybody. Popo came out running.

"I told him not to go for mini lunch now. We will provide them with a meal. He will trace the files, prepare papers and hand it over to us so that we can go to the minister and get his signature. This normally takes two to three months. As per the rules, the minister or his secretary has to come along with us and carry out the procedure in front of him. You see!"

"How long will he take then?"

"We will get the papers by 4 pm today. They will go for suali, you know. I told them I will get them a taxi."

"How much is he asking for all this?"

Popo raised his index finger to denote one million shillings, approximately $ 1000.

"One million! Is it not too much?"

Popo smiled faintly. "That you will recover in an hour when you start the hotel here."

Zuly smiled and asked, "How much time will the ministry take?"

"You said you know him? I also know him very well. My advice to you is pay them off and forget it. Do not carry a monkey on your back."

"But I committed…"

"No commitment. I know him. I know his Mama Ndogo (mistress). He will also need the support of small people like us to be a minister again. Look, it is election time now. You pay something to the party and something to him. This is Zanzibar. Keep a low profile and make your money, Bwana."

Both smiled at each other.

"Come let me introduce you to the registrar."

Popo introduced Zuly, "He is just like my brother…"

The registrar shook hands and immediately pointed out a technical glitch, "You see, these days revenue authority has become very strict. You have to get their clearance on your deed, before I sign. I do not know anybody there."

Popo cut him short, "Mzee, they will ask so many queries like a professor. He is not from Zanzibar. You have the powers. Your signature is final. You sign, we ignore them."

The registrar disagreed, "No,no. Usi vunje sheria (do not break the law)."

Popo smiled, "Usi vunje sheria, kunje tu (don't break the law, just bend it)."

"You Muhindi, you know too much. You are asking me to do all these shortcuts in my office, during office hours, in front of this mageni (guest). You go," The registrar frowned.

Popo and Zuly left immediately. Zuly thought the game was over.

"Don't worry, Bwana Zuly. When he says get out, means work is done. After mini lunch, there is always a big lunch. Hakuna matata (no problem)."

Popo was smiling as ever. They went to the bank and walked straight to the manager. The teller was called; Zuly thanked her for saving his money and said, "Pick a bundle of your choice." Each bundle contained about $100.

Popo declared on his client's behalf, "And one bundle for the manager and staff, Bwana. You are very lucky." Zuly's enthusiasm faded away slightly.

He nodded nonetheless, "Of course!"

His money was transferred without another hitch. They also thanked the police chief, for which Zuly had to shell out another bundle. When he asked Popo about his expectations, Popo gave him a discourse on 'relations'.

Zuly gave him one bundle; Popo was unusually silent and gave Zuly a Mona Lisa smile.

Zuly pacified him, "This is just the beginning, Mr. Popatlal! Do not worry. Now I know you well. You know me well. You are just like my brother…"

Popo was bolshoying in the clouds till now; he came crashing down without a parachute.

"Okay, no problem. Next time take care of me. Let's meet next week. I will call you."

"Khuda hafeez."

"Avjo (bye)."

They shook hands. Zuly was relieved to have found a good agent in Popo. Doktaa Popo was happy to get a prospective client or patient, in Zuly.

Zuly boarded a boat again. This time he made sure that there was no boy next to him, who could puke in his lap. He looked behind at the vanishing island of Zanzibar.

Chapter 2 : Time for change

Mumbai, a city of twelve million people, was going through its daily routine. Roads were flooded with buses, taxis, rickshaws, cars, and handcarts. The local trains were purging and gulping crowds of people every other minute. Everyone was on the run to earn and get home by the end of the day. People walked body to body in crowded railway stations and in narrow streets packed with street vendors and small shops. It was a busy evening in the city's suburbs.

Under all the hoi polloi are hidden seven islands that have been reclaimed and connected. The story of the metamorphosis of this tiny hamlet inhabited by fishermen, dormant for centuries, into India's commercial capital within decades is interesting to say the least.

A series of minor events sometimes changes the entire course of history.

Many races ruled Mumbai. As a part of Emperor Asoka's kingdom, it was ruled by Hindus till the thirteenth century. The Muslims ruled it from the early fourteenth century, till the Portuguese took it away from them in the early sixteenth century. It then came to the British as dowry from the Portuguese, when King Charles II married the Portuguese Princess Catherine in 1662. It was never a prominent place till the British got here. They ruled over it till 1947, when India shrugged them off.

The locals called this place 'Mumba' after a revered deity, the Portuguese called it 'Bom Baia' (GoodBay), the British called it 'Bombay' and the local state government finally christened it 'Mumbai'.

Modern Mumbai was born in the hands of the English East India Company, who took over from the British Government for an annual sum of 10 pounds in gold! The British encouraged the Hindu and Muslim traders from the mainland to establish their businesses in the port town. Soon ships started coming in with British goods; textiles, ammunition, steel and many other finished products. They would load Indian commodities like cotton, wood and spices. Along with external trade, inland trade developed. More local traders started settling down in Mumbai. Infrastructure like schools, colleges, courts, roads, hospitals, railways, etc were developed to make it a commercial and administrative hub. Ever since, it has maintained its prominence as a commercial and westernised modern city. Southern Mumbai, which used to be a grazing ground for cattle 150 years ago, is now one of the most expensive chunks of real estate in the world.

***

Raj, a bubbly young lad in his twenties, was sitting in a small restaurant. Over a cup of steaming coffee and toast, he was looking for jobs in the local newspaper. He sighed and felt that except for him, everybody was on the run.

He was stirred from his despondent thoughts by his friends, Leena and Vicky.

"Hi, Raj, what's going on?" asked Leena.

"Nothing. One more flop day. No ads. How is your job, Vicks?"

"Fine."

Realising that Raj was feeling low, Vicky suggested a movie.

Raj was a civil engineer. He was intuitive, cheerful, but too sensitive for the city. Although, he was passionate about his career, he did not seem to be getting anywhere. Leena was a business graduate and had a well-paid job as a customer relationship manager in a financial institution. She was logical, a perfectionist, and fussy about everything. Not only had she done well in college and in her profession, but her bold beauty had made her very confident of getting her way.

Vicky was a commerce graduate. He worked with an accounting firm. He was quite an introvert, and depended on his two friends to have fun. The trio were very close.

Most of the time, Leena and Raj would keep up an unending battle of wits, much to Vicky's delight. The two would be egged on by Vicky who usually took a neutral view of everything, unless a good fight was in the making. Then he would switch sides, provoking Leena and Raj in turns to fight amongst them. And through it all, the friends never lost their temper.

After the movie, they started walking towards a restaurant. Vicky started,

"Good movie. Wasn't it?"

"Yeah, A very good one," said Raj.

"Frankly, it was too tense and a little boring," said Leena.

"Why?" asked Vicky.

"Look, I mean…they have shown a dedicated teacher who brings up a blind, spastic child. All for a good cause, it's a good effort, but there is too much teacher–child monotony."

Raj could not let this remark go by, "What the hell! It was quite emotional. Different from the song and dance stereotypical movies, or the hero-fights-villain kind. Come on yaar(friend), I never knew you were so dull-headed!"

"Shut up! We go to the movies for entertainment. Not to face real life drama, as we see everyday. Why pay for it?"

"Well, if you think entertainment is only laughs and stunts, then it is not worth discussing. But in my opinion even a tragic story or a documentary could be pretty entertaining, if narrated well."

"Yes! Raj is right. Look at the actors, the music. It was a good movie," Vicky offered.

"Another good thing about the movie was the story, based in the colonial era. The setting, make up, hairstyles, buildings, roads… everything is so perfectly represented. You feel you really are looking at an earlier century. One telephone or electricity pole or a poster on the wall would have pulled down the whole show! That's the beauty."

Leena retorted, "You are confusing the story with the direction. The direction may have been good, but the story is so-so."

"You have no heart. You are a cruel Cleopatra. I pity your husband, if some one selects you at all."

Leena retorted, "And I pity your future wife who will have to carry a box of tissues, if she comes to the movies with you."

"A wife with a tissue is better than one with issue." quipped Raj.

Vicky burst into laughter. "That's a good one. Come on, Leena."

"What 'good one'? He is stupid."

"Aunty! In this world, there are two types of people who are stupid. The first, who actually are and the second, who think others are," Raj said in a sombre tone.

"Uncle! You belong to category one," Laughed Leena

"I may, or may not, but you definitely belong to category two because you think others are stupid!"

Vicky intervened, "Hello, stupids! Where is the restaurant?"

They suspended their argument and looked for an eatery. After settling down and placing their order, Vicky resumed the discussion, "but the story was different."

Leena agreed, "Yeah, I think so too. It is not the run-of-the-mill kind. It may win a few awards. It may be a good entry for the Oscars, in the foreign film category."

Raj shot back, "That's what I am saying, Maasi (aunty)! It is a classic movie."

Leena did not give up, "It may be good for the awards, but not good for an avid moviegoer. There can be films on lepers or AIDS victims or a rape victim but people like me will be scared to go to the cinemas."

Raj lost his cool, "Madam, in this world, very few people make a real contribution to society. Scientists, who invent new things that change our lives for the better or affect society, are real contributors. But, there are very few people like them. You can count them on your fingers. It takes decades for a handful of people to make a discovery or invention that changes our lives radically."

Leena quipped, "That has nothing to do with this movie."

Vicky could sense a tornado coming. He relished it. "No, no. He has a point, let him continue!"

Raj gulped his tea down. "Thank you. So, as I was saying about social contribution, the next category is social workers like Mother Teresa who helped millions and eased their suffering. Or political leaders, like the father of our nation, Mahatma Gandhi, who fought against so many social evils, who taught non-violence to the world and so on. They are very, very few, but they score next. The rest, like you and me, are parasites."

Leena wondered where Raj was headed with this.

"We wake up, we shit, we eat, we work, we reproduce, and we die. We expect society to give us protection, good roads, good schools for our children and good hospitals near our home. We may even expect multiplexes nearby. We throw money everywhere, buy things and sleep at night. If there is global warming, that's not my concern. If the oil wells of the world are drying up, that's not my concern. 'You know, I bought a new car, very spacious'!" Raj continued.

"Okay, cut it short. What has all this blah-blah to do with the movie?" Leena said impatiently.

"He is coming to it. Be patient. Swamiji (holy man), please continue," Vicky said. Raj looked around and waved as if there was a large crowd listening to him. His friends laughed.

"So, what I was saying is that we are all parasites who leave behind shit and our dead bodies and go for good. If one of these parasites tries to do something good by educating society, we should cheer him on.Like parasites, we should not think only about 'my fun', 'my enjoyment', 'my entertainment', 'my career', and 'my bank'..." Leena finally knew what Raj was driving at.

"Raj, among the parasites you are talking about, there are two categories: one who mind their own business and the other, a few, who are boring. You belong to the latter category," Leena said quickly.

They continued arguing all the way home, way past midnight. The parasites finally called it a day.

***

Civil engineers were not in demand in the city. Added to that, Raj was not exceptionally brilliant. He would have been happier working in the films or the media, but his educational and professional qualifications and his parents, would not allow it. He did work on private projects, but his employers were of the uncouth, illegal, corrupt and manipulative kind.

Anyone who had made black money made through dirty politics or extortion would get into the construction business. His employers would get slums on government land cleared by bribing officials, threatening slum dwellers and then, if they didn't move fast enough, by burning their dwellings. They would also give money to politicians, the police and the local "social workers" to acquire the whole area at the low government price. Their clients wanted cheap houses, and no one wanted to pay tax. So by profession, practice and preaching, they were "bypass surgeons" who bypassed everything — taxes and construction norms included. They would flout agreed terms with clients, completion commitments, agreed price and allocation. They would dodge a client while returning the advance money from a client and money owed to small, innocent, harmless people like Raj.

Raj worked till late at night at the sites, surviving on a roadside tea and cheap food from roadside shanty. His employers would ill-treat him and yet, delay his monthly salary. Raj would chug on for some time, occasionally borrowing money from his father and would quit when the employer abused him too much, or his salary wouldn't stretch through the month, or if the work was highly illegal.

His father was a successful executive in a large pharmaceutical company and his mother was a physiotherapist; both were earning well. His elder sister, Milie was married and lived in the UK. His father had suggested several times that Raj go abroad for further studies and then better jobs would come his way. But, Raj did not think he was in a position to decide and act.

Like most people in this world, Raj was a mediocre person. After his education and his experiences as a civil engineer, he felt that he was destined to live an average life. He did not mind getting a lean pay-packet, but he wanted a job that made him happy. He also thought that he would have a good love life and get rich at the end of his professional life.

One Sunday, Raj's father invited a friend home for lunch. Right after dessert, the conversation veered towards Raj's career.
Mohan suggested, "I have a friend in Africa; he is setting up a cell phone company. He is looking for a hardworking engineer who would set up the project and then be involved in running the business."

Raj's parents found the idea of Raj in Africa funny and started joking about it. But Raj could not stop thinking about it. He found it challenging and exciting to work in a place like Africa.

"Think about your future," Raj's mother counselled, "Your marriage, the lifestyle in Mumbai, children, their education, their future…"

His friends told him not to be so desperate for a job and be patient. They were sure that he would surely get a job in the burgeoning city. After all, India was one of the fastest growing economies in the world. After a couple of unsuccessful interviews in large companies, Raj was depressed. He just sat near the window with his guitar, thinking about his successful friends and his own misfortune.

His father was sympathetic, but didn't know how to comfort his son. On one such morose evening, he walked into Raj's room and watched his son strum the guitar while looking at the horizon despondently. It was not the first time his father had seen him so very unhappy. Raj had always been a very cheerful child. He would abide by the rules set by his parents, never once questioning their authority. His parents spent a lot of time with him and Raj did quite well in school.

But, as he grew older, he faltered in his studies. He was very sensitive and would be deeply embarrassed by a reprimanding teacher. He wanted a positive, parent-like response from a teacher and looked for constant recognition.
His parents tried different approaches from gentle encouragements to harsh words, and finally punishments, like depriving him of things he wanted to have, till he achieved his goals.

Raj never stopped being cheerful. He was popular with everyone. Even when he was going through hard times, he would never stop listening to music or watching his favourite films. He was also well-known in school and took part in several extra-curricular activities.

As he reached Form 4 levels, his parents started yelling at him for his careless attitude and low scores. His mother would breakdown in frustration. His father would be upset all the time and treat him with sarcasm. Later on, both parents would confess to each other that they repented of the way they had treated their child.

His father realised that his son might never be a winner, but also that he had never misbehaved. He must treat his son better. He realised that his son would be a child only for a few precious years. Once he went to a college or a hostel, he would never be the same again. Then he would find a job in some city and have his own life. Raj's parents did not want to lose the precious time they had together. He felt that Raj had no bad habits or criminal traits. His behaviour after all was inherited in some ways. Raj's father shared his logic with his wife. They stopped whining and scolding. They involved themselves topic-wise, subject-wise in his academics. They arranged private tutors for Raj and reviewed his progress. They also treated him with warmth and love. Raj managed to do reasonably well in the final exams and just scraped into an engineering college. His parents were happy since they had accepted that their child would have a mediocre career. Raj felt sorry that he could not meet his parents' expectations and knew what they must have been through. He did not want to lose their love.

His father stood close to Raj and ruffled his hair. "Upset, son?" he asked.
Raj stopped playing the guitar, gave his father a blank look and then looked down. He could not conceal his sadness. He asked his father, "Why me? I am mediocre, I agree, but I deserve a decent job that I enjoy. I work hard. I am honest. I execute instructions well. Everybody is happy with my work but either I do not get paid, I get mistreated, or am asked to do wrong things…why me?" His throat was choked. His father was moved.
"When a situation defies logic, do what your heart says. Do not think too much. Do you want to go to Africa?"
"Yes"
"Do not worry. Go to Mohan, give him your papers and visit the place. Do not worry about the money. I want you to fight. Do not give up because of your mom or me. Do not give up, you are so young."
Raj got up and hugged his father. He was excited. The chords of his life changed from sombre Jazz to Reggae - Ragga.

The next day, Raj met his father's friend. He submitted his papers and within days he got a call from Africa, "Send him by the next flight."

It was a two-year contract initially. Raj was ecstatic. But his parents were not; his mother frowned, and his father had a Mona Lisa's smile on his face. He was happy because his son was happy. He felt bad as he knew he would miss his son terribly. Raj called up Leena.

"Are you mad? Only monkeys go to Africa. Do not rush into a decision. I know a client here in Mumbai who is a very reputed builder and has a huge housing scheme that will run for at least five years. He will take you."

Vicky also asked him not to rush into a decision. His mother had a series of sessions with both, the father and the son, discouraging them from taking such a decision. Raj stood his ground.

After marriage and childbirth, life becomes rhythmic and flowing. Parents love their children, sometimes they scold, sometimes they exert their power and sometimes they let go in favour of their children's wishes. All these interactions spin a web of emotional relations between them. The parents, do not realize till the chilren decide to go on their own way. The rhythm and flow of family life is broken. The parents feel that they have lost a part of themselves. Life always looks better in reminiscence than in the existing condition. It is like being in the clouds and not experiencing it. When someone is on the peak of a mountain and the clouds pass by him, enveloping him all around, he does not experience as much as he does when he looks at a cloud-covered mountain peak from the ground. Life is better enjoyed as it is lived than in retrospect.

One has to consciously remind oneself that the current phase of life could be the best one so let one make an effort to enjoy it.

***

It was a difficult phase for his family. His farewell at the airport was very emotional. He hugged his parents and friends. His parents were silent, although his friends were having a great time, joking about life in Africa.

Leena was smiling, but she was very upset. She had realised, just as he was leaving, that Raj was not just a friend. She wondered if he felt the same about her.

Education and stature make you sophisticated. Sometimes, sophistication in nature makes us less expressive and a little defensive or subdued. Before executing a radical or a bold thought, you argue against your own wisdom, scold your heart as if it was a small child, and justify inaction as maturity and sensibility.

Ever since she had heard about Raj's decision, she felt lonely. Although they had continued to meet each other frequently, their usual Tom-and-Jerry sequence of cerebral chasing or outsmarting each other had stopped. Debating his decision was more important than teasing each other, arguing and having fun.

Whenever they met, Vicky and Leena would end up counselling Raj who, in the end, would go on arguing in favour of his decision. For the first time, Leena knew that she would miss Raj. She had many friends, but Raj was someone she would love to report to about everything that happened to her every day. She wanted Raj to tease her. She was accustomed to his companionship and now realised that she was addicted to her friend. But, it was too late. She wanted to hug Raj and cry like a baby, but she could not. She had to smile superficially in the company of their friends. She kept her emotions in check. It was like a mother locking her crying baby in a room and attending a party in the courtyard.

***

Inside the airport, the African counter of the airline was neglected while the queues at the Europe and Middle East counters were moving quickly. Raj had rarely seen Africans in India. One family stood next to him in the queue. The little girl in a pink frilly frock was very cute. She had curled up hair and two little ribbons tied on two short pigtails that stuck up like the two little horns of a calf. Even though it was past midnight, she was running around and falling over the luggage all around her. The parents were silent and tired. Probably the Indian heat, dust, smoke and the crowds had left them half-dead.

Suddenly, the little girl tumbled and grabbed Raj's pants. She looked up with a smile on her face. Raj looked into her eyes.

She said "Shikamoo." (Asking for blessings. 'oo' in Kiswahili is o in more not 'oo' in loose)

Raj said, "Hi! How are you?"

He sat down cross-legged and held her shoulders.

"What's your name?" She just smiled, uttered a few childish words in her native tongue and immediately her father apologised and carried her away.

He boarded a flight to Africa.

For most people, Africa is like a single nation and Africans a single clan. In Tanzania alone, there are hundred odd tribes not to talk of other African nations. It is creditable for the Africans that they have a single identity as a continent. Elsewhere, nations and not continents have distinct identities. Mexicans are Mexicans and Americans are Americans. Chinese and Indians are not commonly treated as Asians. It could be that the Africans look identical to the rest of the world as 'Blacks with curly hair' or could be a sheer neglect of poor Africans.

Once airborne, the cabin crew kept everybody busy with food and drinks. Raj looked out of the window. He was above a sea of clouds. He could not see a single open patch of sky or land. Streaks of sunlight would brighten the contours of the clouds trying to race with the aircraft for a while before giving up.

Despite the fact that they were flying, the ride was bumpy, just like travelling by road. Raj wanted to see the great Indian Ocean and the African continent, but the clouds enveloped the earth and made it look and feel like a road trip. After a couple of hours, the pilot bravely rattled lots of statistics about the speed and altitude as if he had achieved them against all odds or he had done something that none of his counterparts in the world had done before.

Raj wondered whether such stats were really called for. They create more panic in a traveller's mind, he thought. He would prefer to fly as close to the sea or ground as possible rather than at a height of 30,000 or 40,000 feet to have better chances of survival in case of a mishap. Or, why not add more gory details? The pilot could announce, "At this height, if the air craft crashes, the chances of survival are nil. In the past 50 years, on this route there have been seven air crashes, two due to bombs, three due to engine problems and for two, the flight data recorder could not be traced..."

When the aircraft flies at the usual 35,000 – 40,000 feet, the outside temperature is minus 600 F. At 16,000 ft, the temperature outside is a freezing 320°F or zero degree Centigrade. An ultra thin layer of Life around Earth, equivalent to what human air is to a five-storey building, exists for past 1.8 billion years when oxygen built up in the atmosphere and algae were born first.

Educated people gather a lot of information whether relevant or not. The more they are fed with information, the more they go on asking. But, they shun action. A person may have all the stats of the football world cups but is too lazy to play football with his child, who longs for someone with whom he can play. A person may know about various cars, particularly stats of Formula 1 cars, but never opens his own car's bonnet to check the battery or radiator. A lady makes her husband's life miserable narrating all the features and advantages of vacuum cleaners and then when he buys one with the whole range of attachments, she won't remember when she used it last. An Urdu poet has rightly said 'It is soil if you get it and gold if you do not'.

***

Raj had an uneasy sleep as thoughts about past jobs, rude teachers, his friends, Leena, and his first overseas assignment chased through his mind. The excitement of a new world was negated by his memories of the people he had left behind. They stopped at Nairobi, Kenya, for about an hour or so. When the Kenyan airport service staff came into the aircraft for housekeeping, Raj had his first experience of Africa. He found that their mild, smiling faces were always willing to acknowledge him. He got out of his seat and stretched a little to relax. He found that there were more Asians, Chinese, Whites and Arabs than Africans on his flight.

On the way to Dar-es-Salaam, he looked out of his window. It was bright and sunny. He saw a green carpet of trees interwoven with brown patches of lava soil. A rift valley could be seen in the distance. *He could see rivers encircling hills like snakes. They symbolized accommodation and adjustment without any expectation. There were fields, human settlements and life all along a river, settled permanently. He could also see straight, light brown or pink roads connecting the hills, valleys and plains. They indicated need, motive and the transient aspect of humanity.*

Here was the cradle of mankind. Despite plenty of food and water and friendly tropical weather devoid of extreme cold, people had moved further and further away. They struggled against hostile weather, uncertain livelihoods and life-threatening mountains, plains and oceans. The farther they went, the richer they became. The more they struggled, the more they progressed.

***

When they were about to land, Raj was amazed to see the blue ocean and white sandy beaches and islands. Small patches of land, submerged under seawater were revealed by green and brown shadows underwater. They looked like huge green whales just under water or like the body of a white lady showering in her opaque bathroom. His excitement mounted.

As they landed, Raj kept wondering where all the huts or city buildings were. Instead, he saw a thick grove of coconut and other coastal trees all over the land, as far as his eyes could see. He felt guilty about being a civil engineer who replaces such breathtaking nature with concrete jungles.

As he got off the aircraft, he marvelled at the quiet airport and the wide open spaces. The local officials greeted him with smiles. At first, he felt a little awkward with all the attention and polite mannerisms, and then he started smiling and waving right back.

***

Dar-es-Salaam has a lot in common with Mumbai. About 500 million years ago, India and all of Africa were one with South America, Antarctica and Australia as one super continent known as Gondwanaland in the southern hemisphere. India separated from Africa and Madagascar 90 million years ago and drifted north towards Asia. After 40 million years, India collided with Asia forming the Himalayas. They still share the Indian Ocean and a lot of history.

In Africa and in India, the Moslems ruled first, followed by the Portuguese, and later the British, till Independence. The British settled Hindu and Muslim traders and working class people from India in both the places. Persians known as Shirazis in Zanzibar and Parsis in India left their homeland, Iran and settled in both places to save their religion from the onslaught of Moslems. They played an important role in the growth of the British Empire.

The name, Dar-es-Salaam, meaning 'Haven of Peace', was given by an Omani ruler from ZanzibarIsland. It developed a lot under the British in the early part of the twentieth century so it has not been maligned in the slave trade unlike the towns of Kilwa in the south and Bagamoyo and ZanzibarIsland in the north.
Unlike its distant cousins, Nairobi in Kenya or Kampala in Uganda, Dar continues to be a laidback city. In Mumbai, it is 'chalta hai' (that's how the things are). In Tanzania, it is 'Bahati Mbaya' (bad luck). People are not tolerant because they are oppressed. They are tolerant because they are lazy, selfish or keen not to waste time.

Dar is still a 'Haven of Peace'. Due to the power shortage, the electricity would be turned off from morning to evening for six days in a week.
Once or twice in a year most parts of the city would be without water, due to pipeline breakages and breaches. Shops and malls start late and close early. The whole city observes a self-imposed curfew on weekends. Here, you drive your car by looking at the traffic and not at the signal because at every signal there are three variables - power, traffic policemen and condition of the signal. It throws up several probabilities. The signals may be working but still the policeman directs the traffic. A policeman will be there but only as a watchdog, or the signals may be switched on, but the lights may not be working. If you follow the honks, you maybe caught for

illegally crossing an intersection. Commit a blunder and then make peace with the policeman.

The railway passes through the city at many points. At every junction, like a shepherd crossing the road with his cattle, the railway guard gets down from the engine with a red flag or lantern and stands in the middle of the road directing traffic. He blows his whistle and gesticulates wildly at errant drivers till the train starts slowly protruding across. At nights, a solo engine would not bother to follow the ritual. Without streetlights and after a few cans of beer, a car would run into the 'road crossing' train. The guard makes peace with the victim or wishes peace to his soul.

A presidential convoy consists of just two siren-blowing motorbikes, a police car, several Benzes and armed patrol unit, all moving at high speed. Suddenly, one of the motorbikes would branch out to another road on the wrong route only to join the convoy from behind.

One may lose a car's windscreen or headlights that are difficult to find in shops. He would go to a special street, even identify the very same stolen part, bargain with the thief and get it fixed. Make peace with the thief. After all it is a haven of peace.

The best way to enjoy Dar is to go to its unspoilt beaches, enjoy the quiet roads on weekends, enjoy its polite and mild-mannered people, have your own water tank or call for tankers when water is scarce, have your own gen-set when there is no electricity and be at peace. Dar teaches you not to have grievances in life. Do not plan in advance, just live for the day and enjoy it.

Like a drop of water falling on a plantain leaf, life will find its own path.

Chapter 3: Work begins

Zuly shrugged off his Zanzibar hang over and attended his office next day. He had arranged an introductory meeting for his new Indian Site Manager with Hans Moritz, a representative of the telecommunication equipment supplier, to provide technical backup. Moritz was obviously disinterested in the proceedings and it was immediately clear that the Dutchman did not like Zuly's methods of working and his short-term way of thinking. He had seen several project in-charges who came and went. None of them was willing to venture out of Dar. He was frequently called to monitor the project and teach the basics to the new project in-charge. He was also involved in ordering the equipment.

There was gentle tap at the door. The door opened gently and a young smiling face peeped in.
"Come, come Mr. Raj". Zuly introduced young incumbent to Moritz. For Moritz, Raj was just another sacrificial goat.

Zuly explained his plans on a map of Tanzania. — his company, Tancell, wanted to erect two main switching centres(MSC), two base station controls(BSC) and about 250 base tower stations (BTS) all over the country, in 60 months. Raj was supposed to erect the stations and towers in at least four sites in a region, co-ordinate with local government officials and get approvals for various sites. Due to the remoteness of the areas in question, Tancell would use the microwave mode of transmission rather than underground cabling.

Zuly then turned to the Dutchman.

"Hans, you want to say something?"

"No, let him go through the drawings first. He can ask me his questions then."

Zuly got busy making phone calls. Hans had dumped a pile of drawings on the table, Raj glanced through them.

"We want to erect three kinds of towers — 70 metres, 50 metresand 30 metres. Wherever we have large clusters - you know clusters?" Hans asked.

"Yup, we have many in India," Raj smiled.

Hans thought the young man was bluffing and this irritated him, "What clusters do you have in India?"

"There are clusters of villages; there are clusters of shops in the city, clusters of computers in cyber cafés and a cluster of mountains in the Himalayas. In India, you name a thing and it will be in clusters."

"Okay! Now don't cluster my mind with too many examples," Hans resumed, "a 50 metre tower can transmit microwave signals up to 35 kilometres in all directions like an umbrella. So, in remote areas we may go for 70 metre towers to have wide coverage. But in the cities we may have to have smaller 30 metre towers to pack more coverage without interference between them. You understand?"

"What interference?"

"If towers are too close, their fields interfere with each other. The more they overlap, the more we have transmission problems like this," Hans drew two circles overlapping each other.

Raj added, "You mean like in cities, you have crowded railway stations and if people use smaller umbrellas, they can move better together than if they use bigger ones and bang into each other."

Hans laughed out loud, "Now, you are talking."

Raj tried to ask Hans more about the project; about soil quality and importance of seismic or wind speed data in designing a foundation for the 70-metre towers. Every time he was told, "That is your job. I am not a civil man. I am a technical man. You first go through these drawings."

Raj studied the drawings and made notes. He also started getting in touch with the Civil Engineering Office for all the information he needed.

The next day, Zuly introduced Raj to the local contractors who would fabricate, transport and erect towers, and other telecom equipment at the site.

"Raj this is Mr. Bonde, our contractor. Bwana (Mister) Bonde, Mr. Raj."

Raj could see Iddi Amin in Bonde. He was a huge man, with big nostrils, a big smile on his face and a very loud voice

."Karibu (welcome) Mistaa Raji,"

He shook Raj with hands.

Bonde had many sons, all huge and identical, so huge, that Bonde would prefer to bring only one son at a time to the site in his Toyota hilux pick-up. None of them worked. They would sit idle at the worksite, gossiping with the masons and workers. Bonde had an army of masons, welders and workers who would treat him like a father or a village chief, accepting anything and everything that he said. He had one or two partners cum estimators who would help him prepare quotations or estimates; one of them was Juma. He would keep track of material receipts and their usage on the site. However, in the final negotiations with clients, Bonde would put all paperwork aside and accept the client's figure, if the client would boost his ego or appeal to his sentiments.

Bonde would speak very loudly and keep nodding his head. He would digest only a few sentences at a time. The longer one spoke to him, the more he nodded and said 'haya' or 'sawa' meaning okay. He had to talk to his army all the time. He had to download whatever information his limited memory would retain on his ever-attentive army. If silent for a moment, he would start snoring.

One could get Bonde to work if he was told about the plans and objectives of the work and not just the instructions. Shorter instructions would help his mind and a longer dialogue would appeal to his heart.

Raj managed to ride over Bonde's head versus heart problem by joking with him before giving him instructions. He would allow Bonde to recite what he learned to his army.

Another idiosyncratic character attached to Bonde's army was nicknamed Profesaa. The word 'Professor' in Tanzania means someone very learned who talks at length. This Profesaa would always ask questions and offer such arguments of convoluted logic that people found it difficult to answer or contradict him. In fact, people would avoid talking to him and even asking him for advice even by mistake.

But Poto, Bonde's eldest son, would always call him Profesaa in public and mock his weird logic.Profesaa was tall and lanky and wore thick glasses. He would lean like a palm tree and looked very untidy. Two teeth protruded beyond his lips and he always wore the traditional Moslem cap. The trouble was that he would never wash the cap, which was sweaty and stained.

The Profesaa would sweat profusely through the day and like a good rain water collection system, the sweat would finally trickle down to his socks and shoes. The shoes were gifted to him by an Englishman who was very happy at the way his terrace floor had been levelled by Profesaa with his water filled plastic tube. Ever since then, like the Falkland Islands near Argentina, he had stuck to wearing the British shoes by repairing, re-stitching and gluing them. The shoes no longer looked British, but looked more like a horse's hooves. And again, the trouble was that he would hardly wash his socks.The workers joked that if a lion dared to roar in front of him, he would just have to remove his shoes and the lion would start sneezing and run away. Profesaa's socks could be used instead of defibrillator electrodes if someone was having a severe cardiac arrest. If placed near the nose, the stench from the socks was so strong and terrible that the patient would have two or three severe convulsions and get up from the bed.

One reason why Bonde's men were free from illness in malaria-prone Africa, particularly at camp sites, was that at night the Profesaa would remove his shoes and hang out his socks for drying.

Zuly asked Bonde about the progress in the construction of Zuly's farmhouse, "Wipi ile kazi (what about that work)?"

"Tayari (over)."

"Tayari?" Zuly did not believe this.

"E..e…en."

"Umeme (power)?"

"Bado (pending)."

"Maji (water)?"

"Bado."

"Rangi (colour)?"

"Bado."

"Roofing and ceiling?"

"Bado kidogo (slightly done)."

"Everything is pending. So why are you saying that work is over?" Zuly demanded.

"Do not worry, Mistaa Zu-u-uli. I will finish this week."

"Raj, we have to be careful with this man. He always bluffs. He will always start by saying 'over' to everything. "Except for payments. For money, he will always say Bado."

Bonde burst into laughter. "Kweli (really). This is Tanzania, Bwana! Mistaa Zu-u-ulialways joking, joking, joking. Ha, ha."

After Bonde left, Zuli told Raj. "Raj, why don't you go to the farmhouse and give me a report of pending things? Also, give me an account of how much he has purchased. At least, major items like steel and cement, and how much more will be required to finish the thing. I have a feeling that we are dumping the materials and this man has no control over it."

The next day Bonde came to pick Raj up and they drove to the farmhouse. On the way, they saw Bonde's truck loaded with building materials.

Bonde said, "That is our truck. I bought a new one."

Raj looked at it and asked, "Is it going to our place? Or you have some other contract?"

Bonde watched the truck for a few seconds and then said, "No, no, I am doing only your work. But... why does it have so much material, Bwana?"

Raj asked him to follow the truck. The truck left the usual road and set off towards the city's densely packed suburb that was home to the lower income citizens.

"Mistaa Raji, something fishy. Where are they taking the materials? We have not ordered any material today. We do not need anything. They have stolen our materials. I will screw them."

"This means not only the driver and the turn boy but the store keeper, the askari (watchman) and even your engineer on the site are involved," Raj said.

"E-en he-en. You just see now what I am doing."

They followed the truck. They waited till the truck was unloaded into a wholesale shop. Bonde left Raj to keep watch on the truck and rushed to the police. When they saw the police, the driver jumped out of the truck and ran away. The turnboys were caught. The shopkeeper argued that the material was sold to him by the owner. He did not know it was stolen. Bonde slapped the turn boy, it shook the ground.

"I am only turn boy. They asked me to go with this vehicle so I came. I do not know it was chori (theft)," the boy pleaded.

The truck, the material, the boys, and the shopkeeper were taken to the police station. They also went to the site to arrest the store-in-charge and other accomplices. They would be produced in court for evidence in two or three days.

For the next few days, Raj was busy with the fabrication of towers, material estimates and helping Zuly order equipment. He would go to the beaches for short holidays or call up his parents and friends in Mumbai. He liked Dar as the city had an open skyline, unlike his home city. Except for a few multi-storied buildings in the centre of the city, he could see the wide clean skies wherever he went.

***

Zuly had a swanky office overlooking the Indian Ocean. It had classy interiors. The walls had a couple of frames with religious scriptures in Arabic and a photograph of the Aga Khan. The glass walls facing the sea gave one a feeling that he was the captain of a ship. Oblivious of the majestic look this cabin gave him, Zuly was busy on the telephone. Zuly's father Karimji had fractured a leg and was reading a newspaper. Karimji and his ancestors changed businesses depending on financial viability and had amassed a lot of wealth.

Zuly's ancestors were from western India. Arabs traded with East Africa and India as early as the seventh century BC. The lack of prospects in their homeland and the lure of riches they had heard about, brought Zuly's ancestors to East Africa and they converted to Islam.

The British, who were already ruling India, took the reins of large parts of coastal East Africa by the end of the nineteenth century. East Africa, like India, provided cheap raw materials for factories in Europe, such as timber, rubber, minerals, ivory, pulses, cotton, tobacco, tea, coffee, and so on.

The British developed railways and other infrastructure in Tanzania. They also brought in Indians to carry out administrative work. East Africa was under Arab domination for several centuries. The Arabs settled down and married locals. The Portuguese gained control in the early fifteenth century; they were followed by the Germans and British. As a result of invasions by the Arabs and Europeans, Tanzania has African, Arab and Asian populations speaking a common Kiswahili language and sharing the Swahili culture.

Nations have gained independence from colonial powers but the white –brown- black equation continues. Arabs continue to trade. They bring in Indians, Pakistanis and Bangladeshis from Asia, for all kinds of jobs. Whites continue to invent and economically dominate the world, browns execute and work and blacks slog in forests, farms and mines to supply tobacco, tea, sugar, sisal, minerals, agro-commodities, and cotton and so on. Human society has only redefined boundaries and added more ethnic or racial identities but the basic biological roles remain unchanged.

There was a knock at the door and Raj walked in with a smile on his face. Zuly nodded curtly and kept talking on the phone.

Raj walked up to Karimji and said, "As-salaam Alaykum, uncle."

Karimji smiled, "How are you beta (son)?"

"Fine."

Zuly ended his conversation on the phone and said, "Raj, how are you? Enjoying Dar?"

"Fine, yeah."

"So, your first experience of *chori* (theft). Never trust anybody. Not even Bonde."

Raj nodded.

"But work is falling behind now. Why don't you leave in a day or two to the site with Bonde and start work?"

Raj tried to explain, "Tower assemblies will take a week more, concrete poles about 10 days more to cure…"

"No…no... but you go, give the list. I will send it across."

"Mr. Zuly, but after four days we shall be sitting at the site. Bonde will have to pay his labour for nothing."

"Why are you worried about Bonde? He will get millions from me in this contract."

Karimji interrupted and spoke to his son. He agreed with Raj and declared that Raj would leave only after a week.

Raj was upset by this exchange. He wanted Zuly to have faith in him. He wanted Zuly to treat him like a family member and use informal and not intimidating language. But he was quite used to such encounters with employers in the past and brushed aside his worries. He rolled out a few drawing sheets on the floor so that Zuly's father could see it too.

"If we want to build 200 base tower stations in sixty months, we must target four stations per month, allowing for delays by government officials, bad weather, and other unforeseen problems. We must have ten tower assemblies, ten power supplies, ten micro-wave antenna, and ten generators in stock at all times. What we have today is fifty antenna sets, fifty power supplies and two or three incomplete tower assemblies. To my mind, the most critical activity is the tower assembly, which we are doing locally." he said.

He them showed them a bunch of drawings for ready-to-assemble tower assemblies that could be made in Dubai and brought in containers by sea. It was faster and cheaper to erect with the help of chain pulley blocks at many sites simultaneously.

"Who gave you these drawings?" Zuly was surprised.

"I got them done through our structural engineer. I showed them to Hans also. He says there is no problem with minor modifications."

Zuly got lost in phone calls again. He finally said, "Okay. Leave these papers on my table... but you go next week."

After Raj left, Zuly muttered, "He does not want to do the work I give him and brings all these papers to me."

Karimji said, "You are badly mistaken Zuly. You will save millions if you follow his advice. Just get quotes from Al-Zameel in Jabel Ali in Dubai.

We want lightweight but strong towers; install them and forget about it. If they are the nut-bolt kind, they can be assembled at the site much faster."Zuly had to obey his father.

Chapter 4: Tancell Oye

Their D-day had finally arrived. Early in the morning, Raj, Bonde and his army gathered outside Zuly's bungalow. Raj was driving a pick-up. Bonde had two pick-ups and three 10-tonne Chinese trucks. The army had formed a circle around their general, who was talking about the work at hand and the bad roads they were going to encounter. As usual, he was gesticulating, waving his hands and moving his bulky frame.

Africans live a very simple life, probably, because they do not have money. They talk about earning money (hela), having food (kula), cattle, roads and places. They live for the day and for themselves. They are not infested with philosophy or ideologies. They have no hang-ups about their status or nature of work. Children carry brooms with their school bags and reach school early to sweep the compound. Even an office manager would pick a broom and clean the office without any reservations.

Unfortunately, this is a race under the threat of extinction due to diseases, poverty, drought and wars. Nature wants to call them back, like many other species. It is a challenge for the modern world to make them competitive and strong in their battle for survival.

A servant informed Raj that Karimji wanted to see him. Raj went into the house, the 10 million dollar project was about to take-off. Karimji, his leg still swathed in bandages and seated like a king on his wheelchair, was brought in by a servant. He offered Raj tea and said, "Beta, remember one thing. You are going to work with these people. They are very nice, plain and sentimental. Get to know them. Try and talk in Kiswahili. Treat them as your fellow human beings. Give them respect and they will give their life for you."

Raj touched Karimji's feet, asking for blessings. Karimji leaned over and grabbed Raj by his shoulders.

"God bless you."

Raj came out. The sun had started climbing in the sky. He looked at the huge gang of workers and felt excited. However junior he had been in his earlier assignments, he would now begin as if it was his project. He needed to know that the contribution he made was valued. He wanted to be exceptionally organised, reach his completion target and gain the affection of people around him. His excitement at the start of every project till now would wane as soon as his boss would start flogging him like a bullock harnessed to a cart.

People with logical minds can rule the world. They may run successful business empires. But behind their success lie people who are emotionally intelligent; people who love to be physically engaged in the world; they are ad-hoc, intuitive, slightly messy but constantly involved in work. They do not separate family or their personal life from work; they give everything they've got to the job. They are like the engine of a car; they suffocate in their own scorching heat and do not know where the road will go. Once turned on, they are all fired up; the man at the wheel, however brilliant, can do nothing if the engine does not work. The world looks at the car and the man driving it and appreciates his success. They pay for the look of the car not for the noisy mules that make it run.

The very first assignment, he thought, outside my country, that too in Africa. Raj was not very religious. But he looked at the sun and remembered his parents. He vowed to make them proud of his work in Africa. Had his mother been around, she would have put a spoonful of sugar and curds in his mouth, since that was believed to bring good luck to new ventures. She would have blessed him and remembering her love, Raj felt his throat swell up with tears.

He smiled at Bonde and said, "Let's move Mr. Bonde."

Bonde turned around and shouted like an army general launching an attack.

"Haya, Jamaani (people) tuna ondoka (we are leaving)!"

He raised his hands and said, "Tancell oye."

His army raised their fists and shouted "oye".

"Tancell oye."

"oye".

"Tancell oye."

"oye".

Bonde's son Poto took Raj's pick up. Keys turned. Bonde's vehicles said 'Oye' with smoke and noise as well.

Raj was quiet as the city gave way to the lush green thicket of trees. A thin streak of road was going up and down in the middle through the thick fur of cashew, mango and other tropical trees.

It looked as if an artist had drawn a line with the back of his paintbrush on a canvas covered with green oil paint. After a few hours, the coastal vegetation was replaced by wide grassy plains. Raj was thrilled; he wished he could show this beautiful place to all his friends.

After a while, Raj's train of thoughts snapped when Poto turned on the radio. Raj liked the music and talked about Congo music, local pop stars and Zanzibar's Tarab music with Poto. Later in the day, they all stopped for tea, although most workers did not have anything to eat.

Raj pulled out his guitar from the back of the pick-up and continued playing a few chords through the journey. Poto joined him in singing along and the two ended up shouting, yelling and singing all the way.

On reaching the site they cleaned away the shrubs and dry grass. A generator was started late in the evening and a common shed was erected for everybody to sleep.

Mama Rose, a fat middle-aged lady with huge buttocks and breasts had been brought in as Raj's housemaid and cook. She would cover her head with a scarf most of the time. She made plain but delicious rice and vegetable curry for Raj, placed the food and a bottle of water on the office table and waited at a distance to serve Raj. Raj took the plate and sat with Bonde who was eating with his people sitting on the ground. After a few mouthfuls of food, Raj shouted, "Mama Rose, chakula kizoori (food is good)." Rose smiled and thanked him.

After dinner small fires were lit and everybody settled down to sleep. Raj's place was a house without walls and a roof. His bed, his table and other household goods were piled up together.

Raj looked up into the open sky and after the generator was switched off, it was very quiet. A cool breeze swept all over the place. It brought him sporadic sounds of insects and nocturnal birds. Raj looked at the vast expanse of stars. He started thinking about his life, his childhood, his parents, his friends, his hardships at work, his clamorous, glamorous city and Leena.

He felt thankful that his father had helped him get this job that he enjoyed so much already, and for the opportunity of spending a lot of time with nature. Thoughts about his father led him to some precious memories.

The Hindus celebrate their new year by lighting lamps, letting off crackers and feasting for about five days. When Raj was a child, he was crazy about crackers. His father would spend almost all his monthly salary and buy heaps of crackers.

His mother would prepare dinner and wait for them to get home after shopping. She would always find Raj unhappy that he had not been able to buy all the crackers in the market. His father's wan smile would move the mother and she would try to pacify Raj by telling him that he had more crackers than any of his friends and they would last him a full five days. Milie would remind him to appreciate that his father was not as rich as others in the building, but still he was spending almost all his salary on crackers only to make him happy.

After dinner, Raj would open all the boxes and tell his family about what was great about each firework. The family would appreciate the crackers as if they were Raj's creation. At night, Raj would sleep next to his father, talk about his crackers and finally hug him and sleep.

Raj also remembered the time when he was representing his school for a science exhibition and had to travel to another city by road. It was the first time that he was travelling without his parents. The whole family got together to pack his suitcase. He was given lots of advice and several instructions. Raj was very excited and Millie told him about her experiences travelling alone. They finally went to sleep after midnight.

The bus was crowded and on alighting he realised that he had lost his suitcase. His friends suggested that he forget about it for a while and enjoy the exhibition. But Raj felt very guilty.

The next day, Raj was walking home when he saw his father walking towards him. Something is amiss, thought Raj's father, "All well son? Was the exhibition cancelled?"

Raj hugged his father and broke down.

"What happened? Why are you crying?"

Raj could barely speak.

"I lost my suitcase."

His father's first question was, "Were you hurt? Did any one harm you?"

"No."

"Then why are you crying? Cool down. You have come back safely, that is important. We will buy you new clothes. Relax son."

Raj felt even worse. He wanted his father to scold him or slap him to relieve him from the guilt. In fact, everyone at home was very kind and they felt sorry that the child had not enjoyed the exhibition.

A sense of gratitude and indebtedness engulfed Raj. He felt sad that he had not made his father happier by getting better marks. What was worse, he had decided to leave India, and live away from his father. He promised himself that once he made it big in

Tanzania, he would take his father on a tour of the US and Europe. He would insist that his parents stayed with him in Dar for a few weeks and show them all the comforts and pleasures that they had been denied.

The next morning, Raj had no choice but to relieve himself in the open. He was nervous and uncomfortable about answering truly nature's call behind the bushes. But he enjoyed the refreshing, cool air. While getting up, he felt that somebody was watching him. He ignored the feeling and started walking. After a few steps, he turned around to find a dog, almost a skeleton, with many bruises on its body. It followed him, but kept a safe distance between them. Raj was surprised; stray dogs were not common in the country.

It was an abandoned or a lost German Shepherd. Raj whistled to the famished dog. It stood still for a moment and then gently wagged its tail. Raj went close to it, but it started walking away.

The dog had obviously started distrusting people, in whom it had once had so much faith. Raj went back to his hut and asked Rose if there was any food left over. She showed him the garbage can. He picked up some food and found the dog standing a few paces away. He called the dog, cajoled it and finally managed to give it food. Everybody was watching Raj while they were working.

Poto spoke up, "We should kill the dog. They are very dangerous."

Raj patted the dog's head and said, "He is going to be my friend, just like you."

"Aaa..Bwana wipi (what is this mister)? Am I like this dog to you?"

"No. He is thin and hungry; you are fat and overfed."

The site was ready by evening. Temporary houses with makeshift toilets and low fences made from the bushes that were cleared away had been set up.

The next day Raj gathered all the workers together and called Bonde there. Bonde said, "Mistaa Raji, I think we should make fencing first."

"No. the tower foundation will take two weeks to cure completely, so let's dig first. After casting the concrete you will have enough time to do fencing and other things."

Bonde turned to his men, "Aaaahaaan..Ana sema hivi (what he says) …" He translated Raj's words into Kiswahili.

Raj spread out a Pert chart on the ground and held it in place with four stones. He explained to the workers what needed to be erected and showed them photographs of what the tower and station would look like. Everyone nodded and looked at Raj as if he had made a major scientific breakthrough.

Bonde concluded, "Hawa Muhindi akili bora saana (these Indians are intelligent)."

Raj tried to explain the project using the few Swahili words he knew and resorting to sign language when words failed him.

Bonde would translate all this by starting with, "Aaahaaan..ana sema hivi..." but most of the time his translation did not necessarily match with Raj's words. Bonde's army would nod their heads and look at Raj as if he was the creator of the earth. Raj attempted a few witty remarks which Bonde would attempt to narrate while still laughing. The workers would smile in anticipation of the punch line and laugh after Bonde and Raj had finished.

Work began and Raj started developing civil work simultaneously at four sites in a radius of a hundred kilometres. However poor and underdeveloped, Tanzania is not lacking when it comes to well-implemented rules at the grass roots level. Raj had to get through a lot of paperwork to install a tower on a farm. If the sale of land was from one farmer to another, they would execute the sale and hand over a copy of the deed to the village council, which would discuss the matter in a meeting, regularise the transaction and record it in the minutes of the meeting.

A meeting of the village leaders was called to regularise the non-agricultural use of land, such as Tancell's plans. Raj had to pay 'transport and tea' to each attending member, because the meeting was specially convened for Tancell. Everyone took the money although each person had walked from their home, did not drink anything or order water during the meeting.

After a few days, another meeting was held at the ward level and council members from various villages in the jurisdiction of the ward attended. Raj had to again give money to each person. He and Bonde were also invited so that the council members could ask them questions. The meeting was attended by a chairman, a secretary and executives from the environment, school, development and dispensary departments. Women were also represented in the meeting by a member, as was the teaching community.

Starting from the Chairman and his secretary every member of the ward got up and introduced him or herself. Bonde and Raj also introduced themselves to the group. Various members started asking questions though half-heartedly.

Someone asked, "What does the tower do?"

Raj started on a technical answer when Bonde got up and said, "You know simu ya upepo (radio. Simu means phone, upepo means air)? Like the towers for those gadgets, this tower brings waves for simu ya mkononi (hand phone or mobile phone). Like the TV tower brings TV pichaa (picture)."

Everybody nodded.

"So now things come from the tower. Can they bring electricity like that?"

The chairman was very impressed by this technical question. He looked at Raj with a beaming smile. Raj did not know how to answer that but Bonde was quick enough.

"Let's first bring simu then we shall see about umeme (electricity)."

One youngster got up, "These phones will be used more by kampuni (companies) and serekali (government) because they talk a lot." This elicited a lot of smiles. "But what is the use for us? Will it be free?" the youngster asked.

Raj was stunned. Bonde answered slowly, "It will bring development to this area."
"Development by talking! We have been doing that for the past so many years."
The chairman's smile vanished. The youngster was anti-establishment. He was a traitor.

"Ndugu nani (Dear who)? Chale. Let's stick to our subject. This people want to erect tower in small area. Should we allow them? Let us not talk of matters that are above your understanding and mine."

People did not like heated arguments and started talking amongst themselves. One old man remarked, "These youngsters do not want sound or TV but they want Tanzania shilling by air from their towers." Amidst laughter the chairman concluded the meeting without asking people for their opinion.

"Haya Jamaani (okay folks). If we are together, then let us invite this investor by clapping." Everybody clapped.

The third and last meeting was convened for the wananchi, general public, and their leaders. Raj's attention was drawn towards two old men who seemed to be at least eighty years old. They were waze-e wa busara (old men of wisdom). Raj was wondering what role they would play in the meeting. After the introduction, Bonde got up and explained their objective. The site, which was on a hill, was a grazing area and there was no farm there. Raj and Bonde thought that by declaring a liberal $100 contribution to the village and $10 tips to the chairman and secretary, they could walk away with the approval.

But the villagers had a lot of questions.

"The waves from the tower will not create problems for those who stay nearby?"

"You will compensate us only once, but where will our cattle go everyday for grazing?"

Bonde argued, "We need a very small area just like a small room, Bwana, even one lamb will not go hungry."

"How safe it is? What if it falls down?"

One drunk, untidy looking man got up and asked the council leaders, "My question is to the council members not to the wekejazi (investor). I am staying in this village for past… I do not know how many… maybe twenty or thirty years. I still do not know how much spare land our village has. Tomorrow some other company may come. If you give to one, you can't refuse the other. Will there be any land for our cattle to graze or will they call for their meals on mobile phones!"

Everybody started laughing. The man wanted to continue but he was pulled down. Raj and Bonde started feeling anxious.

The chairman got up, "let me answer you, Bwana Nani? (Mr. who)…Enhe-e-e, Ndugu Bakari."

"Do not drink for one day. Have a bath and start walking all around the hill and check how much area we have. Go and ask this question to the young boys who take their cattle for grazing. Next question?"

Bakari was relentless. He got up again. People started laughing again. "You called me in the meeting to ask question. So I am asking you. Okay I give up my first question because you don't like it. But I have second question. You can't stop me."

The chairman looked at his secretary; they decided to let the man go ahead.

"Kwa fupi (briefly)," the chairman cautioned.

Bakari said, "Asante, mwenye kiti (thank you, chairman). My second question is that these people will put up a tower and the tower will give them so many customers. Every year they will make more and more money. What will we get? My neighbour may get a beautiful wife but how will I benefit?"

Some youngsters started clapping.

Bonde got up laughing, "Ndiyo (really). Bwana Bakari you are very right. If my neighbour gets a beautiful wife, what is my gain? Trust me, your wife will start looking after you well."

People started joking about Bwana Bakari's concerns.

"The company will give a good amount to the village council."

"But that these council members will enjoy. Not me. Not wananchi."

By now Bakari had many supporters. The chairman was furious at the allegations.

"Our salary comes from the government. Who built the primary school? Who painted the dispensary? That is village council money. Not my personal money."

There was silence. Tanzanians, by nature, do not like too many arguments, even if it is for their own good. Some people started shouting, "Give up, wewe, Bakari!" Bakari got up and went away. But his question was to be minuted and concluded meaningfully. Katibu, the secretary pointed out. The chairman looked around and saw that the council members were arguing amongst themselves. Bonde looked at Raj impatiently.

The chairman invited the waza-e wa busara to speak. "Silence, Jamaani. Let's have opinion from these, Waze-e. Mzee karibu (welcome sirs)."

One old man asked. "I want to ask this investor. This tower will also have some machines and fencing and wire and some room."

Bonde said, "Yes, yes. Even a generator will be running the entire day, as there is no power nearby."

"So you will need someone to guard your towers and things around?"

"Yes, yes."

"Why do you not employ our youth?"

Raj nodded immediately. Bonde said, "Good idea!"

"You give one year's salary to the council, every year, in advance. The council will put one person from each house on duty for one month, so everybody will benefit."

Everybody nodded at this and the chairman was all smiles again.

"Na shukuru mzee (I am thankful to you sir) I think it is a good suggestion. E-e-e-n h-e-e-n, Jamaani. Tuko pamoja (are we together)?"

Everybody agreed. The minutes of the meeting were written and each person signed. After the people had left, one council member apologised to Raj for the 'misbehaviour of that drunkard'.

Just as Raj and Bonde were leaving, a council member brought the two old men to their car and asked them to drop the men home. Raj obliged willingly. Raj asked Bonde softly, "Where do these old men come from? How far, I mean?"
Bonde asked them, they could not answer how many kilometres away they lived, but said that they started walking at 6.30 am and reached the meeting at 10.
"Do they get paid for attending?"
Bonde asked them in Kiswahili. They just smiled and did not answer.
"How do they go back if there is no car?"
"They start homewards at three in the afternoon and reach home before it gets too dark."
Raj was aghast. He failed to understand where the motivation lay.
They would just get a ball of cooked maize dough called ugali in the afternoon. He felt really bad and gave them some money when they got off. They were happy and thanked him profusely.
Raj wondered, "So little money for a lifetime of invaluable wisdom!"

***

Raj went to the nearest town, 120 miles away, to buy building materials, make phone calls to Zuly and his relatives in India and get the dog vaccinated in a government veterinary dispensary. Poto bought grocery, cassettes to play in his pick-up and some medicines.

Bonde and his colonel Jumma took over the execution of work on the main site and would visit other sites and give the leaders there instructions. Raj would also visit all the sites and check the progress of construction.

Mama Rose recruited some boys from the nearby villages to get milk, vegetables, eggs and poultry to the site where Raj stayed. She would always keep chai (tea) ready for Raj when he returned from long trips or took a break from work. She would serve him roasted peanuts or dry toast in the evening with tea and fresh fruit for dinner. As if she was wired to Raj's mind, she would bring water just when he felt like having it, in a clean and pretty china plate holding the glass and bottle. Raj would sometimes just take the bottle and have a big gulp, spilling a lot of it on his chest to her amusement. Later, she would tell this to the fellow workers and laugh.

Raj acknowledged her dedication and would spend time talking with her in the evening. He talked about India and learnt a few Kiswahili words. He had only one problem, while she cleaned his room, did the bed or swabbed the floor; he could not enter the room because of her wide body. He would look at her huge wobbling buttocks and feel awkward standing there.

One day, Raj brought a cake from town and declared that a small ceremony would be held to name the dog that had by now regained some fur. Its wounds had healed and it now looked active and lively. Rose put some nyama (meat) in the rice and made green salad. Soft drinks crates were bought from the village. While having dinner, Raj asked Bonde to ask his people to suggest a Kiswahili name for the dog.

Somebody said, 'Juma tatu (Monday)' because he was found on Monday.

"Simba (Lion)."

"Clinto-on."

Poto turned to the Profesaa.

"Profesaa, wipi (what)?"

"We have to first see whether he is an English dog or Tanzanian or chotara (mix breed)."

Everybody shouted together, "ndiyo-o-o (correct)."

The chorus was typical of the people whenever Profesaa would utter a few words. Some would shout in a high-pitched voice, some nasally, some in a simian or bovine way. The Profesaa would smile and continue with whatever he had to say.

"Name also depends on how you want to use him. Mistaa Raji keeps him like familia (family). We want him to be askari (watchman). So let's decide all this first."

To this someone muttered, "Leave the Profesaa alone." Someone started barking like dog.

Suddenly, Mama Rose walked into the centre of the group and said she wanted to say something. Everyone clapped, cheered and shouted karibu-es (welcome). She said she had noticed that whenever the dog was called, he would wag his tail huku-huku (from here to here), she indicated this by putting her hands on her buttocks and shaking her hips from side to side.

"Whenever you give him food…huku-huku, whenever you shout…huku-huku."

Poto interrupted, "whenever he sees Mama Rose…huku-huku."

He danced around Rose and they slammed their hips together.

Rose summed up, "Hence, the name should be Huku-Huku."

The crowd christened the dog Huku. Raj put a cap on Huku's head and escorted him to the centre. Huku was shy and overwhelmed by the crowd's attention. He was walking reluctantly beside Raj. The cake was placed in the centre. Raj grabbed the knife and one of Huku's paws and cut the cake. The first piece was offered to him, the second to Mr. Bonde, then to Raj and finally everyone got a piece. Some village songs were chanted in a shrill voice, buckets were used as drums and the workers danced in a circle shaking their hips- huku, huku. Huku simply wagged his tail.

Tearing a fried chicken leg with his teeth, Bonde asked, "Mistaa Raji, what happened to our chori case. Any news?"

"The judge did not come for three days as he was sick. Then he gave bail to everybody except the turnboys. The next date is after one month. Still the public prosecutor has not framed the charges."

"Now you just see. There will be dates after dates. Our material will slowly-slowly disappear from the police station. After few years even if we win the case, you will find nothing. If I had left the truck there, I would get only a rusted frame after few years as scrap."

"Good, you reminded me. I will have to call up our advocate soon. He wanted us both to appear in the court."

Finally, the generator was switched off, leaving the wide open starry sky to bear down on them. The glow of the bonfire and sweating, shining bodies made the night exotic. Raj felt as if he was back in the Stone Age.

Chapter 5: Success at last

The rains delayed work. The tower assembly arrived late. Bad roads and unreliable transporters added to Raj's woes. There were minor thefts at a few sites. One worker's group was mixing less cement, adding more sand and selling the remaining cement. Raj was restless and worried. Zuly was getting impatient and insulting. Some masons suffered from malaria. Karimji was hospitalised for high blood pressure. Raj wanted to visit him but the incomplete work and Zuly's behaviour discouraged him.

Raj's parents were doing well, but they were missing him. While talking to them, he felt guilty that he had ignored their wishes and left them. Leena and Vicky were still talking about job vacancies in Mumbai. Raj felt that he would never have a peaceful life. Why was everything going wrong with him even in the jungle?

In the beginning, he would laugh at any kind of incompetence or at lethargic workers by joking about it. Gradually, under stress, Raj started losing his temper, becoming sombre and frustrated.

In Kiswahili they say - *Sikuya kufa nyani miti yote huteleza.*

The day a monkey is destined to die, all trees become slippery.

Sometimes, he would share his problems with Bonde or Poto. Bonde continued to cheer him up. He would use all the superlatives in his vocabulary and say that Raj was doing something very difficult and yet he was very fast, very successful. He wished Bonde were his boss instead of Zuly.

Late in the evening, once the generator was switched off, Raj would place a chair outside his quarters and strum a few chords in the cool breeze. His only listener would be Huku, who would constantly watch Raj. Occasionally, he would sleep with his head on Raj's feet.

During the day, Raj would be very busy, he would travel to surrounding regions to carry out procedures to accquire land for future installations. Poto was his interpreter. Soon Raj developed a knack of getting along with bureaucrats and getting things done. The country had a very small population and was one of the least developed. There were no queues, no prior appointments required and he was always treated well. People were simple and plain about their needs. Their expectations were meagre.

A Tanzanian's Shangri-La, when he retires, would consist of a small house with a little backyard wherein he would plant a couple of papaya trees and a small patch of mchicha (spinach). He would tend one or two cows and a few hens to take care of his needs for milk, eggs and meat.

Finally, the very first tower was nearing completion. The control room was ready as were the fences and main gate. The ground had been levelled.

It was late in the evening; people were trying to fix the last assembly. It was dangling high in the air from a powerful pulley block. A few people were just under it, standing on a makeshift platform. They were manoeuvring the ropes and slowly moving the conical tip of the tower to its right place. Bonde was impatient after working hard through the day to complete the tower.

Everyone's patience had been stretched to the limit. Raj looked pale and worried. The workers were taking too long to disentangle the chains and arrange them in the pulley. The pulley was squeaky and wobbled. The chain slots were worn out. Despite Raj's persistent reminders, Bonde had not bought a new pulley.

Suddenly, a rope slid out of one pulley. The entire structure slipped down three feet. The workers had a hard time holding on to the other ropes.

The structure swung a little and crashed into the main tower. A loud metallic gong reverberated through the site, like a huge bell ringing in a cathedral.

Some workers lay down on the platform; some hung on like monkeys from below the platform; those who were on the ground simply disappeared. This included mighty ones like Bonde and Poto too. Raj was frozen to the ground, looking up.

Huku's incessant barking stirred Raj. He started shouting orders. The workers on the platform regained their senses. The conical top was slowly lowered to the ground. A few people laughed nervously.

First, one of the team leaders narrated the whole story with actions and sound effects. "I was slowly pulling it up...kikikiki...he said take it on right...then..fffaappp..rope came down..then...taaannnngg sound...I was shaking...tikitikitiki..."

After a while, people were taking a break in small groups. Each one had someone narrating the same story with identical action and sound.

When everyone had settled down, Poto asked the unusually silent Profesaa.

'Profesaa, wipi?'

"We should ask how they are erecting such big-big towers in other countries like Dubai, India, Ulaya (Britain)."

"Ndiyo-o-o-o."

Poto agreed, "Really, Bwana. Let us ask Mistaa Raji."

"Secondly, instead of making one big tower, they should go for two small towers at shorter distance for safety of people."

Someone shouted, "Ina maana (that means), a whore should sleep with two young boys rather than one man."

Everybody burst into laughter. Professa grinned. His theory of relativity (of towers) had triggered a chain reaction in the crowd.

The next day, Bonde decided a celebration was called for. Raj wanted to invite Zuly to inaugurate the very first Tancell tower. He also wanted to visit the ailing Karimji. Bonde would take a day to clean up the site and make it tidy. He wanted a day more to decorate the place and make arrangements for food, chairs and music.

Raj left for Dar early in the morning in the pick-up with Poto and Huku. He reached Zuly's house in the evening. The dusty, rugged pick-up entered the lush green compound and circled a tiny pond. Raj parked the vehicle, patted Huku and asked Poto to wait. He found Karimji sitting in the veranda of the palatial house with the whole family. Raj was looking dusty and untidy.

Karimji was sitting in the wheelchair. His eyes opened wide and gleamed when he saw Raj. "Oh! Raj...Beta aav (come)."
Raj asked, "How are you uncle? Pole-saana (very sorry for your ill health)."
Somebody offered him a chair, but Raj preferred to sit on the ground next to Karimji holding on to the old man's hand.
"How is your project?"
"I have come to invite you to inaugurate the very first Tancell tower."
"Great. You did it finally, Raj. You know my condition. But I would love to come."
Zuly arrived, "Oh, Raj! How come you're here?"
"Tancell's first tower is ready. We are celebrating the day after. We want you to inaugurate."
"You must be joking. Raj, there are 21 more towers and then I will inaugurate the Tancell network countrywide. Take a few tins of beer from Dar, Bonde does not drink. He is a Moslem like me. You drink them off and pack off to the next site the day after. You know how late we are."
Everyone was taken aback at Zuly's cold words.

Gratitude of a donkey is a kick - Fadhila ya punda ni mateke.

"Mr. Zuly, the beginning is always small. When a baby is born it is small and beautiful and then it grows up to become a complete human being. It is never born big. We always celebrate the birth every year, not his personal milestones or achievements every year," said Raj.

The women smiled approvingly, Karimji also liked the answer and smiled. Zuly's mother agreed with Raj, "He is yet to find a girl to marry but still he is talking about a baby's birthday celebration."

Zuly's wife asked, "Where is the place? Is it very far?"

Karimji declared his wish to go. But still, Zuly refused and Raj left the house.

The next day, Raj returned to the site. The place was decorated with balloons and confetti brought from the town 120 miles away.

Bonde asked, "Is tajiri (owner) coming?"

"No," said Raj.

"Why?"

"He will come when we finish all 22 towers."

"He should have come. He is making a mistake. Even if it is a small job, no other maneja did it. It looks simple when you sit in Dar but when you come here and work, you will know how difficult it is."

"True," Raj sighed.

Bonde tried to comfort Raj.

"That's why they are tajiri, Bwana! Don't w-u-ori Mistaa Raji. We are going to celebrate bam-bam (perfectly well)."

In the evening, the music was turned on and everyone had dressed for the party. The workers had taken a bath and the women had applied jelly cream on their body and seemed to be shining.

A few people were dancing and the first round of drinks had started. Raj was happy just watching everyone have fun. He wished Karimji could have come.

A popular Congo song started. Poto pulled Mama Rose to the centre and they started dancing together to everyone's cheers.

Bonde pulled Raj to his feet. "Mistaa Raji, let's dance."

"No...no, I do not know," Raj spluttered, but no one was listening to him. He had no choice but to imitate the moves of those around him.

While dancing, Bonde said to Raj, "Tajiri should have come. Today is a big day, Bwana."

Raj smiled, "Didn't you say he is tajiri, because he is not sentimental?"

"Ha, ha. You remember it well."

They saw a small cloud of dust moving towards them. A gleaming Toyota Hiace van was approaching the site. People stopped dancing and watched the van as it pulled to a stop near the gate. The gate was opened by the watchman and the vehicle cruised to a smooth stop near the workers. The driver stepped down and on the other side someone else got down as well.

"Who is that?" asked Bonde.

The driver opened the rear door. Raj saw Karimji, seated on a wheelchair, smile and wave at him. Raj ran to the van.

His eyes turned moist. He helped escort Karimji. Everyone started clapping and shouting. They gathered around him and bowed as he passed each person and a few men shook hands with him.

The music was turned down low and Poto announced Karimji's arrival. He thanked him profusely for having come to their party in spite of ill health. Poto cheered,

"Tajiri oye."

"Oye-e-e," the crowd replied.

"Baba (father) oye-e."

"Oye-e-e."

"Tancell oye."

"Oye-e-e."

Although Zuly had not come, his children and younger sister had come and had joined the dancers.

Karimji said, "Good job Raj, You will make it. Tancell is born now." Karimji looked up at the tower and was lost in the sky on the wings of his memories. He remembered how he had inherited a small hardware shop from his father. He savoured memories of his career, his major customers, his peers, his struggles in Africa. He felt proud to have progressed from a mere shop owner to a 'high-tech' business owner. Bonde, Juma, Poto and the other workers waited to have a few words with Karimji. They were all full of praise for Raj.

Karimji left after half an hour to rest at the nearest hotel. He could not say much about how good he felt but conveyed his feelings through his eyes and smile.

***

Site clearance started at three places simultaneously in the northern and western regions. Zuly had ordered pre-fabricated structures from Dubai on Raj's suggestions and Karimji's requests. Bonde increased his manpower to erect four towers simultaneously.

Arusha, a cool, not very crowded town was located near the north-western border. It was well-known, since Africa's largest mountain, Mount Kilimanjaro, was to its west and the famous Serengeti wildlife sanctuary to its east.

It was planned that a mobile switching centre (MSC) would be installed in Arusha along with a back service centre to cater to the northern regions and those along the border with Kenya.

As the workload increased, Bonde's team worked with more and more enthusiasm. One day, Bonde asked for a few minutes of Raj's time. "Mistaa Raji!"

"Yes, Bwana Bonde."

"If you have extra money, there is a good chance for investimenti!"

"What?" Raj was surprised. Bonde was talking like an Indian.

"Minister for land is my close friend. They are going to make Bagamoyo a free port. I have bought a piece of land there. After a few years, the price will go up when it is a free port. Now it is very cheap. You can buy a football field in just 10,000 dollars."

"How many football fields did you buy?"

Bonde smiled, "Only one Bwana. If this work goes well, I will investi more and more. It is a good chance, Mistaa Raji. You get your money from India. Borrow from your father for just two or three years. You will be rich man. Minister is from same region. Elections are coming. He wants to be in power again. So he will declare free port. I give you guarantee Bwana!"

Raj laughed, but shook his head.

"Tell me what can go wrong."

"This government will lose in Zanzibar. The ruling party will find it very tough to win an election in Zanzibar. For many years, they have promised a free port in Zanzibar. If they do it in Bagamoyo, they will be thrown out of power in Zanzibar and they will demand a separate nation."

Bonde looked worried on hearing this and looked at Juma and his son for support. Poto agreed with Raj and explained further 'Ana sema hivi….' He translated Raj's logic. Their faces became pale. He told them in the end, "Muhindi knows our politics well."

Raj's logical perspective shook Bonde's dog-like faith in Raj. It hit him like a bad nightmare and he wished fervently that it was wrong. For a few moments they did not know how to prove Raj wrong.

Bonde smiled feebly at Raj and said, "You just see!" He left with his deputies. They were confused. They were busy arguing on various possibilities.

In Kiswahili, there is a saying 'Ndege mjanja hunasa kwenye tundu bofu,' (A smart bird will end up in a trap)

Chapter 6: First Attempt

A visit to Arusha's government officials and donor-funded agencies was next on the agenda. Raj decided to take Poto with him. On the drive there, Raj realised that he would pass by Mount Kilimanjaro. He had not had the privilege of seeing it yet. Poto and Raj talked during the journey about all kinds of things from girls to family traditions; road accidents to bandits.

Poto asked, "Bossi, how many girlfriends you have in India?"

"Three or four maybe."

"Kuna (any) special one?"

"Yes, one."

"How much special?"

"Indian special is different from African special."

"'Special' is 'special' Bwana. Everywhere. Bossi, I agree that you are good with your work, maybe also with money, but when you want to be mapenzi (lover), please consult me."

Raj asked Poto, "Okay, tell me how to be a good mapenzi?"

"There is no textbook. Where is the girl? Show me, then I will tell you."

"That one crossing the road."

Poto pulled over close to a woman standing at the side of the road. "Haalo, habari (how are you)?"

"Fine." she replied, politely answering Poto's enquiries about her health. Poto asked for directions to a town they had already passed by. The woman was surprised and told him that he had come too far and that he should go back.

They talked some more and Poto told her that he was having a problem with his vehicle and couldn't go back. He needed to stay somewhere till the next morning. The woman had caught on and smiled. Poto asked her if he could stay in her house.

She laughed and said, "Uliza Baba yangu (ask my father)."

Poto jumped at the invitation, said "Let's go. Get into the vehicle."

Raj did not know what to do, he felt uncomfortable listening to this exchange. He tapped Poto's head and pointed towards the main road.

"Mapenzi, drive there or I'll throw you out of the car," Raj said firmly. Poto waved at the girl. She waved back giving Poto a broad smile as he drove away. "Bossi, today was Day One. Always remember – *Cheleva, cheleva utakuta toto sio yako.*"

"What does that mean?"

Poto answered, *"If you delay too much, your wife will have someone's child!"*

After sometime, Poto pointed out of the window, "Bossi, Kilimanjaro."

"Where?" asked Raj, he looked at where Poto was pointing, but it was a cloudy day. There were a few hills on the horizon, but they didn't seem to be too big.

"Where is it? That one?"

"No, there... look behind that big tree... kule juu (there up)."

The sky was sparsely filled with clouds in the direction that Poto was pointing to. He could see some distant hills on the horizon and tried to figure out which one could be the mount.

Suddenly, Raj's eyes found a mountain peak way above the clouds. Mount Kilimanjarowas above the clouds. It looked as if it had just finished spewing lava and the smoke had gathered like clouds around its neck. It was standing like a monarch surrounded by an army of clouds.

Raj exclaimed, "Oh, my..." It was magnificent. Raj stopped the car and stood looking at the mount in silence.

But for an occasional vehicle passing by, there was no sound. Poto made his way through the bushes to relieve himself. He came back and sat inside the car, banging the door as if the sight of Kili meant nothing special to him.

Kili mesmerised Raj. A mountain that stuck its neck out. A mountain that clouds could surround, but not conquer. A mountain that proudly holds its head high in the sky, above the clouds. During his childhood, Raj had drawn pictures of two mountains resting side by side, a river flowing through the valley and one or two motley clouds and a sun blazing in all glory, well above the mountains.

Raj now wondered if his art teacher would have accepted a painting of the Mount Kilimanjaro, a mountain above the clouds. How would the world look from up there?

It had been standing there for millions of years, holding its head above the clouds watching mother earth changing her colours. Towns and more towns came up. Roads and bridges were built around it, part of the earth's skin was bleached and farms were laid out. But for Kili they were still not noticeable. It was like a colony of ants in one's house. Nature is huge. Kili was a giant.

Raj had an urgent desire to climb the behemoth. He had lost too many battles in his life. He was unhappy with his mediocre self. He wanted to prove his worth to himself. He wanted to do something extraordinary and hold his head high, like Mount Kilimanjaro, in front of his parents, friends and the world. Kili was not as difficult as Everest, but it was still the fifth largest mountain in the world and many people had died trying to conquer it. It would be a feat. If not anybody else, he would at least respect himself.

"Bossi, you like it very much?"

"Yes, I want to climb it."

"I cannot."

"Let's go." Raj was silent. He was brooding about his life again and kept looking at Kili for as long as he could.

Raj stayed in Arusha for a week. One evening, they drove down to Moshi, a town close to Mount Kilimanjaro. Poto took Raj and a friend to a popular pub.

It being a holiday, the band was playing the current favourite music. Poto, as usual, was in his mapenzi mood. He had his eye fastened on two unescorted girls in the pub. The girls were also interested in Poto and his friend. Raj turned to look at them; one girl was breathtakingly beautiful. She was slim, slightly fair and her sharp features indicated her Arab or Asian heritage.

Poto and his friend got on to the dance floor. The girls also got up; Raj liked the music and was beating his foot in time to the rhythm. Poto got talking with the girls and very soon they were all dancing together. Raj could not take his eyes off the girl for long. She seemed to be watching him too. Beer was flowing. Bartenders were running around like fire tenders.

The singer of the band was trying to get Raj to join the dance. Raj smiled and shook his head, but the singer would not take 'no' for an answer.

He called out on the mike, "Haaloo... Mistaa nani (who)... Mistaa Muhindi (Indian) ...njoo (come) Bwana... come and dance..." The crowd started chanting the words 'come and dance'. The crowd cheered.

Raj had no choice but to get up. He went over to the band and took a guitar and started playing in tune with the rest of the band. The singer stopped crooning into the mike and danced for about five minutes. The rest of the band seemed to take their lead from Raj and pretty soon the crowd were on their feet, having a great time. An Indian playing African tunes for a dancing crowd was an impossible sight. Poto was calling out, 'Bossi, bossi', with great pride and telling everyone that Raj was 'rafiki yangu (my friend)'. After a few more minutes, Raj handed the guitar back to the band, but the singer would not let go of him. Raj stayed on the stage, swaying to the music and clapping to the beat.

Once the song was over, the singer asked Raj to sing. Raj obliged by singing a popular Kiswahili song, mostly relying on his chords. People shouted and laughed at his pronunciation, and sometimes Raj would fill in words he did not know with 'lalala' or 'naninani', but these words had meanings in Kiswahili, 'lalala' was the word for 'sleep' and 'naninani' meant 'who'. The crowd laughed and applauded. A few people took out money, circled it around Raj's head thrice and put it in his pocket. One middle-aged lady enjoying a drink with her husband went over to Raj and gave him money while shaking her body in front of him.

Raj finally bowed and started walking back to his table. Poto drew him to his group and introduced the girls. The one whom Raj liked was Salome and her friend was Tunu. Both of them knew English well. Poto introduced Raj, "My bossi, Mistaa Raji. He is my rafiki saana."

Raj watched Salome closely. She had curly hair that she had left loose; her broad smile broke into a laugh easily, revealing perfect small teeth. Her eyes were her most beautiful feature. Her thick eyelashes and thin brows gave the impression of unparalleled loveliness. She had a slim frame and delicate bodyline. Nature had not been stingy when it came to endowing her chest and hips.

While taking breaks between dances, the youngsters exchanged important personal information. After a while, Raj declared that he would like to relax with a drink and looked at Salome expectantly. She understood his unspoken request and walked away with him. Poto and Tunu were dancing relentlessly as if they were in a gym.

Salome was well educated, inquisitive, and smart. She belonged to the learned, business-oriented Chaga tribe. They got along very well. They did not once feel like strangers. She was a school teacher and taught social studies.

Raj and Salome seemed to hit it off really well; soon they were talking to each other about things they never shared with anyone else.

"I want to climb Kili tomorrow," Raj declared.

Salome smiled, "Are you serious?"

"Yes, yes, why? You think I can't make it?"

She shrugged her shoulders, and said, "The way you sang and played music here, you may do anything!"

"Oh, thanks. You liked it?"

"Yes, very much," she said. "How long have you been in Tanzania?"

"Um… a few months."

"How do you like the people here?"

"Good, friendly, I enjoy dealing with them."

"You do not miss your country?"

"My country misses me!"

She laughed.

Poto, Tunu and his friend joined them and ordered food. Soon after dessert they parted from the girls.

Poto said, "Bossi, people liked you very much. You are a hero. Even these girls..."

"I am going to climb Kili tomorrow, you want to join?"

"Me? I am very tired, but I will drop you."

"No. I'll manage. Marangu (entry) Gate is not too far away."

Poto wished him good night and asked, "Bossi, you liked that girl?"

"Yes. Good for friendship, but nothing special... African special... Good night. Keep all the girls for your dreams."

The next morning, Raj walked to the entrance of the Kili trail. Mountaineering gear and guides were available there and many tourists were waiting to start their climb. Raj would not be able to see the peak until he made his way through eight kilometres of thick forests. Raj chose a guide and started his ascent.

The first landmark, after a strenuous journey, was Mandara. The road was covered with shrubs and trees. Except for the sound of streams and a few birds, it was very quiet. Only a few sunrays could make their way through the thick green canopy. A few monkeys were seen occasionally but they were high above them jumping from tree to tree.

Raj started panting; he still had a long way to go. He realised that he was still struggling to reach the top, while several tourists he had seen at the gate were on their way back down. They seemed to be well-equipped for the trip, with ski sticks in each hand and a bottle of water or energy drinks. Porters with kerosene stoves, groceries, food, tents and other camping gear, followed them.

Raj wondered if he could spend the night in some hotel on the way up and complete the climb the next day. The guides had started giving him information only after they were sure that Raj would walk for at least half a day thus ensuring a $10 minimum porter charge.

Raj still had a reservoir of enthusiasm to draw on and forged ahead. They stopped for a while every now and then, but Raj did not want to quit.

Their pace slackened. Raj stopped talking. His endurance had been severely tested. Competitive pressure (to complete the climb) and thought of time and distance pervaded over the mood of excitement and enjoyment. He struggled for another three kilometres and reached a clearing in the forest. It was a relief to see the open sky after such a long time. A few other tourists were occupying the ancient wooden benches and tables.

Each group of climbers was accompanied by one guide, one assistant guide, one cook, and six or more porters. Raj was thirsty and hungry. There were no hotels, not even roadside vendors. He was looking around him and cursing everyone silently for not sharing their food with him. He wished they would suffer from a painful stomach.

He asked his guide, "How far is Mandara?"

"Four kilometers."

"Is the route similar to the one we have come over?"

"Yes."

"Any hotel there?"

"No. It is like a dormitory or hut."

Raj realised that if he decided to go back, it would be evening by the time he got down. "We are going back," he said sadly.

The guide was only too happy. As such, he was not very keen to slog further with an unequipped Raj.

Raj started his descent. He thought it was an experience inevitable before making it to the top. Standing above the clouds was not so easy. It required planning, training, equipment and a back-up team of porters, guides and cooks. It was not merely a fun trip as he thought.

Kili was wonderful. He wanted to enjoy it like a butterfly or a small bird that flies from tree to tree without bothering about distance and time. Instead, he was required to be a hawk, concerned about what was distant rather than fascinated by what was close. A hawk would first fly high, look for the target or objective, observe it, get closer, and grab it.

This reminded him of any other endeavour in his mundane world where competition and objectivity would replace fun and excitement.

Enterprise was important, not entertainment. What could have been an enjoyable excursion turned out to be a failed mission.

Raj felt hurt. Though none of his bosses of the past and present were around, he felt as if he had fallen in their eyes. The odour of mediocrity engulfed him. He resolved to fight back. He decided to prepare well for the next time and scale the peak. He consoled and reassured himself that someday he would rise above the clouds, rise in his own esteem.

Next morning, Poto, as if certain that Raj would not have made it, came to the hotel.

"Bossi, wipi... Kili?"

"Next time. It is not a one-day job."

"Just take one pichaa (photograph) and be happy. Why take trouble to climb, Bwana?"

To Raj, it sounded like mockery, although he knew that Poto was innocent.

"I will give you a pichaa of Tunu, so when you see her in a bar next time, don't talk to her or dance with her, just look at her pichaa tu (only)."

Poto laughed. "Aa Bwana! You are comparing mlima (hill) with msichana (girl). One is dead, other is sexy! You climb on mlima, me... on gael (girl)."

Chapter 7: When it rains...

Raj was spending some time wandering in the market place in Moshi. He found a telephone booth and decided to call his friends in India. As soon as he stepped out, he was nudged by Poto, "Can you see them? Our new friends!"

They saw Salome and Tunu talking to a garment seller. Raj was reluctant to approach them. He was not sure how they would react. Before he could make a move, Tunu saw them. She waved and spoke to Salome. Salome turned around and smiled. She was wearing black capris and a sleeveless pink top. Poto started walking towards them.

Raj said, "You go, I am coming."

He pretended to be interested in the locally made artefacts displayed in a small shop beside him. In moments, Poto and the girls were beside him, Raj greeted them and they went into a hotel. They ordered drinks and chatted about the night in the pub. Raj would not look at the girls for too long, preferring to look at his drink rather than stare at the girls like Poto was shamelessly doing. But Salome was watching Raj intently. Raj's clothes, his style, his accent, his expression, his smile... she noticed everything. Raj invited them to his hotel for dinner.

Salome prepared for the date by going to the beauty parlour. She changed her hairstyle to a ponytail. Since she did not have long hair, she could manage only a

'Doberman tail'. She liked Raj and was quite infatuated with him. She wished she could go on meeting Raj and enjoy his company.

She was not bothered about the future or the usual logical parental reasoning that should precede but always follows an affair. Like a true African, she lived for the moment and strove to enjoy it.

When it rains, do not bother about where the water flows after hitting the ground, just bathe in the rain and enjoy the moment.

Do not worry about how long it would last or what will you do with wet cloths on. Just bathe! There will be shivers. There will be sneezes. One craves for warmth. One feels the need to be cuddled and wrapped.

They met in the evening. Raj started the conversation by asking the girls about their families. He ordered a sweet lime soda for himself. Salome opted for Fanta. Poto looked at both of them disapprovingly and said, "Bossi is treating us today so let's drink beer or whisky. Soda we can always buy from our pockets."

He went to the wine counter with Tunu and sat there. Raj and Salome were left alone. They chatted about their day.

"Could you climb Kili?" she asked.

Raj just shook his head shyly and confessed, "It was a flop. But I shall try next time after preparing for it."

She told him about what he needed to do to climb Kili. How people die climbing due to altitude sickness. They talked about their lives, parents, their jobs, nature, and their own good and bad memories.

They were lost in their conversation. When people get along well, energy, not just the words, flows. They do not have to hunt for a common topic. They just talk endlessly. Salome asked Raj how she could get in touch with him. Raj offered her his card, "The card gives my Dar office numbers. Whenever, I go to the nearby town, once every week or 15 days, I call up people."

She gave her number and said softly, "Raji, can we be good friends?"

Raj was slightly taken aback at the question, "Yes, why not? We are... are we not?"

"No... what I mean is, people remain friends as long as they meet or they are in the same place... but once they separate... the friendship fades away..."

"True... but let's give it a try."

"How often will you come to Moshi?"

"Well, when I come to climb Kili, around Christmas. But I may come to Arusha a couple of times before that."

"Promise me that you will let me know whenever you come to Arusha."

"Oh yes, definitely."

Raj realised that although she hardly knew him, Salome was demanding a relationship. He decided that he should behave in such a way that she could not look beyond friendship. But he admitted to himself that he liked her — her confidence, her body language and her simple and plain nature. He could see that she adored him. She was beautiful, her smile was infectious. Her charming smile would tempt you to keep on teasing her.

After two more days, Raj had finished his work in Arusha. Salome called up one day; she wished that Raj could stay on and meet her everyday. Raj left for his work site. She went back to her school. Her lesson was on the evolution of earth and mankind. The discussion in the class went on to different regions and their people. "About 20 million years ago, Arabia was separated from Africa and the rift valley was born. Earth got grass, elephants and horses then. Mankind started in our rift valley about 1.8 million years ago along with large animals, and moved on to upper Africa and moved over to Europe."

"Ma'am! You mean Muzungu (Europeans) are also from Africa?"

"Yes."

"Then, why are they fair? They look different."

"Climate, sunrays," she pointed out.

A boy asked, "Why are they so rich?"

The children laughed, Salome smiled at the student.

"They are rich because they were not happy with what they got in the jungles. They were inquisitive, adventurous and went away from the jungles. They struggled to survive. They learned to farm, to build houses, to wear clothes for protection…"

"How are Maharabu (Arabs)?"

"Nature is very hostile to them. No water, no food, only sand, extreme cold, extreme heat. They moved from place to place, they connected east and west. They became experts in trading. They sold spices and textiles. They sold humans. Now they sell petrol and diesel. Now they are into airlines, they are building big-big cities where people from all over the world come and stay and enjoy the modern city life. This world will not have petrol and diesel after some years. It will have something else. But, money will not be replaced. This world will need money and Maharabus will have money then. They learned to survive by grabbing opportunities."

"And Muhindis (Indians)?"

Salome was surprised. "They are good at computers, finance, management, medicine as professionals."

While talking she felt as if Raj was sitting on the last bench and smiling. She could not describe what he was good at but she found him a good companion.

She fumbled slightly but recovered.

"Every race has its own ability, its own strong points. Any country or society, if it utilises its natural talent well, then it becomes successful and rich."

A boy asked, "Why we are poor compared to them? Why we can't be them?"

Salome smiled again. "We can be them. We are good at sports. Europe is looking for African footballers now. We have nature and wildlife. We can do well in hotels and tourism. We have rich minerals like Arabs have petroleum. We can export minerals. We can be good at agriculture. Our tea, coffee, cotton, cashews and many other crops are imported. We are good at heart. We are good at service. We can serve as good nurses or supporting staff in hospitals. The world needs all kinds of people."

The class was over, but she could not keep Raj out of her mind. She remembered what they had spoken about. She could not stop smiling while walking down the corridor.

Chapter 8: Technical man

Things weren't running smoothly on the sites. Everywhere work was stuck either for want of material, equipment or technical information. Zuly had already asked Hans to visit the sites and activate four towers on trial. Raj tried sorting out the mess. The Dubai-made assemblies started arriving at all the sites after being held at the port due to congestion. Raj had to visit all the sites within a week, with Bonde or Poto, Rose and Huku. Heavy rains, malaria and a shortage of material were severely slowing down the pace, but thankfully, the workers were as hard-working as could be hoped.

Raj made use of his simple Pert chart for each work site and started chasing critical activities. He would share his priorities with Bonde and his team. Huku would follow Raj like a shadow and lie down on the ground flat like a crocodile when Raj would stop or sit somewhere. Sometimes Raj would get up from his chair and call Bonde and his masons or welders for some work. They would make a semi circle around Raj. Raj would spread out a sheet of paper on the ground or take a small twig or a stick and draw a sketch on the soil. At these times, Huku would simply get up to sit next to Raj. Sometimes he would push his nose ahead to the smell the sheet or the stick in Raj's hand as if enquiring about the drawing, much to the crowd's delight.

One day, Poto, got into an argument with his father after Raj raised a point about their technical deviation from the drawing. Bonde defended himself by pointing to Huku,

"Look, Bwana, technically you are just like him. He is still better. When he does not know anything, he does not bark."

The workers hid their face behind each other's shoulders and silently laughed as they were scared of Poto. Poto was fuming and walked away.

Raj said, "No, Mr. Bonde, but when it comes to chasing females, Poto is better than Huku." Ferocious Bonde's face underwent a transformation; his cheeks blew up like balloons, his eyeballs popped out and he laughed out loud.

As usual, he turned to his army and General said 'Anasema hivi (what he says)..' and he narrated Raj's comment in Kiswahili. Since the general was laughing, the army also laughed. Poto also overheard Raj's comments and smiled reluctantly.

Raj looked at the Profesaa standing at the edge of the crowd, "wipi, Profesaa!"

People were pleasantly surprised that now Raj also knew Professa well.

After some hesitation, Profesaa said, "Poto should think about marriage."

The crowd shrieked, "ndiyo-o-o."

Poto got back in the fray. "I don't want to marry your daughter, because she will be just like you, Professa."

This comment amused everyone, even the Profesaa was grinning.

"Mistaa Raji, even this dog may have questions but it can not speak, you see!"

Raj forced a smile on his face and said 'Kweli (Really).'

He tactfully shifted away and started talking with Bonde.

After supervising the workers for an hour Bonde drifted away from the work and walked towards Raj.

"Mistaa Raji. You know that storekeeper who was involved in chori, he has tortured his lover with burning cigarette. It is in the newspapers. These people, Bwana, they cheat. They loot money. They do chori. Mahakama (court) does not give punishment. They bribe and escape.

But Mungu (God) is watching. They spend their money on making love with so many ladies. Their own children steal their money. Finally they die of Ukimwi (AIDS)."

Raj added, "Last time the judge came to hear the case, but he was called away to the high court, so he gave new dates and left. Before that, when the prosecutor was framing charges, he said he is not feeling well, so he gave dates to all the cases on hand. People come from far away places. They spend on transport. They lose their daily wages, and they go back without any result. It is frustrating, Bwana."

Bonde asked, "Is it same in India or betaa (better)?"

"Not so bad, but still it takes years to complete the case. There, judges are far more responsible but advocates are the culprits. That way, Muzungu (white men) and Maharabu (Arabs) are faster and better."

"Kweli. Mzungu, Bwana, before they do any thing, they write sheria (rules) or procedure. Before you make even a small house, they will make ramani (map). I say!"

**

Raj went to receive Hans. By now Hans had heard about the speed with which Raj had tackled work and he was impressed. He had never expected that he would be back in four months. Raj was always attentive to Hans even if it was a matter relating to electronics or telecommunication; something not related to his civil engineering field. Raj could easily see the change in Hans's attitude.

Hans got the new telecom engineers involved in the work as well. Raj involved himself in any kind of physical work — from handing over tool kits to splicing or lugging a wire or arranging for fags and mineral water for Hans. Soon they became friends and they started eating and drinking together.

After the switching centre at Dar was commissioned, Hans and Raj visited the sites. Hans was happy at the way Raj had organised everything. The power connections and earthing had been carried out correctly; the equipment, tool kits and facilities were all in place and in order. Hans did not need Zuly for any help for the first time. He forgot Raj was a 'civil man' and started teaching him about start-up and debugging procedures.

The equipment had been almost set up. It was already de-cased and kept in a tidy condition. Hans started connecting the power cables. He took Raj's help and also go a newly appointed engineer to complete the work.

He checked the insulation, voltage, the power supply panel, the microwave system circuit and the connection to the generator and in a few hours the centre was ready to start.

Mama Rose brought black coffee for everyone. Hans and Raj took a break. Hans narrated his funny experiences while commissioning the equipment in the past.
"How long will it take now?" Raj asked.
"We are almost done. Yes… oh, microwave antenna! Oh! That will take time."
Anchored to ropes, the antenna disc was being raised up slowly by two men. Hans climbed up along with Raj and two other men and taught them to position the euqipment. The disc was clamped down after a while. The workers were curious. Curiosity mounted. Bonde and his people were going close and watching the proceedings in turn. Someone was peeping from the window. They did not know the subject but every one coming out of the room would meet the group outside and whispered to the others that the Muzungu (white man) was a real Doktaa.

The Professa was looking at the tower and discs intently. Poto asked, "Wipi, Profesaa! What are you looking at?"
"Why have they put both discs facing Dar-es-Salaam?"
"To receive simu (waves) from Dar."
"They should also put more discs in the direction of Mwanza, Dodoma…"
Poto did not have an answer to that, so he went away saying, "Kweli, Bwana."

At long last, Hans Moritz declared, "We are through…"

He pulled out his mobile phone, switched it on, and handed it to Raj. "You just watch this screen. When you get a connectivity bar here, let me know. Okay?"

"Okay." Raj stepped away from the equipment and held the phone a little higher so that the workers surrounding him could also join in the fun. Hans started barking out commands to the engineers.

"Supply on, mode manual."

"Check power supply, LED, okay?"

"Yesaa (yes, sir)."

"CheckDC output, 24V, Okay?"

"Yesaa."

"Connection from DDF to STS?"

"Sawa."

"What?"

"Yesaa."

"Is AC working?"

"Yesaa."

"Check alarm, okay?"

"Yesaa."

"Check antenna, sweep RF feeder. Done?"

"Yesaa."

"Check power on transducer. How many watts?"

"20 watts, saa."

"What?"

Hans rushed over to confirm.

"I knew something like this would happen. It should be 36 watts. We have to replace the trans-receiver."

His declaration had everyone worried. They stood still watching him check all the connections, the process of system integration started. STS switched on. System software was loaded.

Before he could look at Raj, the crowd yelled, "Tume pata (we got it)!" Raj raised his thumb as a symbol of victory. Hans looked at the tiny blip in the bottom corner of the phone screen.

"Now you will see this dot will become a big bar. Okay?"

"Sawa," said Bonde.

Hans switched off the BTS and looked for loose connections. Time passed by. People shuffled their feet, but did not want to go away now. Hans was sweating profusely. After tightening all the connections, Hans switched on the BTS and asked, "Is it big now?"

"Hardly," said Raj.

Hans asked that the power mains be switched off. His assistant switched off the panel as well as the mains. Hans was lost in his thoughts. He started investigating each wire again by pulling it individually. Time was ticking by. People were half dead by now. Mama Rose brought water for Hans and Raj. Finally, they found the problem, a cut in a tiny wire; it was replaced.

This time, Hans switched on the power himself. Since the mains had been switched off, it gave a signal to the generator. The generator started with a sudden roar. People were not expecting this. Workers ran out in alarm, Bonde missed a step and fell down. Juma was right behind him and fell over him as well. They quickly realised what had happened and started laughing. Someone came forward and helped Bonde and Juma get up. Bonde was laughing uncontrollably.

Hans went to the mains and switched on the mains. Normal power resumed. The gen-set stopped.

As usual, Bonde turned to the laughing crowd and started narrating his side of the story, "una juwa (you know), I was looking at that hand phone…" He was moving body and making signs.

Hans came out of the room and looked at the crowd, everyone fell silent. He asked them to stay out for a few more moments.

He gave the phone to Bonde, pointed at the symbol showing connectivity and said, "You stand outside the room and tell me when you get this (blip) ..full, sawa?"

"Sawa, Bwana."

Only Raj and the engineer were inside the room with Hans.

Within minutes, the blip grew to become a bar.

Bonde was excited and shouted, "Tayari! Haalo..Saa (sir)."

Hans rushed out, saw the screen and raised his fists as sign of victory. People started clapping.

Bonde turned to the workers, "Bismillah i rahim."

Hans dialled the phone number of the office in Dar. It was answered by the company engineer.

"Hallo, Mr. Charles, can you hear me?"

He could hear Charles' voice very clearly. He gave some instructions to Charles. He handed the phone to Raj and the waiting crew. Almost everyone spoke with Charles and his team in Dar. Then Hans dialled Zuly's number. Zuly had left the instrument on the table and gone out of his room. Karimji was in his wheel chair. He heard the phone ring and wondered for a minute what was ringing. He thought it was alarm clock. Then it struck him.

He smiled and pushed his wheelchair towards the phone with all his might. He lifted the instrument and connected. Hans gave the phone to Raj.

Raj fumbled, "Mr. Zuly? I am Raj here."

"I am Karimji, beta... how are you?"

"Oh, great! Uncle, what a surprise! Tancell is born, uncle!

"Al ham dulillaah (by grace of God) I am very happy. Congratulate Hans, Bonde and his team on my behalf. Good job, Raj! Keep it up!"

Raj was moved by the older man's encouraging words.

"I will ask Zuly to contact you," Karimji promised.

The first tower was activated by Hans, Raj watched while the second and third towers were activated and he activated the fourth tower by himself.

Hans gave his cell phone to Raj as a souvenir. "I may have to take it back for a day to transfer my contacts. Sorry, you deserve new and better stuff, but I felt like giving it to you to remind you of this day. If you don't like it, just give it away. Do not worry."

"No Hans, I am very happy that you consider me close enough for such a gift. This will be a good souvenir."

While leaving, Hans told Zuly, "I do not think you will need me next time. That civil man is good enough."

Zuly wanted to start his network in the coastal and central regions. He started to push Raj harder. Anything that Raj achieved was just "not enough". He would talk aggressively with Raj but the bite was toothless. Raj did not feel hurt or humiliated. Ever since the success of his first project, he felt as if life was a river, smooth and flowing.

It had twists and turns and sometimes ran through an unpredictable course. He was happy floating and moving like a log.

Bonde asked, "Mistaa Raji, can I get some money as advance?"

"But we did hisaabu (account) last weekend?"

"Sawa. But you know I told you about my investimenti in Bagamoyo."

Raj smiled, "Buying another football field?"

Bonde said shyly, "No Bwana! We are contributing for minister's election so that he wins again in his area."

"So first you put your money on land. Now you are putting money on the minister. I am telling you; sell your land before the election, whatever the price."

Bonde shuddered. For him, the money was too much to lose. He found Raj's warnings a bad omen. He left with anxiety.

Chapter 9: First Love

Back home, Leena was upset. Eight months had gone by. Raj was in touch with her, but that was not enough. She realised with sadness that Raj was much more than just a 'close friend'. She could not stay away from him for long, although she was too reluctant to confess this to him. She thought it might ruin their relationship. She waited for some heavenly sign or a God-sent intermediary who could bridge the gap between them. She could not tell this to anyone, since everyone thought that Leena was only focussed on her career and her independence.

One day, during a training session on 'customer sensitivity', Leena had a revelation. She was participating in a role-play. As usual, the subject could be explained in a line or two but the trainer had arranged many role-plays and sensitivity exercises. She had to enter a room and of the six people seated there, she had to find who her 'Mr X' was. She had no information about Mr X, and yet she had to quickly and correctly, with the fewest wrong attempts, find that person. Most people went up to each person and asked if he was Mr X. Some would walk up to the third or fourth person, taking a gamble that they would be lucky and locate Mr X immediately.

However, the winner was the one who called out for Mr X from the door. The trainer pointed out, "It pays to talk straight and loud, to get what you want."

It struck Leena that she must call out to her favourite Mr. X that she loved him, but wanted him not in the jungles, in the cities. She decided to break the ice herself. She wrote to Raj and said that she wanted to come to the jungle where he was. Mr. Tarzan was thrilled.

Raj went to Dar to receive his very first guest. Zuly had a house that was used as the company guesthouse. They stayed there for two days. Raj wanted Leena to settle in before giving her jungle shock.

Leena also did not want to confess to Raj at once. Both wanted to spend a little time with each other. Raj wanted Leena to like Africa and probably take back a better picture of his new home to his parents and friends. But Leena's task was more difficult. Firstly, she wanted to convince Raj that they could be more than just friends and secondly, to convince him to return home.

Raj took her to a quiet beach in Dar. Leena found it a welcome change from the hullabaloo of city life. There were no queues, no waiters or visitors intruding on their privacy. They caught up on each other's lives and soon fell back into their old routine of teasing each other.

After several hours, they got up and ran into the water. Leena loved the feel of the greenish blue ocean water and the clean white sand. Seeing each other's wet bodies aroused them. Every time they touched they felt more and more alive.

They decided to walk back to the guesthouse and started talking about their families
to keep their minds of the erotic thoughts that were stoking their desire.

Suddenly, Raj asked, "When are you planning on getting married?"

Leena was taken by surprise, "Well, I should by now, but... I am not sure..."

Raj persisted, "What kind of person would you like?"

Leena said quickly, "Any good person, I mean a sensible person you enjoy being
with. Of course not a monkey a like you."

"So you need a guy who keeps your coffee ready when you come from work, late in
the evening, pulls out some junk food from the fridge, heats it up in the
microwave...and says, 'Honey! Food is ready'."

"Shut up! I did not say that!"

It was obvious to each other that they were not really saying what was on their mind.
To Leena and Raj, it seemed to be too soon to seriously venture into that subject.

Raj started talking about Africa--the people's habits and customs and his experiences.
Leena couldn't help but notice that he was crazy about the place and the people. It
would be very difficult to convince Raj to return to India.

The next day, Raj took her to the site, near Dodoma, the capital town, in the
afternoon. They left Dar behind and reached the site late in the evening. A thick grove
of tropical trees including cashew, coconuts, and mango trees impressed Leena
immediately.

"So green and cool!" she exclaimed.

Raj was elated that she liked the place.

Initially, she talked about their common friends, their college, her job and her clients and so on. She was so involved in talking to Raj that she did not notice the scenery or the up and down, rope-like straight highways. When she went out of steam, there were silent spells. After two hours, he took her to a small eatery by the road. Leena was amazed at the juicy pineapples, watermelon slices and passion fruit juice served for breakfast. It was a quiet, pleasant and bright morning. They watched the interplay of mountain range and white and grey clouds unspoilt by city smoke at a distance.

Raj couldn't resist asking, "How do you find the place?"

"Very nice, the breakfast was great."

"This is just a beginning, M'aam! A trailer. You will see the movie in the evening."

Leena smiled. She realised she should not have praised the place so much; it would be even more difficult now to convince Raj to leave.

They drove towards the site, singing and laughing like they used to back home, For Raj, it was a much needed change from his routine. He felt that since Leena already liked Africa, she would like it more as time went by.

After lunch, Leena fell asleep and Raj was lost in his thoughts. He was overwhelmed that she had come all this way, spending money and time to see him. It was true affection, he decided. He looked at her; the hot sun had burnt her skin. There were a few drops of sweat on her upper lip, but her windswept hair, dark eyelashes and long mace-like earrings made her face pretty. She was looking beautiful.

Raj recollected what she had told him that evening on the beach. She was not seeing anyone, or she would have told him. She could be his life-partner. Had she come all the way here to propose to him?
What if she did? If she didn't, should he? Would that spoil her mood? He was sure that she had a great affection for him. It was evident by her body language. Should he try to pass all these happenings through a prism of relationship to see connubial colours on the other side with her?
He was sure that their parents would readily approve the marriage though they belonged to different castes.

But then, would she leave her career in Mumbai, and live with him in Africa? Was it not unfair to ask her to do that? He sighed and wished he knew what to do.

Leena woke up and saw Raj's tanned and sweaty skin gleaming in the afternoon sun.
"How far?"
"About an hour more."
"You must be tired."
"No, I am used to long drives now."

"You do not have a driver?"

"Yes, I have, a friend who is also the driver, Poto, but I did not bring him with me."

After a while, Raj slowed down the vehicle.

"There is the site."

Leena watched the people scurrying around as Raj parked the vehicle near his hut. She got down and immediately Mama Rose greeted them. Bonde, Poto and Juma, came forward and Raj introduced them. "Mzee (elder)! Leena, rafiki (friend) yangu (mine)."

He looked at Poto, both of them recollected their earlier conversation about 'special friends'.

Leena greeted them with a smile. Africans have long greeting rituals.

"How is India?"

"Fine."

"How are your parents?"

"Fine.'"

"How was your safari to this place?"

"Fine."

"How did you like Dar-es-Salaam."

"Good."

Bonde pressed ahead with more questions. After every question, Leena would respond briefly by saying "Fine" and he would respond her answer by thanking god, Shukuru Mungu (thank God)'. or 'Al-ham-dulillah',every time.

Poto interrupted. "And how is Mistaa Raji?"

Leena laughed and said, "Um… not bad, okay-like."

Bonde burst into laughter, "This mama janja (smart) saana."

He turned to his assistant and said "Ana sema hivi…"

He narrated the whole dialect between Poto and Leena. Juma nodded head and smiled.

Mama Rose brought out a neatly arranged tray with a bottle of water and glasses. They sat down on plastic chairs, but Raj and the others were called away for work, leaving Leena alone.

Leena looked around her and nearly jumped when she felt something soft touch her feet. She pulled back her leg to find Huku trying to lick her toes. She jumped up and hid behind the chair.

Huku was surprised and raised his ears and eyebrows as if alarmed. At that moment, Rose came out with tea and biscuits, understood what had just happened and shouted at Huku. She reassured Leena that the dog was harmless. Huku lay down flat, like a crocodile, and kept an eye on Leena, staring at him. He could smell the biscuits but stayed still even after Rose left to call Raj.

Raj and Leena had tea together undisturbed and watched the sun set. The sun was setting. Shadows from the distant hills were stretching far ahead. The machines and the men became silent, only the generator kept humming.

"Do you run the generator for 24 hours?"

"No, it will be put off at nine."

"What? Then the whole night…? Without fan and light?"

"You don't need them in Tanzania."

"I will go to the loo, before it gets dark then! I do not know what I am going to do if I have to go again at midnight."

"Call me, or Rose. There will be a lantern burning."

Rose escorted Leena to a small thatched hut with just a one-foot hole in the centre. Leena was shocked, she felt like running away. But Rose's presence and her own disobedient bladder forced her to enter the hut quickly. She banged the door behind her, but it did not make a sound, since it was made of neatly knitted twigs and grass. Gritting her teeth, she managed to relieve herself. She was fuming when she came out.

"Raj… how far is the hotel?"

"A good one is about… 90 kilometres."

"Let's drive. I can't stand all this."

"What's wrong?"

"This blessed place! It is much worse than the slums we have in Mumbai."

"Take it easy…"

"No I cannot. You finish you work here and come there. I do not mind staying in a small hotel till then."

"Let me explain what I have planned for you…"

Raj told her that he wanted her to stay with him for three days after which they could go on a safari in the famous SerengetiNational Park. While talking, Raj led her away from the site and the noisy generator. Leena forgot her annoyance for a while and when they came back, Mama Rose was arranging a table for dinner. The mixed vegetable dish, steaming hot rice, salad and pineapple slices, soothed Leena's mood.

"Wow! What food, Mama Rose, food is great!" she exclaimed.

The generator was switched off soon after they had finished eating. In the quietness that ensued, Raj and Leena gazed at the stars.

"Have you ever seen such a clear sky and big bright stars, like diamonds in the sky? Raj asked.

"Yeah, it is wonderful, but where are we going to sleep?"

"Under the sky! You will be inside the hut. I usually pull my bed outside."

"Don't you feel lonely at times, or get bored of all this?"

"No. That's why I remember you folks more than you remember me."

Leena liked the answer. She wanted to ask him whether he remembered her specially. Did he miss her? But, she could not. They talked into the night, oblivious of the time. There were no buildings around them and no one watching them from a window or balcony. With their hearts full of contentment, they whispered 'good night' to each other and fell asleep.

Chapter 10: The Lion sleeps tonight.

Raj had to get to work early and Leena was also up before her usual time. They had tea together and a long walk. Mama Rose asked Leena if she would like to accompany her to a nearby village market. Leena accepted the invitation gladly.

As soon as they stepped into the village, the children surrounded them, wanting a good, long look at the 'Muhindi (Indian) mama'. She smiled and waved at them and learnt Kiswahili words for common vegetables and fruits.

When they got back, Rose wanted to learn how to make Raj's favourite Indian dishes. Leena was very happy to oblige and by the time the afternoon drew to an end, the two women had become close friends. Rose told her everything that she had learnt about Raj's idiosyncrasies, his absentmindedness, his sentimental nature and his funny ways. Leena loved to hear every bit of it. She told Rose about things that had happened in India.

Soon after, Rose would prepare and improvise on the Indian recipes she had learnt from Leena. Raj loved the change in his diet and would try to tick off Leena by saying that it was 'much better than anything made by any woman in India'. However, Leena would deflect the comment by reminding him, 'Your mother also cooks well Raj'. The witty repartee that defined their relationship soon become the talking point with all the women who worked on the site, thanks to Rose's narratives Rose would also prepare cooked maize dough (ugali) and banana curry with tomato puree, a local favourite, especially for Leena.

Raj felt that things were going well. His mood was upbeat and cheerful. Bonde's workers were happy too and very curious about Leena's precise relationship with Mistaa Raaji.

On the fourth day, Bonde invited a local tribe to perform 'Ngoma', a folk dance. A few men beat the drums while a small troupe of young dancers sang along. Each member would sing at the scale he or she was comfortable with, making the chorus funny, distinctive, and loud. After a few moments, a dancer would blow a whistle and the steps would change. Most of the time, the dance consisted of shaking the hips. But, even that required considerable skill as the torso and legs would hardly move while the buttocks swung in a semi-circle. Leena joined the troupe too. She had been given a 'khanga', a printed cloth tied around her waist that covered half her body and her hair had been braided the African way. She tried cheerfully, but desperately, to keep up with Rose and other ladies in the troupe, trying to shake her relatively tiny hips in vain. Raj, Poto, Bonde and others joined the fray a little later. She took snaps and also got some one to take her snaps with the troupe, Mama Rose, Poto, Raj and others.

Later, Raj and Leena set out on a safari. Raj had arranged for a Land Rover with a convertible top. He had also hired an experienced driver and guide. Against the backdrop of the mountains, they drove through the plains dotted with beautifully distinct acacia trees. Raj talked to his driver for some time.

Leena was mesmerised by the beauty of the country. For miles there were no highway shops or motels, nor humans. Except for the tarmac road and an occasional vehicle, there were no signs of modern civilisation. Soon, the grassy plains gave way to marshy reeds, climbing the valley that runs from the Red Sea to Lake Nyasa in southern Tanzania. Soon they were surrounded by huge mahogany and fig trees. It was getting cooler and cooler. They could see large flocks of flamingos around the huge LakeManyara.

The guide said, "If you are lucky, you may see a lion on an acacia tree here."

Leena was wondering what she could do in this wonderful land to pursue her career. Forget the ground; she would settle here if her customers were found even on treetops.

"What are you thinking?"

"Trying to locate my customers on acacia trees."

"Lions do not need your bookish advice. They know where to invest well."

"Where, if I may ask?"

"In good lionesses."

"Why?"

"If you see their lifestyle, you will realise that the lion just lies down the entire day and relaxes, while lionesses find food. They manage the cubs too. Then they entertain the lion."

The driver laughed. Leena retorted, "My foot! To hell with such a customer!"

"That's why; stop looking out for customers on treetops. Enjoy the jungle."

For a while Leena switched to Hindi. "Shut up. Tell me, are you going to follow a lion in your personal life?"

"No."

"Why?"

"Because I am a monkey. You have been saying that."

Leena smiled. After a while she said hesitantly, "Raj… it's a wonderful place. I liked your jungle."

***

Laws of Nature are timeless (long term to the extent of infinity), rhythmic re-occurring and perpetual. It does not have quick fixes. It does not pester individual areas or a clan. Nature has a very wide canvass from Alaskan seal to tropical Passion fruit.

Sun heats up ocean. Ocean gives clouds. Wind blows them over and till they deliver rains. Water flows back to ocean or into landmass. It goes on for millions of years.

Mankind has grown up from 2 to billions but still nature sustains. It is not just the vastness of mother earth. Nature also does not mean heavens. There are deserts. There are earth quakes. There are Tsunamis. Species evolve and become extinct. Animals starve.But still it runs life for millions of years and it will continue to do so.

Vested groups run a society or a government. The solutions are short term, area or clan specific and less comprehensive. Nature forbids humans to stay in deserts. A powerful group defies it, puts air conditioners, carts fertile soil from tropics, melts Alaskan ice and flies water and harvests wheat and claims to have conquered Nature. Animals will not visit desert. They will migrate to better areas abiding by the laws of nature. The so-called powerful group can scoff at them only till power or money lasts for a few decades or a century. 'So what! We did it?' Ask people whom they left behind when power fades.
They will perish. They will be misfits in the society. They will be victims of internecine war or hunger or mass epidemics.

***

Late in the afternoon, they reached the ridge of the famous Ngorongoro crater 110 square miles wide and a 2000 foot high crater all around. They parked the car on a spot high above the crater from where Leena took some pictures.

Raj watched her for a while and said, "Put away your camera. You just can't capture this magical view in a frame. You can only experience it."

Leena was about to retort, thought for a second and then agreed, "Yeah, true."

The driver said softly, "Ma'am? You are from India?"

"Yes."

"You have a zoo in your city?"

"Yes."

"This is God's zoo. Whenever he is free, he comes here and watches his animals."

Leena smiled at the thought, "Well, it must be true."

"Tomorrow, he will find one new animal in the crater…," muttered Raj.

"Yeah, some crazy monkey," Leena laughed.

But the pun was lost on the driver. "Generally animals do not migrate in and out as in Serengeti, once they are inside the crater," he explained, "Can you see those trees on the other side? You will mostly find lions there. That water hole. That is the place to see rhinos and hippos…"

The safari was better than what Leena had expected. No sooner had they entered the gate, than they spotted wild fowls, deer, and monkeys. They drove down into the crater. Foxes, hyenas, gazelles, bucks and hordes of zebras and wildebeest excited them. They stood shoulder to shoulder in the Rover, standing on the seat to have an all round view from the open roof. Both were enjoying the bumpy ride and the fleeting moments when their bodies would touch.

Leena and Raj had never felt so close in all the years they had known each other, as they did then.

Leena took pictures of a pride of lions she spotted. The lion family was lying in the tall grass, swuatting flies with their tails. Their curious cubs were playing. They were intermittently climbing on the tree bark while others were trying to pull them down. Hordes of wild buffalos, zebra and wildebeest grazed just a few feet away, all in close proximity, watching each other.

***

With evolution, the humans left honesty and natural behaviour in the animal kingdom behind. A lion pounces on a Zebra only when he is hungry. He does not do it to have dominance of Lion clan in the jungle. If you serve him food in jungle like you do in a zoo at a fixed place and time, he will stop hunting. Animals believe in peaceful co-existence. Humans do not.

Organizations can grow on their acquired or inherited skill. They can be run on a reasonable fair play. A Jiffy (giraffe) has a long neck. It will go to those areas where it can nimble tree leaves. It can graze on thorny bushes. It leaves the tree behind for the next season. If there are no bushes or trees, it will rather perish than start eating lizards.

Animals like humans have to play survival game but still they are innocent, straight, and honest, relying on their natural ability.

Jiffy does not cry over why he cannot be a lion or ponder 'grass is limited so let me kill zebras'. Jiffy can collude with hyenas and lead them to a mother antelope that is just delivering a baby to remove competing grass eater. Better still, the Jiffy clan will negotiate with lions and act like informers if other herbivore come to their area and bargain their security so no other animal can prey on them.

Lions may think that they get easy food so let clumsy Jiffy be spared and go for the deal. The agreement may be labelled as JALTO (Jiffs and Lions Treaty Organization).

Evolution also made humans ambitious unlike their counterparts in animal kingdom.

A Rabbit is happy eating berries on the ground. It does not have complexes when he sees Jiffy plundering leaves from tall trees. A human rabbit is ambitious. He wants his son to eat from top of the tree. Then start the manipulations. Son looses charm of being with the community and the berries. He is prone to risk from vultures and leopards that rest on the tree. His clan can hide in the tall grass and run away as they are on the ground. After facing all odds, the son realizes that berries were tastier and juicy compared to leaves.

His father could manipulate every thing so that he climbs to the top but could not give Jiffy' taste buds. It is too late for him to retract as he is worried about his social pride

and of course father's wrath. Father Rabbit had ego, accepting blunder of his lifetime.
High expectations make a man tentative and prone to short term quick fixes.
In a society where individuals shirk pretence and dishonesty, a society that thrives on
natural ability is a Natural society. We scoff at jungle rules or society running on laws
of jungle but that is an ultimate utopia or Shangri-La.

The sun climbed up in the valley, watching the two creatures who were unable to
admit their love to each other and hid beyond the edge of the valley casting long
shadows.

It was time to return. Both were tired. On returning to the hotel, they had relaxed hot
baths, pondering over the events during the day in the bathtub. They were confused
and unsure about what to do next. In their own rooms, they pondered the same
question — How to stay together? The more they thought about it, the more vexing
the issue became. Marriage and career, nature and modernity, just could not coexist.

They met for dinner. Both of them were unusually quiet. The dining hall overlooked
a swimming pool with a few chairs strewn around it.

"Tired?" Raj asked.

"Yeah, but the bath was very relaxing."

"Did you like the safari?"

"Yes, just out of the world!"

"Do you like Africa?"

"Yeah… as a tourist."

"You can't get your bank job in some town here?" Raj's tired mind gave way.

"I can… but... why are you asking me this?" Leena couldn't believe what she as hearing.

Raj fumbled, "No… no... I mean, I can have company…"

"Be honest, Raj! Is it just 'company' or something more? I want you to say it. I am sure you are thinking about it. That's why you said it. What is it Raj? Please."

Before Raj could tell her the truth, they heard the kitchen doors swing open and the entire staff seemed to be singing. The chefs and the waiters in their spotless white uniforms formed a line and walked towards Leena while singing a traditional Kiswahili welcome song. All the guests in the hotel looked at the young couple. The chef at the head of the line was carrying a huge cake and some of the waiters danced and clapped to the rhythm of the song.

The group passed between the tables all around the hall and circled around Raj's table. Notes changed and the group started singing 'Happy Birthday Mama Leena'. Leena laughed in surprise and Raj stood up to join in the chorus. As soon as the song ended, Raj borrowed the guitar and played the national anthem 'Munguibariki (God bless Afrika). The guests and the staff were delighted and joined in the cheerful song.

The best part of the Tanzanian national anthem is that it is less martial and informal. One can enjoy it as a song or prayer. Once the song ended, the hall reverberated with whistles; African shrilly shouts (gelele) and claps (koffi).

After the cake had been cut, and they were left alone, Raj saw tears in Leena's eyes. She said softly, "Silly, you never told me you were going to do all this, love you."

"Raj, I can't believe this. I will remember this forever. A birthday in the middle of a real jungle and in front of the whole world! Thanks so much. Can we just go out and sit?"

"It will be cold."

"Let's chill!"

They took their drinks out and on the pool chairs, neither wanting to be the first to speak.

They stared each other. Raj finally broke the silence, "A jungle has its own charms, you see!"

Leena replied immediately, "And a monkey has his own stunts."

Both sipped their drinks for a moment and looked in different directions. Their faces became a little serious and their mood turned sombre.

"Raj, tell me..."

"What?"

"Why do you want me to take up a job here?"

Raj took a little time to answer. Leena was looking at his face expectantly. He was staring down on the floor. He took a gulp first; he took a long breath and said, "We have been good friends.

We know each other so well. We like each other very much. I thought I could propose. I mean... you know what I mean."

Leena smiled approvingly at him. "I don't know what you mean," she gently teased.

"Leena. What do you feel?"

Leena whispered, "I could not have asked for a better time and place to confess that I love you Raj and I want to marry you."

Their secrets revealed, the young couple finally drew closer. Raj held Leena's hands while she cried tears of joy.

But, later, during dinner they fell silent again. Who would give up their job?

Leena spoke up first, "I know, Raj, that we have to solve this issue about your job coming in our way, but we will think about it. Together. Isn't it?"

"Yes, we have time. What's important is that we love each other."

Dinner was over. Once again they sat by the pool and held hands. But as the night enveloped them, it got colder. Raj reminded Leena about the safari early next day. She confessed that she would rather spend the night and the whole of next day with him, in their room, than leave him now. Raj got up and gently ushered her towards their rooms.

Leena rested her head on his shoulder while walking, which made Raj feel a little uncomfortable. When they reached their rooms, Raj patted her head and said, "Good night, madam!"

Leena was unwilling to let go, "But we decided to marry, so why have separate rooms?"

Raj coaxed her hands away from his arm and gently shook her, "As we know we have to sort out some very vexing issues before we do that, Mama!"

"But how can we sort out anything without staying together?"

"Okay, the one who forgoes the room has to forgo the job. If you come to my room, you have to settle down in my country."

"No. Then why don't you come to my room?"

"I can't."

"Very mean you are!" Leena looked into his eyes and pleaded for his company. Raj was also smiling teasingly. Finally, she let go of his arm, "Bad night," she wished him. They gently walked away from each other looking at each other.

They had settled down on their respective beds. But they could not resist the temptation of staying close together. Leena banged a can of mosquito repellent on the wall that parted their rooms. Raj responded by banging his fists on the wall. Like heat, emotion transferred by conduction first and then by electronic radiation. Unable to wait any longer, Leena called up Raj. They talked, laughed and whispered sweet promises on the phone for about an hour till the generator was switched off.

After a few moments of silence, Raj heard a knock on his door.

"Oh gosh, this lady!" he muttered.

Leena was standing outside, with a candle in her hand. Raj could see an armed guard waving her to go inside, since it was dangerous to be out alone in the dark. Raj pulled her in and shut the door.

"You stupid girl, did you hear what that fellow was saying. It is risky."

"But I was scared."

"Liar. You..."

"Sorry. But can I stay in your room?"

They were standing very close to each other and in the light of the flickering candle their eyes betrayed their passion for each other. Leena placed the candle on a table and they both slowly moved closer and hugged each other.

Leena whispered, "It is time to celebrate, isn't it?"

"Yeah, tonight is a very special night."

"Love you, Raj."

Leena took a step back to look into his eyes; he smiled at her trying to reassure her. They were both slightly nervous. Raj put his hand around her waist and she put her arm around his neck. They walked to the bed. Again they turned to each other and hugged. They closed their eyes. They could feel their warm breath. Raj slowly moved his hands from her waist to her shoulders. With every nudge of Raj's finger, Leena's excitement mounted and finally left her lips half opened. She held Raj's robe tightly. Raj held her face in his hands and gently brought her close.

He whispered, "May I..."

"No need to ask. Do whatever you want to."

Raj kissed her lips. This was the first time they had ever gotten intimate and they were nervous. It was not a very thorough but little shaky and short kiss. Excitement and lust took over their minds and bodies. The front of the robes they were wearing had slipped open and Raj was thrilled to see Leena's bare shoulders and breasts. In the dim candlelight he looked at the beautiful young woman in front of him; her flat stomach, the lacy panties and her shapely thighs; her fair skin glowed and he grew bolder.

Leena felt shy but moved closer. She could feel Raj's chiselled chest and tight stomach muscles on her skin.

Raj brought her face up again, nudged her nose with his, kissed her lips again and pulled her close. They both stroked each other's skin and lay down on the bed side by side.

"Oh, Raj you are so exciting. Give me a long, long kiss," whispered Leena. Raj licked her lips and thrust his tongue inside her mouth. His hands stroked her chin, her neck and finally found the soft smooth skin of her breasts. Leena was in flames. Raj understood her desire and kept stroking and pressing her breasts. She cried out in pain and Raj let go of her at once. "Sorry! Sorry! Did I hurt you?" he asked.

"Silly, I was saying there are two of them, not just one," she laughed.

They burst out laughing. Raj felt a little guilty when he realised that lust had taken over love. "I think we should leave something for our honeymoon, right?"

Leena nodded and pulled the blanket over them and rested her head on his chest. She closed her eyes and Raj kissed her forehead. They were lost in their dreams before they fell asleep.

The next day, they went to Serengeti. Raj wanted Leena to witness the amazing migration. Serengeti is world renowned for the wildebeests' migration. About 1.5 million wildebeests, 500,000 zebras and 200,000 gazelles migrate over a stretch of about 200 miles across two rivers. Carnivores would also be spotted, since it was convenient for them to catch food.

As soon as they got there, they saw animals covering every inch of the land. They were stopped by herds of wildebeest and zebras crossing the red lava soil. They could see a pride of twelve lions right beside their vehicles. But despite the awe-inspiring spectacle all Leena and Raj could think about was last night's erotic experience.

Generally people tend to adventure while in love but here they were romancing in adventure. It seemed that they were not watching the animals but the animals were watching them.

Chapter 11: Missing you

Before checking in at the airport, Leena told Raj, "We shall really work out something that makes us happy. We have plenty of time. Let's work with an open mind, if we cannot, we shall just toss the coin, but we cannot stay without each other. Should I inform our parents? Although, they might be expecting this."
"Yeah. We should. I shall call them up too."

Raj felt very lonely driving back to the site. The road that was so exciting a few days ago was now gloomy and deserted. He remembered how they had talked, teased each other, and sang old favourites while travelling together. He started missing Leena. Despair and frustration choked his mind. Why me? Why can't I get a good job in India? Something is wrong with me. Maybe I am mediocre, he kept telling himself.

For a few days, Raj was not quite himself. He avoided socialising with people and Mama Rose knew why Raj was so sad. So did Huku. Every now and then he would trot over to Raj, give him a quick lick on his feet and sit beside him, looking at him with his large, sympathetic eyes. Raj would pat his head and remember Leena and Huku had gotten along after the first day. Mama Rose continued to make Raj's favourite Indian dishes that Leena had taught her. She also missed the girl.

After three weeks, it was time to visit Serengeti again.

Unlike Raj, Leena had lost herself in work. Catching up with her family and friends in Mumbai and the pressure of increasing work made her forget Africa. However, she did tell everyone about her feelings for Raj. His parents were relieved with the thought that the marriage might bring Raj back to India. For them Leena was like a family member for so long. Leena would drive Raj's mother to the shopping mall or simply visit and talk about her African safari on weekends.

Leena's aggressive and dominating nature at work put her ahead of the pack. She became the preferred presenter and delegate for the company while negotiating financial packages, particularly with large companies.

Within weeks, Leena was an expert at presentations. She could rattle of the sales pitch in her sleep, "We are the fastest growing... 35 per cent on Y-O-Y growth consistently for seven years... our EVA is... third most preferred scrip on NASDAQ amongst Asian corporates... value driven... concern for people and investors... as part of social responsibility..."

She was promoted and she spent a lot of time and money in the world of beauty salons, designer stores, financial developments, data analysis, presentations and meetings in exotic locations. Eventually, her communication with the monkey in the jungle was severed, as she had to wait for Raj to visit a village to contact her.

Mankind has invented two wonderful, yin and yang (opposite) gadgets; a deep freezer and a microwave. Food is cooked and put in a deep freezer.

When the need arises, the microwave will not only shake it up from deep hibernation but vibrate the frozen water particles in it, thousands of time in a second till it starts fuming and becomes steaming hot. It tastes as if it is cooked fresh. Very soon, there will be deep freezers and microwaves for humans.

A time will come when a dear one departs; the wife will dress him up nicely and put his body into a deep freezer. On wedding anniversaries and birthdays, he will be put into the microwave. He will be pulled out, looking fresh. The wife will put a knife in his fingers and make him cut the cake. After the ceremony, he will be put back into the deep freezer. Instead of videos and photo, one will have 'lively' memories of his or her dear ones.

Issues may arise afresh but they are conveniently put into a deep freezer to suit our so-called 'busy' life and at a convenient later date they are microwaved to look hot and fresh in spite of losing their relevance.

***

Leena was not alone in her flight to success. She had a handsome, tall and suave pilot in her boss, Binoy. Binoy had an MBA in finance from the best management school in the country. Leena was impressed with his qualifications and visions.

Binoy's intention with having Leena head customer meetings and presentations was paying off. He would guide her.

He would also apprise her about possible queries from customers. He believed that when a woman, particularly a young and beautiful one like Leena would make a presentation, the client would tend to try and impress her with his technical queries. By doing this, the client would be 'hooked'. He would be responsive in subsequent follow-up calls from Leena, ultimately paving the way for acceptance of the proposal.

Binoy would be silent for most of the time during discussions with the client and ask a few questions only to display his own prowess with data analysis and knowledge of businesses across the globe. His logic worked. Success followed him, Leena, and their team. They were loaded with more and more responsibilities and had to sit late after office hours. They would eat out in restaurants or call for food in the office. Binoy had started dropping Leena off at her home. Although he was four years older than her, he was 'hooked' by her beauty and intelligence.

Leena was intoxicated by her work. She could not discern if it was her work or her smart boss that had cast a spell on her. The issue of leaving her career to marry Raj was put on hold.

Chapter 12: Serengeti adventure

Raj's army of workers had shifted to Serengeti. Being a wildlife sanctuary, the work in the area had to be finished speedily, with minimal vehicular movement. It was decided that the workers would finish the job in shifts. The noisy generators would ensure that animals stayed away and a few Masai, the local shepherds who were known to fight lions, were hired to ensure the safety of the workers. The Masai were getting paid in free meals, local booze and $100.

It took them two days to find the right site and mark the area. The Masais cleaned up the site and put up a fence of thick thorny bushes. The whole area had only one wooden gate wide enough to allow a truck inside. Fires were lit in several places outside the fence, to scare away any animals, while the Masais and the workers would sing and dance through the night.

One day, while cleaning the area, Raj and Bonde were pegging the area with their team. They were walking through tall grass.
"Mzee, Bonde! There are no snakes here?"
Like a heavy Patton tank coming to a screeching halt, Bonde stopped.
"Aan, aan. Don't talk about snakes when we are in the field," he warned.
"Why?"

"If you remember them, they will come, Bwana. We never talk about it while we are clearing the site."

"Are you serious?"

"Very much. You know the snakes in Serengeti? Go to Arusha Snake park and see. Have you heard of Kali (deadly) snake Mamba?"

"Really?"

"Wewe (you) Mistaa Raji! If Black Mamba comes now, he will stand like you and bring his face to your level and then he will spit in your eyes. You will be blinded immediately. Then he will bite you on your face and everywhere. You will die immediately."

The workers walking close behind them seemed immobilised. Raj could see the halo of death around Bonde's face. He could not smile and pass this off as a joke.

"There is one more snake, Green Mamba. He will always be sitting on the tree. Veli komfotaboli (very comfortably). When you pass by the tree, he will hang upside down and come…"

Bonde lunged forward, grabbed Raj's head with his hands and brought his face close to Raj. His eyeballs seemed to pop out of his head; his mouth opened wide and he hissed with incredible force… 'ffffaaahh'.

Bonde's imitation of the Green Mamba's hiss was so perfect that Raj could almost see the huge python-like creature hanging down from the tree to kill him. The foul smell from Bonde's dry mouth almost made him vomit. Bonde decided to take a break and asked the staff to get him tea and water.

When they had gone, Bonde continued, "In a jungle, there are two deadly things you should worry about, which even the Masai cannot stop. Snakes and bees. They can be any where. They can come at any time and you cannot escape, even if you have a gun or a Masai with you." People nodded heavily.

"If Simba (lion) comes, this Masai will stand here. He will not run away. He will fight. But if bees come, you will not find him. When bees attack you, they go into your ears, eyes, mouth, and any hole in your body. They bite like dogs on your cheeks, stomach, chest, *hiaa dheya evere whia* (here, there, everywhere). They are so many that you have no time to push them away."

"When I was young, I was in the jungles looking for firewood with my friends. We were throwing stones on the mangoes in the tree. We did not see the beehive inside. One big stone hit the beehive. They came down on us like smoke from a gun. Luckily, I fell down, as I was heavy. The other boys ran so the bees chased them. Two of them died. They removed bees from inside their stomach and intestines!"

The listeners grimaced as though they had bees in their intestines

He lowered his head to show scars left by bee bites. They looked like patches of burnt land on a hill.

Raj tried to ease the tension, "Mzee, you are scaring me now."

"Haaki ya Mungu (I swear by God)! These two, snake and bees, are deadly. Never remember them, otherwise they will remember you."

The silence after this statement lasted for a long time. Then Poto asked, "wipi Profesaa?"

Professa, as usual, was ready with a comment.

"Kweli! If you call Mungu, he may or may not listen to you, but if you call bees and snakes! Halleluyah! They will come. As we say in our language, *Ukitaja nyoka, shika fimbo mkononi. (When you mention a snake, have a stick ready in your hand.)*"

For the first time, everybody around did not respond with the customary 'Ndiyo'. They started dispersing after listening to the bee-like words of the Professa.

Within three days, the huts were ready, and work on the foundation had started. All the necessary material had been piled up all over the site. The trucks would make only one trip in a day, bringing diesel, cement, gravel, and other construction equipment.

It was a quiet afternoon and everybody took a short break for lunch. They were eating quietly. Poto was teasing Rose. Others were watching them and commenting in between. Raj enquired. 'Hey! Why are you teasing her?"

Bonde said, "Mistaa Raji, Rose is very rich now. She will leave our work."

"Why?"

"Her big mother died a few days ago."

"What do you mean 'big' mother? Grandmother? And what is there to celebrate?"

Bonde explained that Rose belonged to the ferocious Kuria tribe living on the border of Kenya and Tanzania. As per the Kuria rules, a rich lady with a barren womb can marry another, generally younger, girl by giving some cattle to the father. They stay together in a house and the arrangement is called Nyumba ya Ntobo. The younger girl then conceives children on behalf of the rich lady and hands over the children to the lady who uses them to perform household chores, such as getting firewood and looking after cattle.

An old widow had married Rose's mother who had been the fifth child in a large family. Her grandfather could not afford her. His need or greed was cattle, not Rose's mother. Rose's grandfather had agreed to this marriage for barter. He had received two cows, two lambs and five bags of maize for his daughter. After the marriage, she had to do all the work around the house. She would go for cattle grazing. She would fetch fire wood. She gave birth to three children following a long relationship with a truck driver. She could not get married to the man, since her husband was the old lady!

When Rose grew up and had children, the old lady had the first right to them. The children started working around the house. Rose's husband left her when Rose was diagnosed with tuberculosis. Her brother sent her to Dar-es-Salaam so she could get medical attention.

After a few months, Rose was feeling better and started working in Bonde's house. Her mother had died and now the old lady had died, leaving behind cattle, a big house and a small maize farm. Rose and her two siblings had inherited all this.

Her brother was asking her to meet him to decide the division of the inheritance and take care of her grown-up children.

Raj heard all this in silence and turned to Rose. "What will you do now?"

Rose replied shyly, "I do not know."

Poto stood up, "I am going to marry her. *Ukipanada mboga, lazima upenda ua lake.(if you want vegetables then first like their flowers)"*

Rose screamed with laughter, "Wewe toto (you kid)!"

"What did Poto say?" asked Raj quickly.

"If you want to marry a woman, better accept her children first," said Bonde.

Before Raj could react, he saw a Masai running towards them shouting something they couldn't hear. As he got closer they realised he was saying "Climb on the trucks".

People left their food and ran towards the trucks. Raj and Poto climbed over the roof of a truck, but still had no idea why the warning was issued.

"Shida gani (what's the problem)?" Raj asked the Masai.

In reply, the man pointed at the nearby hills. Raj could see nothing more than a cloud of dust on the horizon. Within moments, under the cloud of dust, he could see a black rug of a massive horde of running beasts —wildebeests and zebras descending from the top of the hill on the back.

"Bossi, yule nyama (those beasts) can you see them?" Poto yelled.

"Yes but after going down that hill, where will they go?" Before Poto could answer, they saw the first line of beasts crest the top of the hill nearest the site. People were still not clear why they were on the trucks.

Raj laughed, "Ah, wewe Masai! Why are they so scared? Let's go ahead with our work."

Before Raj could jump down, it was clear that the beasts were headed towards them. The earth vibrated under the thundering hooves and now everyone feared for their lives.

Some of them cried, prayed or simply held on to the truck's roof as well as they could. For a moment Raj felt numb. Poto pulled him into the truck and shouted, "Bossi, get inside the cabin."

A few yards away from the fence, the running beasts had gotten divided into two deadly streams. In seconds, the streams closed in and circled the site. Finally they hit the fence, ran over it and started running all over the site. The huts were torn apart, utensils, clothes and light building materials that had been so carefully stored on the site, were now flying in the air and being trampled into the dust. The animals banged into the diesel drums and the generator and toppled them over. They stomped over the cement bags and every thing that got in their way.

Some animals stumbled, fell and were trampled by the others behind them. But nothing could be seen clearly now, the dust that had risen had made everything beyond a few inches from their eyes invisible. The trucks were shaking. The animals banged their heads and bodies on the front and the sides.

Suddenly, a gazelle jumped over the driver's cabin and landed into the open carriage at the back. It fell in the midst of the trembling humans clinging to each other in fear. Their cries could not be heard, but the gazelle's hooves did break a few skulls and cut scars on faces. In fear, it jumped again, but could not jump out of the carriage. After a few seconds, the animal stood quietly watching the herd pass by.

Poto and Raj were hiding under the steering wheel. Raj had closed his eyes waiting for the worst to get over. The animals had slowed down and in a few minutes, they had disappeared, leaving behind the badly mangled bodies of their mates and a shattered worksite that looked as though a particularly devastating earthquake had struck.

The trucks were damaged beyond recognition. The torn out radiators, broken fenders, shattered headlights and the blood on the windscreens made for a ghastly scene. The people gingerly picked their way across the mess only to find a pride of lions merrily picking up their food.

Cries for the Masai filled the air. But the famed shepherds seemed too scared to do what they did best. Raj called out to Poto, "Start the truck, reverse it and blow the horn. Fast!" Poto panicked. He reversed the truck rashly without paying any attention to what was behind the vehicle. People still clinging on to the back of the truck fell down in surprise and the gazelle that had been left behind, jumped out and ran for its life. But the lions became cautious at the sight of this noisy vehicle. They went away reluctantly.

It took them two more days to reorganise the site.

"Mistaa Raji! One more very bad news, Bwana."

"What?" Raj thought Bonde would refuse to get back to work on the site.

"That ministaa did not get tiketi (ticket) for re-election from Bagamoyo. Now they will not declare free port there I lost my money Bwana."

"Pole saana," Raj said. He felt genuinely sorry for Bonde.

"Bahati mbaya (bad luck)," then with his characteristic smile Bonde said,

"Ukimwiga tembo kunya utapasuka mkundu." Juma and Poto standing next them, started laughing.

Raj did not understand "What?"

Bonde refused to interpret, he felt shy.

Poto explained "If you copy an elephant shitting, you'll burst your… (anus)" He could complete only pointing at his bottoms.

***

Raj modified the plans for the site and fortified the fence to prevent any disasters in the future. People worked at an unbelievable speed and worked beyond their normal shift times to get out of the place at the earliest. Raj no longer spent the evening playing the guitar and reminiscing about Leena.

Every now and then, the workers would look up at the hills, where they had first spotted the running hordes. The hills had become the real supervisors on the site, reminding every worker to get back to work.Bonde was also a changed man. He no longer idled his time away and was always on his feet shouting 'Harakka' (fast) to the workers.

Finally, the site was ready, and it was with a lot if relief that the materials were packed up and loaded in the trucks.

A herd of about sixty wild buffaloes was grazing not more than a hundred metres away from the site for a few hours. Suddenly, all of them turned their heads in one direction. They were looking at something and one of the bulls issued a loud cry. The whole herd turned, walked a few paces and turned around again in perfect tandem like a ballet. The Masais once again drew the attention of the workers.

A pride of six lions had appeared. They were cautiously approaching the herd of buffaloes. The herbivores stood together, forming a protective circle around the calves. The lions did not charge but continued to move slowly, never once lifting their eyes from the prey. The buffaloes started to move away from the lions. Two of the animals at the periphery were not quick in keeping up with the rest of the herd.

Two lionesses seized the moment to charge and caught a buffalo that was farthest from the herd and brought him down. The buffalo gave a loud cry and tried to stand up; the lionesses were hanging from his sides. One more lioness charged as well and bit his throat. The herd turned around again to face the lions. One of the bulls leading the pack issued a loud cry. It was time for the lion to act now. He was standing a small distance away. Now, he stalked the herd. The herd moved away as fast as it could, leaving behind the hunted one.

By now, the lion had reached the injured animal, and stood watching the herd move away. It seemed as if they were not in any hurry to kill the animal, but wanted the herd to go away. The herd turned around once again to face the lions.
The buffaloes, with head and ears erect, took two steps in the direction of the lions and stood still. The lions took a step forward as though accepting the challenge.

Raj was moved by what was unfolding in front of him. The people beside him enjoyed watching this battle of nerves. Raj wondered if it would help the poor animals if he would back his vehicle into the lions or at least honk the horn. He urged the Masais to do something, but they were content to just watch.

The herd had moved away again, and had resumed their watchful stance. Both sides were watching each other. The injured buffalo had started bleeding. Three lionesses were trying to gouge his flesh out. But he had not succumbed.
Two buffaloes from the herd took three steps ahead, a few seconds later a few more followed them. Then the whole herd moved a few steps closer to the lions. But they stopped again. The lions were alert and ready to attack.

The injured buffalo fell to one knee, the buffaloes moved again. One of the younger lions, at the head of the pride slowly, took a step back. This prompted the buffaloes to move forward again. They were now just twenty feet away from the lions. The lions held their ground, unfazed by the herd. One of the lionesses let go of the buffalo and joined the pride. The herd was feeling more confident now; the buffaloes leading the herd shook their heads as a warning. Another lion took a step backwards.

Another lioness let go of her hold of the buffalo's neck. When the herd was within ten feet of the lions, the other lioness left the buffalo and moved back. The herbivores reclaimed their ground, step by step. The lion turned back and was about to walk away when two lionesses charged ahead. The herd froze, the lion turned back and roared.

It was too much for Raj to bear. He jumped into his pick-up and sped all the way to the middle of the scene, honking as loudly as the vehicle's horn would let him. Both sides looked at the charging vehicle. Raj took it behind the lions. The pride was now between the vehicle and the buffaloes. They ran away as fast as they could. The herd circled the victim and watched the vehicle turn away from them. The buffaloes slowly moved away from the place with the bleeding victim.

The mood back at the site was jubilant. But one Masai was very disapproving of Raj's interference. "It is illegal to run vehicle like this on animals," he said. Poto retorted, "You are not real Masai, he is real Masai. Get lost."

The team headed back to Arusha. The Serengeti experience had knocked out Bonde and his team. His vehicles needed urgent repairs and Ramadan Eid was a good excuse to recharge everyone's spirits and spruce up the equipment.

After a lot of deliberations and pleading, Zuly agreed for a two-week break. Mama Rose set out to find her new-found fortune.

As Bonde's army headed back for a well-earned rest nobody was in a mood to talk. Some of them were irritated that they could not sleep on the way home because of the bumpy roads. After hours of torture, the trucks rolled on to tarmac roads.

The Profesaa took advantage of the moment to say, "Serengeti is full of animals. I do not know why we were putting simu tower in jungle. Who will use it?"

Glad to be back on their favourite routine again, everyone chorused, "Ndiyo-o-o."

Bonde had dozed off and woke up on hearing the shout. He opened his eyes and said, "Profesaa! Eh!" He fell asleep immediately.

Raj was in his own world, thinking about climbing Kili again. Serengeti had taken him away from rest of his world.

Chapter 13: Second attempt

Raj decided to go to Moshi, a town near Mount Kilimanjaro and prepare for the climb. Poto accompanied him since repairs needed to be carried out on the damaged trucks. Raj found a small, neat guesthouse run by Poto's friend and decided to stay there.

He went to the Mount Kilimanjaro base camp and was stunned at the sight that greeted him. It was a clear day and Kili looked majestic with both peaks, Kibo and Mawenzi touching the sky. Looking at the lush green valleys, and comforted by the distant sounds of ringing church bells, Raj felt happy. He was tired after his short climb and decided to head back into town.

He called up to speak with Leena, but she was busy in a meeting. He spoke to his mother. She asked him when he and Leena would get married. She insisted that it happen quickly, and that he decided the date within six months. After that ultimatum, Raj called up his friends and caught up on their lives. Huku who had accompanied Raj on this trip, settled down for a long nap. When Raj walked out of the booth, he found Salome standing there, waiting for her turn to use the phone.

Their eyes met. For a moment, they could not speak. Raj stammered, "Mama... mama... habari yako (how are you)?"

They held hands and hugged each other. Huku jumped out from under the chair. Salome yelled in delight, "Oooo, Huku! You too are there?"

She sat down to greet him. Huku was wagging his entire body. He seemed to be crying tears of joy and licked her shoulders and cheeks. Salome was caught off balance and nearly fell but she was smiling and laughing throughout Huku's warm welcome. Raj offered her a hand and pulled her up.

In one breath she asked him where he was staying, how long he would be there and how he was. The people milling around the phone booth enjoyed this reunion.

"Let's go and have beer, Mama."

"Don't call me Mama! Call me Salome. You forgot my name too."

They sat in a bar and filled each other in about what was happening in their lives. In the evening, Salome took Raj to her house. Her father, a retired civil servant, belonged to the Chaga tribe, known for business acumen, education and administration. He was very scared of Huku and was suspicious about Raj's relationship with his daughter. As he watched his daughter and the Indian man chat, he found a good companion in Raj. Salome's mother liked Raj too and found him funny. Soon enough, the father started talking about his favourite topic — local problems and politics. They discussed the poor financial state of the local community dispensary and the efforts by some of the members to highlight their urgent plea for help.

Raj suggested, "If Raisi (president) is coming to visit, then instead of asking for appointments with him and then begging for funds, why not present a cultural programme involving the children during the evening dinner being hosted by regional commissioner?

All the senior government officials, local businessmen, bankers, and NGOs will be invited. It would be a good backdrop to appeal for help."

"Good idea! Baba (father)?" Salome chirped excitedly.

Salome's father liked the idea too and decided to meet the other community leaders.

The idea was accepted immediately. It was decided that three songs would be presented. One would have a nationalistic theme and would be accompanied by children dancing to it. Boys from the community would present the other two songs. The regional commissioner was a good friend of Salome's father. He liked the idea as it would add an emotional touch to his high profile dinner.

Raj and Huku continued to train for the climb, walking from the hotel to the base camp twice a day. In the evening he would go to watch the rehearsals for the musical programme. Occasionally, Raj would be invited to Salome's house for dinner. Then they would sit in the veranda and talk. Huku was a passive observer of these endless conversations. Raj told Salome about Leena's visit and their uncertain future together. Salome privately wished she were Leena. She was not upset, since she could not define this relationship. White men and women could court each other, but this was not the case with Asians. But she just wanted to live for the moment and enjoy every moment with Raj. She adored him. It was unconditional, unilateral, selfless love.

The programme was due to take place in three days and Raj was busy with that and his training for the climb.

The programme was due to take place in three days and Raj was busy with that and his training for the climb.

Raj attended training sessions organised by a hotel that conducted Mount Kilimanjaro climbing professionally, every year. Raj approached the owner to book his group of guides and porters. The owner, a white man, was having a drink with another elderly white man, Jonathan. Raj booked his date and told them that he preferred to stay with his friends outside but he would still join the troupe with all the requisite training and equipment provided by the hotel.

They settled for a price. Jonathan was looking for some more members to share the expenses of a guide, porters and cooks. Raj agreed to join him.

"Are you not the one who regularly walks up to the base camp with a dog in the morning?" Jonathan asked.

"Yes, and in the evening too."

"Good. You must get used to the thin air and low air pressure before you climb, particularly if you come from Dar, which is at sea level." The hotelier said. He was a diehard enthusiast of Kili-neering

The evening of the programme was filled with frenetic activity. The lush green lawns, outside the old palatial government guesthouse were the venue. After welcoming the dignitaries and introducing the local leaders to them, a special treat was announced.

Well-dressed children ran on to the lawn and cheerfully sang the national anthem. After that the kids danced to the accompaniment of the audience's applause. The older boys, dressed in white and a blue necktie, were received with warm applause, although the boys tended to forget the words and spoke to each other while they were supposed to be singing.

Raj was standing near the boys and realised that they were very nervous. He walked into their midst and started singing a very popular local song, in Kiswahili. The boys were relieved, since they knew this song really well and they joined him. It was about someone complaining about his lover or wife who threw all sorts of tantrums in their daily life. It had repetitive line 'e mamma e..' , with thumping beats. Their first son looked like an Arab when he asked her about the reason; she said it looked like his father. Everybody laughed.

The chorus was well known and the audience joined in. During a musical interlude, Raj took the microphone, "everyone has a child in their heart. As we grow, we put a cage around it; we shackle it by inhibitions, age, social status, and so-called maturity. The child wants to sing and dance. The child wants to be free."

The people agreed, they said together, "haya."

"Unshackle it, open the cage. Do not worry who is watching you. Do not worry who you are. Do not worry who is next to you. Just do what it says and you will enjoy your life," Raj continued.

He continued with the song again. The second child looked Chinese. Again she said it was like her grandfather and so on. The song narrated his daily life in a humorous way. The boys kept singing, Raj added, "Let the child in you be free. Enjoy yourself and dance. Sing this song aloud even if you do not know the words. Get up and shake your body. Look at that Bibi (old lady). She is thumping her feet. So old, her health does not allow it, but look at her."

He walked to the lady, took her hand and led her to the front. The applause was deafening. The lady raised her hands and tried to shake her body. Most people got up and did the same. The lady hugged Raj and made her way back to her seat.

Though it was a formal occasion with the president in the front row, the straitjacket of decorum had been removed. A group started dancing a little away in the corner. More and more people joined. Heads turned towards them. The president was smiling too and Raj's encouraging words and funny Kiswahili pronunciation made everyone smile.

Once the song ended, Raj politely acknowledged the prominent dignitaries and the crowd. He seized the opportunity and made an appeal, "As you can see, the children and these young boys from the Marangu community are so lively and refreshing like a bunch of flowers on Mount Kilimanjaro, or a pack of birds chirping and reminding us of early morning. They are our future. They are the morning."

"To keep them smiling, they need to be healthy. The community's hospital earlier run by an NGO has nobody to fund it. It is in a very bad condition. Our appeal to all the elderly and lion-hearted people here is to run it or at least donate liberally for the dispensary."

This time everyone stood up and clapped. A well-known, elderly freedom fighter from the community who was supposed tlo make the appeal, rushed to Raj, "You saved me. I couldn't have said it better. God bless you."

The regional commissioner joined the bandwagon and added his pleas.

After the dinner, it was announced by the president that he would help the dispensary and that the details would be announced soon. A missionary NGO head came forward and made an offer to adopt the hospital if the government allowed it to.

While dinner was on, many people came and congratulated Raj. Everybody thanked him for his assistance and his powerful speech. Men, women and children from the community surrounded him. They wanted to pose with Raj as if he was born and brought up in the same community. *Salome stood next to him with pride evident on her happy face. The whole scene looked like Raj's wedding reception.*

The next two days were very hectic preparing for the climb. Raj shifted to the hotel from where he would begin his climb to Kili. Every body assembled. The hotel finalized the guides, cooks, and helpers and handed over the climbing gear to the team members. Jo met Raj over dinner. They talked about the equipment they were carrying. The climb was to start at 6 AM.

Raj woke up at 5 AM. He was not feeling too good, his body ached and he felt like going back to sleep. But he cursed himself and stood ready.

The caravan started at 6 AM from the base camp. It was a very cold morning. The large pine and cypress trees shrouded by giant ferns and old man's beard did not let the sunrays reach them, they climbed in silence.

There were no sounds of human beings, or the distant sounds of vehicles, or the chirping of birds. It was a dead rain forest. After walking for half a mile, Raj started lagging behind.

Jonathan noticed and said, "Young man, what happened?"

Raj assured him that nothing was wrong and asked him to continue, promising that he would catch up soon. Jo went ahead leaving the guide behind. Raj's legs were too stiff and heavy to walk. He was breathing heavily. More than that, he was disgusted with himself. He told his guide, "I have been walking and trainingfor the past one week. I never felt like this before."

The guide consoled him, "Do not worry, you will get used to it."

After another kilometre, Raj stopped talking, except to ask how much further they had to go. He was keen on reaching the first campsite (2723 meters) at Mandara. He felt feverish and took analgesics. He kept stumbling now but finally managed to reach the resting point. He lay down flat on a bench. One of his helpers was ready with hot coffee and sandwiches. Raj could hardly swallow.

He just did not feel like getting up. The guide advised him to return. But Raj
continued to the next camp and crashed there. He started shivering.
Jonathan sat next to him, "Are you alright?" He touched Raj's forehead. "Oh boy!
You have fever. You cannot go any further," the older man pronounced. ' Raj was
writhing in pain. He spent a restless night.

The next day, Jo and the others went ahead, but a guide strapped Raj on to a stretcher
and carried him to the base camp. He was rushed to the government hospital. Malaria
was so rampant in the region that the doctor gave him quinine shot before any other
medication. The guide informed Salome and she rushed to the hospital.

Chapter 14: Lead, kindly light… the night is dark

Raj was running a high fever. Salome talked to the nurse about his condition and took charge of his needs. She constantly checked his temperature and put a piece of wet cloth on his forehead and arms to cool his body down. Raj knew that she was always by his side, but did not have the strength to thank her. He hovered between a state of semi-consciousness and deep sleep. Salome did not leave Raj's side even for a moment. He was unable to keep down any food or water and continued to vomit. As an Asian, he was an unusual patient for the hospital. Not just Salome, the nurses and doctors also tried their best to restore his health.

A boy was dispatched with blood samples to Arusha, about 50 kilometres away. However, it would take at least two days for the report.

Raj finally woke up on the second night of his stay in the hospital. He looked around him and saw Salome's head resting on his forearms. She was holding Raj's hand with both her hands and was asleep. Raj was overwhelmed. When he had left India, he had never thought he would one day find himself in some remote African hospital and be looked after with so much care by an African girl. He gently ran his fingers through her hair and softly thanked her. In moments, he fell asleep again.

The next afternoon, Zuly arrived. He met the doctor on duty and asked about Raj's condition. The head nun in charge of the hospital accompanied him to the general ward where Raj was being treated.

Zuly was surprised to find Salome sitting close to Raj, putting a wet cloth on his forehead. He thought she was a nurse. He asked, "Is he still feverish?" Salome was too worried to say anything and just nodded. Zuly touched Raj's forehead. He was very warm.

Zuly turned to the doctor, "How do we control his fever?"

The doctor tried to explain what Raj's medical condition was and kept asking Salome details about his fever and she replied quickly and unerringly.

Zuly thought Salome was the nurse in charge of Raj. "You think he is improving?" he asked her. She shook her head and broke down. The head nun tried to comfort her but she just could not cope. It was then that Zuly realized that Salome was not a nurse.

While comforting Salome, she told Zuly that Raj was very lucky to have such a dedicated friend. At that moment, Salome's family and friends came into the ward. Zuly wondered what Raj could have done for all these people that had made them so grateful.

The nun said to Salome, "Calm down child. It is prayer time now. Why don't you go to Yesu and pray? He is very kind. He will help."

Salome got up, wiped her face and looked at the crowd around her. She saw her father there with a basket of fruits in his hand; he pulled her close and hugged her. She broke down again but this time the nun led her out of the room into the hospital's church.

The parish priest started "Lord Yesu, (Jesus) you shared in our human nature to heal the sick and save all mankind. Mercifully listen to our prayers for the physical and spiritual health of our sick brother whom we have anointed in your name. May your protection console him and your strength make him well again. Help him find hope in suffering for you have given him a share in your passion. You are Lord forever."
The gathering said 'Amen'.

Salome walked to the front of the congregation and began to speak in a trembling voice in Kiswahili

"O, Lord. He is a very nice man. He is very kind. He helped our community. We need him very much. He does not deserve such harsh punishment. Be kind, my Lord. Please.." She could not continue and started sobbing.

The hall reverberated with a melodious song that came straight from the hearts of everyone gathered there.

"Lead, kindly light. The night is dark, and I am far from home, Lead thou me on."
After a very touching prayer from Salome, people went back to Raj's bed and wished him and Zuly good luck and left.

Zuly was stunned by this genuine concern from people he had never met. He asked one man how so many people knew Raj.

On hearing Raj's role in the community's development, Zuly was impressed. He decided to call 'flying doctors' from Nairobi and take him there. He called up Raj's parents and they instantly said they would come to Nairobi.

On his way with Raj to Nairobi, in a small chartered plane ambulance, Zuly looked out of the window and thought about the young man who had done such good work for him and for strangers. He remembered the days before Raj was part of the team, when the men appointed as the project head would just not go out of Dar and start work on the site, giving him various excuses. They would behave like dictators and distance themselves from the locals. While preparing to go to the site, they would make arrangements to stay in a guest house, eat good food and come back as soon as possible. Raj had not only set up towers but he had also spun a web of relations around him with the locals. And yet, Zuly had been particularly tough with Raj. A strong sense of guilt took hold of him.

Raj's mother made her senior doctor talk to the doctor in charge in Nairobi. It was decided to go for typhoid confirmatory tests since four days had passed and Raj was still suffering from high fever.

By the time his parents made it to the hospital, it was confirmed that Raj was suffering from typhoid. Zuly developed a genuine concern for Raj. He picked up Raj's parents from the airport. He reassured them that the diagnosis and quality of treatment was top notch. Because it was their first time in Africa, Raj's parents were very worried about being unable to help their son and were enraged at almost everything that they encountered.

Raj was very pale when his parents saw him.

"My son, what have you done to yourself?" his mother cried.

The father tried to converse with people around them. The medication was changed and Raj's condition improved. Zuly looked after Raj's parents well. They were friendlier as time passed. In a few days, Raj's condition showed great improvement. It was decided that Raj would be taken back home to India once he was fit to fly. Raj was to board his plane on a stretcher.

On the way to the airport, Raj's mother told Zuly, "Mr. Zuly thanks for saving my son's life. You gave him a job, which for the first time in his life, he enjoyed. He likes Africa so much. But it is time he goes back to India and settles down. His marriage is long overdue. Can you spare him now? If you want, I will send him here for a few months, but… you know... I am really sorry…"

"No Ma'am! If you feel that Raj has a better life or future in India, I will manage. He has done so many things for me. Do not worry. Let him recover. But I will miss him."

On the day of his departure to India, Raj was still unable to sit up for too long. Zuly had made all the arrangements and Raj's parents were happy that Raj was coming back home. Zuly took Raj's hands in his and said, "Raj, I am sorry if I have hurt you, but I will miss you. I hope you are happy with your family. Forget Africa. God bless you. Bye."

Raj was touched and promised, "I will come back, do not worry Mr. Zuly. Sorry for all this trouble. Please give my regards to uncle. Tell him not to worry."

Soon, he was airborne. The monkey left the jungle. All through the long flight, Raj thought about how his life had changed, especially in the last few days. He remembered Salome's kindness. He could feel her soft hair and hands. She had not hesitated once in doing any 'dirty work' for Raj. She had washed his feet, helped him change his clothes and sheets and held his head while he threw up. He did not know how he could repay her at all. He felt really bad that he had not been able to bid her goodbye. Raj remembered Poto, and suddenly thought about Huku.

My God, where will Huku be? I hope Poto takes care of him, he prayed.

Back in Africa, Huku was sleeping under Poto's pick-up and Poto was snoring in the driver's seat with his legs jutting out of the window. A welder was busy repairing the truck's front guard.

When Raj reached Mumbai, he was given a hero's welcome by all his relatives and friends. Leena was waiting for him, ahead of anyone else. Raj was brought out on a stretcher and he had to get back home in an ambulance. Vicky and Leena got in with him and kept up a constant conversation with Raj.

Leena was confused. She was quite concerned about Raj's health and wanted to comfort him, but Vicky's presence ensured that she couldn't really speak her mind. There were spells when she would look at Raj and Raj would just give her a faint smile. She wanted privacy.

Raj felt good to be back in Mumbai. He could see the ever-changing skyline of the city, huge hoardings, flyovers and new vehicle models and all such urban wares with an aura of modernity. The familiar sights and sounds comforted him and reassured him that he would survive all of life's challenges now.

Chapter 15: Swinging in concrete jungle.

Raj recovered quickly. The visits from relatives and friends became less frequent. Leena had to travel out of Mumbai for a presentation. His mother had taken a week's leave from work and made all kinds of healthy vegetarian soups for her son. Apart from being busy in the kitchen, she was busy answering calls from relatives and friends who would end up suggesting 'get well soon' herbal recipes. Milie, Raj's sister, flew down from London not just to see him, but also to convince him to never return to Africa.

Once Raj was back on his feet, his mother and sister would try to get him to talk about marriage. They would sing Leena's praises and tell him all about what she had done for their family.

Zuly called up to assure himself that Raj was feeling better. All Raj could ask about was the work on the sites. Zuly told him that his cousin had taken charge of the work. The older man reminded Raj that his parents wanted him to stay in India. But, Zuly added that if Raj couldn't find a job, his work in Africa was always waiting for him.

As the days went by, Raj became more convinced that he did not want to take up a job in Mumbai. But, under pressure from Leena and his parents, he did apply to a few companies.

One morning, Leena called.

"Raj, how are you, love?"

"Bolshoying."

"What?"

"Nothing, tell me."

"Listen, I have a client who is quite known to me. I talked to him about you. He is looking for someone who can manage one of his projects. It is a resort."

"Is it not cheap to ask favours from a client as a financier? What image will he have about the company and about you?"

"Shut up! This is not a time for a joke."

"I am serious."

"Be practical, yaar. I am not doing any favours for him. He can go to any banker and get funds. I am also conscious about my image and the company's."

"Okay. So?"

"I want you to see him tomorrow in the afternoon." She gave him the address and said, "Raj. Just close your eyes and remember the moments we spent in Serengeti. Just pick up any job. We are going to have a very long and very happy life ahead. For the sake of our future together. I love you so much."

His mother was ecstatic to know that Raj was going for an interview. She went to her puja room (worship corner) in the house where photographs of Hindu gods and deities were hung. She folded her hands and prayed with closed her eyes.

"If Raj accepts this, I will observe fasts on fifty-one consecutive Thursdays. Lord, please take care of my son."

Raj reached the office. He was immediately called into the boss's cabin. He saw a young man surrounded by four people.

"Mr. Raj, can you wait for sometime? We have a meeting going on, I will call you," the young man said.

Raj nodded and waited outside. He took the time to remember the resorts he had been to in India and in Dar. He analysed the consumer habits in India and in Africa. He almost started designing the resort, but was shaken out of his daydream by the receptionist. "Would you like something to drink?"

"Yes. Some water and a cup of tea."

The so called meeting did not last much longer but people were going in and out of the room. After two hours, while Raj was snoring in the bedroom of his virtual resort, he was called in.

"Sorry Mr. Raj. You are working in Africa, yeah? Must be pretty exciting, with all those wild animals. My children are after me to take them there on a safari."

So saying, the interviewer ended up planning the entire itinerary of his safari with advice from Raj. Finally, he got back to talking about work again.

"Well, Mr. Raj, as far as work goes, it may start after two months, but you can come from tomorrow."

"What about my work? I mean, what is the project like and what is my role in it?"

"I will tell you all that, once you join."

"Okay sir, I shall come tomorrow and join work but after about a week or so I may have to go back to Africa, and wind up my work there. It may take about two weeks."

"No problem. As I said, the project will take time. I was discussing the project and Ms. Leena told me about you. I will need someone, so why not take a known person?"

Raj hated this attitude and left. He had almost expected this. He had not been selected because of his experience or qualifications. He had also found the employer too casual in his approach towards work.

But not to seem egoistical, he decided to join the next day. Leena's and Raj's parents were only too happy. Raj did not do anything on the first day, except answer questions about Africa from his new colleagues.

"Had you been to the place, which National Geographic channel is showing films about this week?"

"Yes, Serengeti wildlife area in Tanzania"

"Have you seen any hunting?"

"Yes but not in Africa."

"Where then?"

"In Mumbai"

"What?"

"Yes, head hunting!"

"What is the difference?"

"Well, lions and deer, zebra all move together. When a lions get hungry, they target one animal and hunt it down. Calm returns after the kill. The grass grazers settle down to graze a few feet away from the carnivores. It is a fair natural play on both sides. Intentions are very clear and evident. One wants to prey and the other wants to escape. A human will first tempt his prey to comfort and trust by sheer expression and behaviour and then kill it."

"Is it true, that in Africa, people eat humans also?"

Raj decided to be tangential in his answers as he found people teasing him.

"Yes. But only one at a time. Not the whole community as is done elsewhere."

"Eating communities ? Where?"

"When a nation decides to host Olympics by overspending and borrowing. It can convert a shantytown into world-class mega-polis in a few months and win laurels world over. What happens after the show is over? The massive infrastructure thus built to facilitate a few days' show proves a big drain on finances. Either the city fades or continues to get finances at the expense of rural or under developed society forcing them to further flock the city."

"But where in all this, are communities being eaten, man?"

Raj continued unperturbed "Then comes the waft of criminality, social evils and diseases. Society goes for shortcuts to survive or thrive in so-called mega-polis. Shortcuts in acquiring land, shortcuts in building, shortcuts in jobs, shortcuts in products or contracts. Those who are powerful become skilled at shortcuts and cuts. Again vast section of society undergoes suffering. The city had no long-term perpetual survival kit. The small village community thus gets consummated in the process."

"Uh! You are talking like a politician."

"No, no, He is an environmentalist, the green boy!"

After playing anchor on the private National Geographic channel, Raj went to the same restaurant he would frequent when he was in college. He called up Leena but she was busy.

A waiter recognised him. He smiled and said, "After a long time, sir. Where are you these days? Got a job somewhere?"

Raj did not know how to answer him, so he simply nodded his head. After his customary coffee and toast, he called up Zuly.

Zuly missed his hardworking employee. He told him about the progress on the sites and asked Raj's opinion on a few issues. Raj asked him about the case in court. Zuly laughed and told him that now the court had shifted to its new premises and the files had been misplaced. Raj asked for a number to contact Bonde. Although he could not get Bonde on the line, he did hear about what was happening on the site. He came to know that Huku was not eating well and that Salome and the people from her community were enquiring about him often. He left behind his contact number and tried calling Salome's number at the school, but could not get through. He hung up. He was silent.

Like a screen saver on an idle terminal, Raj's mind was covered with his African experiences. The memories of his recent past emerged on the screen. Salome, Huku, Poto, Mama Rose Mr. Zuly, Mr. Karimji, open skies, mountains and clouds and finally the defiant Mount Kilimanjaro all rushed on his mental screen.

He felt like a coward, running away from everyone and everything that had become so important for him. He was sad.

***

"Raj, good news! One more call letter," his father said.

Raj was in a quandary about his many contradicting commitments. But, his parents and Leena were happy that Mumbai had finally recognised Raj's worth. They would talk about the job offers Raj was receiving each time a relative called.

Raj tried getting through to Leena, but she could not come to the phone and Binoy took Raj's messages.

Later that night Raj took Leena out for dinner. He wanted to put forward his dilemma, but it would upset Leena, so he was keeping mum. She talked about her day, her boss, Binoy, and his many accomplishments.

God made only one mistake while creating or evolving humans. Those, who are innocent and honest to themselves, who go by their natural instinct, who cannot express themselves, are ruled by those who are wily, manipulative, pretenders, dishonest to their heart. But they can express themselves very well.

"How is the job, Raj? Does he spare some time for you?"

"No."

"Okay," acquiesced Leena, "let's see if you like this offer, if you don't, dump this guy. No hassles. He would not mind."

"Yeah, good riddance."

"Come on, honey! Don't be sarcastic. It is just a passing phase. Raj, please cheer up. I can't see you sad. Things will change for the better," she promised.

He tried to forget what was on his mind by talking to Leena about various things. But he found that the only thing she could talk about was her work and her boss.

Raj went for another interview and had to tell the manager why he was hopping out of the African job after such a short time.

"So, you did not do some hi-tech civil job in Africa."

"True, but I have been there for just a little over a year."

"It makes a big difference when you are out of touch with the latest for more than a year, Mr. Raj."

Raj's patience gave way, "You know, sir, when I appeared for my first interview, after college, and started discussing the latest trends, I was told that those things were theoretical. I was advised to be practical and learn the 'realities' before I speak.

When I acquired relevant experience and learned to be 'practical',now I am being asked to be equipped with the latest..."

"Look here. We always go for technical expertise…"

"What is your project like?"

"A township for lower, medium and higher income groups, only seventy kilometres from Mumbai. About five hundred flats, ten floors, buildings and bungalows.'

"Something like what I did before going to Africa. Well, to me, the job of a good civil engineer involves managing work as per the plans, on time, with minimal thefts and so on. If I do not have knowledge about some aspect of the project, I learn it from the architect. Despite technological advances, the top floors of our buildings always leak. When the tenants cry hoarse, we put tar or chemical in the cracks. We still park our cars in the basement and they get submerged during the floods. Our flats will be no more than 500 to 700 sq feet, but we will boldly say that it is a 'three or four bedroom luxurious flat'. If you ask me to work on building a national highway or an airport or a 50-storey building on reclaimed land, I will need a senior like you to guide me. One must have his heart in the job, sir!"

"We shall let you know, if you are selected," was the curt reply.

Amidst all this confusion, Leena's parents decided that the most eligible man for their daughter was Binoy. They started talking to Leena about it.

The monkey did not know how to swing or jump in the concrete jungles of Mumbai.

Chapter 16: Africa calling

Ten days after he had left Africa, Raj got in touch with Poto.
"Bossi! When are you coming back? You forgot us. Huku is crying, Bwana. Ata (even) your girlfriend is missing you a lot. Please Bossi, don't be so harsh, Bwana.Mr. Zuly is also very sad. His ndugu (relative) *don't* know anything, very lazy, shouting all the time. Watu (people) do not like to work under him, wewe rudi (you come back),"

Raj called up Salome too. She was too tongue-tied with happiness to say anything more than 'How are you?' She also kept asking him when he was planning to come back. Her genuine concern and warmth shook Raj. He felt as if he had gone into the past. He felt like going back to the hospital where he left her. He wanted to sit in the quiet ward and talk with her. He wanted to make her smile. He called up Zuly and told him that he would like to come to Dar, to wind up his work.

When his parents were told about his imminent trip, they were insistent that he get engaged before he left. Raj tried explaining to them the issues that needed to be sorted out before marriage. Things were back to square one with him. His parents could not prevent him from going to Africa. Leena cried and made him promise that he would come back in ten days.

As soon as Raj got there, he started handing over approval files, cost sheets and technical data sheets to Zuly's nephew, Azim, and visited the new site at Mwanza selected by him. When he reached the site everybody stopped work.

Poto ran towards him and greeted him with a hug. Bonde was right behind. Raj shook hands with each worker; they all expressed their sadness 'Pole' (sorry) at his illness. Then Mama Rose first shook hands with him and then embraced him. A sudden yelp alerted them that Huku was still tied up and straining at his leash to jump on Raj. As soon as he was free, he shot forward like a bullet and almost climbed on top of his master. Raj sat down and Huku licked Raj everywhere. Raj could not help but cry. Everybody assumed that he had come back.

Later that day, Raj asked Azim, "What happened to that theft case? Any judgment in sight?"

"What judgment? There is a shortage of handcuffs now. The prison where our turnboys are kept needs thirty handcuffs to bring remandees to the court. They have only sixteen. So, after the first batch goes back from the court, the handcuffs are handed over to the next batch. By that time, the judge goes away. The people who supply food to prisons have not been paid for the past one year, so they have stopped supplies. The prisoners are on strike and refusing to climb the vehicle which brings them to court. The whole thing is at a standstill."

"Are you joking?" was all Raj could ask.

"No, Bwana, I am serious. You know the shopkeeper who stole our material is freely moving around."

"Why?"

"He has two cases against him now. Our case is the civil one and his lover's case is the criminal one. So, whenever our case comes up for hearing, his lawyers say that he has a date in another court and vice versa. Now, the director of prosecution will decide which case will be heard first, or which judge will handle both."

"Wait, wait," Raj pleaded, "give me a break now. I will forget my civil engineering and become the law minister of this country." Poto, Bonde and Juma started laughing.

Bonde said, "I told you, Mistaa Raji, everybody will escape and only two people will be very happy — the police and the advocates. Serekali (Government employees)! Duuh! If they were Mungu, a mama will deliver toto after ten or twelve months.Till the child puts his hand out and cries or kicks mama in her stomach."

Everybody burst into laughter.

Poto added, "There is one more problem. The prison vehicles are out for repairs, so they have asked for jeshi (army) buses. How many can they give? So if a traffic policeman charges you on Friday evening under dangerous driving and puts you in the lock-up, you just can't come out on bail, because of all these matata (problems)."

Juma spoke up, "And they will catch Mzee Raji first, because he is a Muhindi. The policeman will have a fat bribe. He will enjoy his weekend."

The Profesaa wanted to have his say, "The UK police is very good, the Mossad in Israel and FBI in US are also very good. The courts are good in USA. We should send our police and judges to all these countries for seminar and training."

The customary uproar, "Ndiyo-o-o," drowned out all other sounds.

Raj forgot his troubles back home and enjoyed being back in Africa.

***

Raj inspected the site chosen by Azim. "We have to change the site," he pronounced finally, "We need to have it on that hill, rather than in these plains. It is too close to the other towers and it will affect our transmissions."

Azim argued, "It will be more expensive."

Eventually, the site was changed and Azim was packed off. Raj decided to complete the Mwanza project and then return to India.

He needed time to decide whether to make Africa his home or not. He was spared the wrath of Leena and his parents as there was no direct phone in that area, but not for long.

Sparks flew when he conveyed his decision to prolong his stay. Tears flowed from India but the Indian Ocean was large enough to drown them. Leena threatened to break off the relationship, saying that Raj was keener about Africa than her. His parents continued to plead with him.

One day, Salome came to the site to meet Raj. Everybody teased Raj right in front of her. She laughed and so did Raj. Raj took her to the lakeside. They sat and talked for hours in very quiet and serene surroundings. They opened their hearts to each other about their true feelings. Salome told him how she had felt when he was in the hospital and then when he was taken to Nairobi. She could not describe how she felt after he left for India.

"I thought you would not come back after that illness."
"Yeah, I might not have, but you know. Kili wouldn't allow me to forget it."
"God! You still haven't forgotten the mountain?"
"No. It used to fascinate me earlier. Now it upsets me that I was defeated twice."
"Take it easy, Raji! Why are you so hell bent on climbing Kili? There are many other wonderful things in your life."
Raj laughed, "Such as the people who stay near Kili?"
Salome could not believe her ears, "Well said, Raji--I hope you mean it."
After a moment of silence, Raj said, "I shall try again, after I finish the next site in Mbeya (town in southern Tanzania)."
"But why are you so crazy about it? Tell me honestly," she asked.
Raj paused for a moment, unable to decide whether he should confess or laugh it off with a joke. He looked at her and saw the intense concern for him in her eyes. She was too soft to argue or insist that he should not climb Mount Kilimanjaro. But he could see in her eyes a wish that he wouldn't do so.

He smiled and said, *"There are two kinds of people in this world. Smart ones, who like horses, are fast and good at jumping over obstacles. They do not remove the obstacles. They are fed well and looked after. They are always in the limelight. People put a lot of money on them.*

Their master may ride them for an hour a day but the rest of the time, he bathes them, feeds them good fodder, keeps scores of people for their health and hygiene, to keep their stables clean and so on.

They are displayed and petted in front of visitors. They comprise ten percent of the entire population. The rest are donkeys. They slog all through their life. They live a hard life, because they are mediocre. They are always abused even though they are obedient and hard-working. They are mocked for their mediocrity. I belong to that category."

Salome could not fathom the self-hatred and wounded self-esteem that made Raj think like this. She could weed out only horses and donkeys from Raj's philosophy.

She laughed, "Donkey and you? Wewe! I thought our forefathers were monkeys!"

But, now that Raj had spoken what was on his mind he couldn't stop. "You know Salome, I hate mediocrity. *A mediocre person can find comfort only with another mediocre person. He is surrounded by mediocre people. I pity his wife who was probably smart and intelligent. Had she married a smart guy, she would be living a much better life. I pity the children even more, who are programmed to be mediocre because they inherit his genes. They are destined to be mediocre.*

They would be smarter and wealthier if they had a smarter father. I want to prove me to myself. I want to attempt something heroic, something extraordinary. I want to stand up and rise above the clouds of mediocrity like Kili," he concluded.

While talking he avoided looking in her eyes. He was staring down on the table. He was looking at her but not into her eyes but when he looked at her face, he found that her smile had vanished. Her eyes were moist. She understood what he meant.

"Please Bwana, do not hate yourself. You are great Raji. Trust me, if you think you are mediocre, then I am very happy to be with you. I am sorry, I will not ask about Kili again."

Raj tried to bring back their shared bonhomie, "Oh, no, Mama. This always happens when I start on my third bottle of beer. Let's order some food."

They dined till late and finally Raj dropped her to her relative's place.

Chapter 17: Rolling Stones.

Lake Victoria, the third largest in the world is, in fact, a sweet water ocean in the midst of East Africa. It touches the Kenyan, Tanzanian and Ugandan borders and is one of the sources of River Nile. Like an ocean, it has several islands, huge waves and big boats ferrying everything from vehicles to bananas. A huge steamer takes the whole night to cross the lake. About one thousand tons of its fish, Nile perch, is air-freighted daily, for European middle class consumers. Mwanza is situated on this lake.

Because it is situated on the lake and has several tall trees, Mwanza has a vast population of birds, such as kites, storks, egrets and spoonbills. Each species has a preference for a certain kind of tree to stay and perch on. Egrets, in particular, prefer trees with a thin leaf cover, such as the eucalyptus, and perch on its branches and trunk. Even the road below was stained white with their droppings. In the late evening, between the hills, the sky was filled with thousands of bats.

Mwanza, with its two million-strong population, was busy during the day but very quiet in the early morning and evening. The city was in the midst of several hills on both sides of the main city centre. The hills were dotted with huge granite rocks, mostly egg-shaped, oval or round, some of them more than two storeys high.

Due to erosion, there was no grass or mud on them and the rock surfaces were neatly exposed.

Many of the rocks rested on a single gravity-defying point. Many were overhanging, like a toad or a reversed egg, looking very unrealistic. Some rocks as big as a lorry rested on the top of other rocks.

They all looked so neat, as if a careful child had washed and arranged the pebbles, sometimes one over the other. It was nature's sand play, rather pebble play, on the beach of the great lake.

In fact, the hills had more rocks than trees or open space. Many people stayed on the hills. The poor ones lived in huts using the rocks as walls. The rich lived in the valley in buildings two or three storeys high. Also situated in this area were banks, markets and other important establishments. The city was divided by two major roads; one, along the lake and the other in the centre of the valley, dividing the hills.

Lake flies were a peculiarity of the area. These were tiny, like mosquitoes starved for one week, constantly flying in dense clouds. They did not bite or buzz, but they clogged mosquito nets and filled every open space with their dead bodies. They got stuck in the hair, in your mouth, nostrils and ears. It was not advisable to attend nature's call in the midst of a cloud of lake flies. The flies formed such a dense cloud over the lake and surrounding coastal areas that it could be seen as smoke or fog from a twin propelled aircraft.

The lake with islands, hills, birds, tall trees and millions of rocks was a true natural delight.

Since the site was not very far from the city, Raj stayed there in a rented apartment. He loved to jog along the lake in the morning and would try to climb one of the hills. He would reach the peak, choose a rock and rest there for a while looking at the majestic lake.

Work progressed well and was completed on time. Raj, Poto, a watchman and Huku stayed back to complete commissioning while the rest of the gang including Bonde proceeded on a long journey south with all their materials.

Raj wanted to start commissioning in the early morning, and so went to bed before midnight after flipping through a few TV channels as usual and so did the whole town. At 3 am, there was a mild tremor. Some husband thought his wife had gone to pee as usual and pushed the bed. Some wife thought her husband changed the side rather too vigorously. Some old people thought their sugar had gone down, some old people got up and enquired in loud voices and were silenced by even louder voices from their progeny. A few dogs barked and the birds chirped noisily. People got out of their homes and into the streets. A police van prowled the roads. One could see how ugly the usually pretty looking, tidy, well-dressed lady or a gentleman looked when they have just got out of the bed.

Huku and Raj were too lazy to get up and the squeaky ceiling fan created a sound curtain around them, not allowing any other sound to enter the room. After a while, panic was replaced by a sense of adventure. Some people stayed up to have fun, while the rest of the town went back to sleep.

But forty miles away, on an island called Ukerewe, people could not have fun or sleep. The tremors were stronger there, waves crashed onto buildings and shops. Roofs vanished, anchored boats collided against each other, and the powerful sound of waves and screams engulfed the island. There were thousands of fishermen all over the lake fishing Nile perch. Boats near the epicentre overturned. Many people died, some managed to stay afloat. But the rest started fleeing towards the coast. The island had no electricity from the mainland. The waves blew two or three transformers on the outskirts of the island and silenced the generator within minutes. The waves dislodged the generator, the transformers, the cables and poles. Those who survived tried to hang on to whatever they could grab and fled with whatever came in their way.

Some died, some survived like ants clinging on to a floating leaf or twig in a stream. Lake struck with vengeance. It removed every trace of civilisation and fell silent as it was millions of years back. Ukerewe was submerged.

Though the lake covered up the Ukerewe disaster because of its huge mass and size, like the Russians trying to cover up Chernobyl, it could not prevent a few huge waves from spilling over the road in Mwanza city. The waves overturned the boats anchored along the coast line. No one noticed. Most of the town was asleep.

But soon there was somebody else silently complaining about Ukerewe. People woke up to find themselves buried under the bodies of dead clouds of lake flies. The news about Ukerewe spread like wildfire. Although the tragedy of Ukerewe was confirmed, businesses, government offices, banks and schools in Mwanza opened as usual. People were talking in groups in the streets and on the main road. They flocked to see damage done by waves to the roads and the coastal areas.

Raj woke up to find a thick sheet of dead lake flies on his mosquito net. He peeped out of the window and saw a thick cloud of flies covering the street. Huku's body had flies all over; he got up and shook them off. Raj came down to his parking area with Huku where the watchman told him about the tremors at night and about Ukerewe. Raj was surprised at the large-scale devastation, but felt something was amiss. He thought it might be because of the flies and smoggy atmosphere. He drove off to work.

On the way, he found the whole city was on its feet. On reaching the site, Poto told him the same Ukerewe story but he dismissed it as a rumour. He got on with his job.

At around 10 am, short but strong tremors were felt. Streetlight poles vibrated and tube lights fell off. The sky was dotted with birds issuing loud cries and circling the city. Billboards fell down, and some hung up precariously, injuring people. Within seconds, people were rushing out of buildings. Shops and business establishments started closing down.

Suddenly, the lake bulged and a huge wave engulfed the city in waist-deep water, which quickly entered the streets, shops, banks and vehicles. Panic had set in and people and vehicles went about helter-skelter banging each other, blocking the streets. The rich were determined to leave town with their families as long as their vehicles would permit it. Some were apprehensive of the masses and the floods.

Most people went towards the hills. The people on the hills watched the commotion down below. The choice was between the flood and the earthquake. Some started shifting on the terraces with foodstuff and bedding.

Groups of vandals broke open shops and started looting. One group entered the bank. The guard had disappeared and so had most of the staff. The officers were closing the strong room and safes. They were pushed aside and the money was stashed in bags. The robbers inside did not leave because of their greed. They were squeezed and squashed as more people entered the bank to take what they could find. It was the same case in the shops.

A few people laughed, while some cried and prayed. Food, garbage, plastic, slippers and the assorted belongings of citizens started floating in the flood water.

The lake flies had disappeared. The sky was clear, the birds had disappeared. The worst was yet to come.

Raj was about to put a tiny screwdriver in the screw slot when his hand was pushed aside by the tremor. Poto jumped out of the room shouting, "Bossi, kimbie (run)." Raj followed.

They ran out of the control room and saw the tower shaking. The antenna and the dishes were vibrating eerily. Huku was barking incessantly.
When the tremors stopped, they were all panting. Poto said, "Bossi, let's leave Mwanza now. It is dangerous."
"Where should we go? It is not safe to drive when the earth is shaking. Wait till it cools down."
"Let's slowly drive and go to Shinyanga. I told you about Ukerewe. You did not take me seriously."
Raj waited for a while and then mocked Poto, "Ahh, wewe mayayi tu (you are soft like an egg). Be a man, dume. I am about to finish my work. We shall go then, okay?"
"You will repent bossi. Hurry up."
They went inside the room again. They did not notice the mercury-like lining on the horizon a few kilometres away. The lake was spilling over the coastal land.

After about half an hour, there were very strong tremors again. Entire buildings collapsed. Electric and telephone poles were uprooted. Transformers burst, sounding like bombs. Vehicles overturned and vandals were entrapped and found their wealthy grave in the shops and banks they were looting. Some just left the booty and tried run out into the open but fell down and struggled to keep out of the water.

The worst was to come now. Bismarck Rock, a famous landmark in Mwanza city, stood like a huge toad on a sharp edge, defying gravity for eons. When the tremors struck, the toad seemed to lower its head as if it had regained life after millions of years of hibernation. It lowered itself gradually further and further, as if to drink water from the lake. It toppled into the water. When the king bowed down, his army followed. The rocks that had been sitting pretty in the hills of Mwanza city for millions of years started rolling down.

People in the hills were still watching the floods and the panic in the streets. When the avalanche started, they did not have a chance to prepare themselves.
In the first tumble, the rocks flattened houses under them and then they rolled down and killed the people who had gotten outside their homes. This took everyone by surprise; just as people from the city crawled up the hills, the hills pushed everyone away.

There were cries, confusion and chaos. Some were aghast and just accepted their stony death. There were many who climbed the hills, fearing bigger waves. When they saw the rocks coming down on them, they ran down. They fell over each other and the rocks made their fossils for the future.

There was no husband, there was no wife. There was no father. There was no son. Every body was looking at the rocks and trying to dodge. Rocks had no definite path. They would roll and hit other rocks and either stop or bring down another one too. They would get deflected by smaller stones or stubborn tree trunks and change their path.

It did not matter whether someone ran or stopped or got behind a solid rock. Death had come with a long checklist.

A mother had gone to fetch water from a tap, leaving behind a five-year old daughter with a three-year-old son. Both children were in their hut under a huge rock that served partly as a roof and one wall. On hearing the loud cries and colliding rocks, they started crying. They fell down frequently due to tremors. The sister came out to look for their neighbours and the brother followed her, holding on to her skirts. They stepped out of their hut. Their backs were towards the hilltop. They were looking down the hill expecting their mother and crying.

They did not know that a huge rock had started from the edge of the hill in their direction.

The rock came down tumbling over them. A half-cut tree trunk about two metres away deflected the rock slightly. The rock fell on one side and hit the rock that formed a part of their hut. There was a big crash. The tumbling rock was stopped by the saviour rock giving asylum to the poor family. The children were frightened at the sound and turned back to see another wall behind them. They did not know anything and the sister pulled her brother along and went back into the house.

Destiny was not kind elsewhere. There was a government hospital located on one of the hills. As the tremors started, the hospital staff ran out of the two-storied building. Some patients, a few helped by their relatives, also managed to come out. The stronger tremors pushed the ground floor underground and the second storey crushed the intermediate one, which it overhung with broken slabs.

An old lady got out of the building but was unable to walk due to jerks. She shouted for help when she saw people running outside the hospital. When the building collapsed, the 10,000-litre tanks burst and let out the water stored in them. The water came down with force and washed away the old lady down the hill.

A young man shouted at his family to look up to the hills and dodge the rocks. He managed to dodge two rocks as he watched his family get crushed by a large rock. As he recovered from the shock, a herd of cows came running on the narrow pathway from behind. The first cow hit his back and threw him down. He was trampled underfoot by the herd of stampeding cattle.

It seemed as though the hills were melting—the small rocks that sat on top of the larger rocks like a baby monkey sitting on its mother's back, began to tumble down with great momentum. Multi-storied buildings fell like a pack of cards. Two petrol pumps, at the bottom of the hills, burst into flames. Several large trucks with long tankers and cargo containers, which were parked close to the pumps, were squashed like toothpaste tubes.

The sounds of falling and colliding rocks were so loud that human cries could not be heard. Rocks formed a barricade around the hills at the bottom. The debris of buildings clogged the streets.

The tremors seemed to have given the lake a life of its own. Within minutes, it looked like a dome made of a huge gas balloon and thrashed the city with two-storey high waves, one after the other. The water found its way through the streets and the buildings. It moved with great force through the hills. The barricade of rocks on both sides of the town and the debris in the street restricted the water mass spread. As a result, the water entered the city centre at great speed and tremendous force like a water jet. It washed away trucks, vehicles, beds, windows, furniture, roofs, trees, animals and people and all that came after the lake was formed millions of years ago. There was nothing left in the centre of the city other than dunes of wet rubble.

Several fishing boats and ferry vessels were anchored on the shores of the lake. Some of the ferry vessels would even cart huge trucks and goods train to neighbouring country like Uganda and Kenya. There was fish auction yard and wholesale market. There was a fuel depot with huge storage tanks. When waves struck the shores, they dislodged the boats and splashed them on houses and near by streets. The waves took the dead fish with them trying to capture them back from humans. The first wave lifted mighty ferry vessels like a mother lifting her tiny child for diaper changing.

There were some foreigners living on the hills, specially carved out to nest these privileged birds. Some were working for mining companies; some, for road construction companies; some, on water pipeline projects and others as missionaries or NGO workers.

When the lower tide swept the city, it surrounded the hills. A middle-aged white couple were curiously watching the lake water surrounding their hill from wide glass windows of their house near the top of a hill.

The panoramic view of the overflowing lake and its water encircling their hill was exhilarating. After the initial tension, they stood on their balcony with their two daughters.

They moved from one side to the other and called to each other to have a look at the goings-on. Soon, the mother brought four mugs of coffee. With a mug in their hands, they looked on.

When the tremors struck their house, the mugs fell down. The father shouted 'Out, out, out of the house'. They tried to come out but fell on the floor and on the staircase. They tried to grab each other and help. The daughters cried. The parents yelled. They saw a crack in the middle of the floor like a serpent. The house tore from the middle. Walls collapsed. The ground gave way. The house came down like a pack of cards. The first giant wave hit the compound wall like a herd of running beasts.

The wall was gone in seconds, as if it was nothing more than a curtain. Wave after wave came but could not touch the debris of the house. They pounded the soil underneath. The bungalow melted into the waves like an iceberg. The mugs of coffee, like a drop in the ocean, were lost in the waves.

When tremors struck the Tancell towers, the tower started shaking and groaning. Raj, Poto, the watchman, and Huku crawled, tumbled and rolled out of the control room. They got up and ran away only to fall down again. In between the tremors, Poto and the watchman ran for the pick-up; Huku followed Poto, while stopping briefly for Raj to catch up. Poto carried Huku into the back of his pick-up and fumbled with the keys as Raj turned behind to look at the tower. He noticed the water shining behind a distant hill, covering the entire horizon. He was frozen into immobility. He realized that the lake had spilled over.

Since it was the first low-height wave, it was fast but smooth. From the tower hill, it looked harmless. Poto started the engine and started honking frantically.

Raj stopped and started pointing out the water behind the hills, screaming that they had nowhere to go. Poto could not see it; he threatened Raj that he would go away, if Raj did not get into the pick-up. Then the final tremor came. The tower tilted slightly like the Tower of Pisa. The huge antenna fell to the ground. It bounced twice and rolled towards the pick-up. Poto could wait no longer; he drove the pick-up down the hill. Raj was left behind.

As soon as they reached the bottom of the hill, the watchman realised what Raj was trying to say. He started banging the top of the driver's cabin and started screaming. "The lake water is coming. Stop the car."

Poto did not listen and increased the vehicle's speed. The watchman tumbled from his seat, reached the window and screamed again into Poto's ears.

When Poto looked sideways, he saw the water coming towards him. He turned the vehicle around and started driving away from the approaching water. Raj could clearly see Huku, the helper and the pick-up being chased by the oncoming water.

A loud sound behind him forced Raj to look away from the impending disaster. A huge wave was about to hit the control room. Raj started climbing the tower. He was not sure if the wave would flow over the hill but he kept climbing. He had hardly reached the middle rung, when the waves passed him by. He looked at the waves as they swallowed Poto's pick-up, which was tossed up like a rubber toy and pushed down by the second wave.

Raj screamed, "Potooooooo." He then closed his eyes and softly cried, "Huku." He stopped climbing and looked around for the pick-up, which had vanished.

There were so many things floating in the water; the debris of vehicles, houses and uprooted trees. There was a deadly silence.

Mother earth probably experienced it for millions of years earlier when it was born and was cooling down. It had a barren womb then, preparing for life on her.

But the outside world was noisier with radios and TVs flashing news of the disaster. Some thought it to be a minor breach of the lake. But soon the news spread fast. The government and NGOs started appealing for help. The army got there first and sent the first aerial pictures of the devastation. They did not find a landing place for relief work. The president, ministers and journalists got there too and were stunned at the extent of the devastation. It was too much to handle for the poor country.

Hours went by. It was getting darker. Like insects coming out from crevices and holes, survivors started making their way out of the rubble. They were looking for their families, for food and water, and for light. People were asking for matchsticks or burning wood to light up their shelters. Children could be heard crying and elders were helplessly pacifying them. It was going to be a long, long night.
Raj slowly climbed down from the tower and started walking around the hill looking for some sign of life. He could not find the pick-up. He held half a bottle of water that he had rescued from the control room. He took one sip and looked at the sky as if he was thanking God for sparing his life. He realised that his parents might know about the quake and the floods by now. They might think he had died. He could imagine their plight, but there was nothing he could do. He was very tired and lay down on the roof of the control room. He fell asleep, only to wake up from nightmares of a fresh onslaught.

Frogs and insects took charge of the night. The noise they made was head-battering. It was like giving various opera instruments to a whole school and asking children to play whatever they felt like.

When Zuly heard about the quake, it took him some time to realise what it meant. He called Raj's parents and promised that he would find their son. He also told them that Raj's home was about twenty kilometres away from the lake. Both the parents decided to fly immediately to Tanzania. Raj's friends and relatives called or met them to give moral support. Leena wanted to join them.

Bonde, on his way to Iringa with the rest of his army, was taking a break in a small eatery. He was laughing and holding forth on many discussions, when Juma shook his shoulders and pointed at the television screen. Suddenly, the eatery fell silent. Everybody including the hotel staff was looking at the TV. Bonde's hands started trembling. "Allah! Mmeona jamaani (did you see, folks)? Mungu, Al–Madad, help my son and Mistaa Raji." After few moments, he got up. He turned to Juma, "'Jamaani, tuna ondoka Mwanza (we go to Mwanza)." He could not control his anxiety and shouted 'Twende..(let's go)'.

Salome and her friends tried to get as close to Mwanza as possible, and find Raj on foot. She asked her parents to request a special mass in church and pray for Raj and his team. While climbing into the vehicle that would take her to the nearest village, she looked at Mount Kilimanjaro with tears in her eyes and whispered. "Wait till he comes, don't go away."

Mwanza airport used to get one or two Russian-made cargo planes everyday, carrying frozen fish from the lake to Europe. The airport was just a few houses and a tarmac road without lights. It was a refreshing change for a visitor who was used to the Gatwicks of the modern era to climb down a tiny aisle from the aircraft and walk down to the single-storey main building with its iron sheet roof. The first room had two open rectangular openings in the wall, facing the airstrip to push the luggage in and a few grill-like holes above to see the baggage cart coming.

There would be a mild commotion to grab the baggage over exchanges of 'excuse me' and 'samahani-s (sorry)' followed by smiles. The second room was the exit. Four flights of small and medium aircrafts, from morning to evening, would make this airport a reality. The Lake was at the end of the airstrip. The airport was not very well illuminated but because the surrounding area was dark, pilots could manage landing an aircraft in the late evening. Such landings were mostly done by four or six-seater charter planes, used by aid agencies, such as UNHCR and WHO.

Once, a Russian cargo plane pilot wanted to land his aircraft in Mwanza after night had fallen. He circled the lake, he mistook the lights on the fishing boats for airport lights and landed a few kilometres away from the airport, in the lake waters, like a swan! Best thing about Vodka is that it's not just the pilot but even the aircraft goes tizzy over it.

There was no equipment to remove the sunken planes and boats.

Once submerged, they would stay submerged. A few divers might get underwater to take away valuables if any but that was a part of their 'hobby'.

When the tremors had struck, the airport had been instantly destroyed. The earthquake pulled down the galvanized roofing sheets of the airport and the control tower tipped on one side. The giant waves had tossed the two cargo planes a couple of times and made them lie like cockroaches on their backs.

They were ripped open in the centre and the wings were broken. The frozen fish were strewn all over the airstrip, making a carpet of ice and dead fishes.

The army helicopters landed first on the muck and dead fish at the air strip and immediately started cleaning up and making room for more planes and food supplies The skies that used to be dotted with a variety of birds all the time had a few small jets and copters from aid agencies, foreign news channels and politicians flying every now and then.

It was difficult to land in or around the town because of the rubble and mud.

Raj spotted a helicopter. He removed his t-shirt, tied it to a stick and climbed the leaning tower. He hooked his legs around a pole and waved the stick wildly. It was a small airplane. He was spotted, but could not be helped. He waited for a while and climbed down again. He was very hungry and thirsty. There was very little water left in the bottle. He felt helpless just sitting there so he walked down the hill towards the closest village. It was the same direction in which Poto had driven away. The water had receded to the extent that it only lapped his ankles.

On his way he saw more ghastly remnants of the flood and the quakes. There were dead animals, uprooted trees, human clothes, broken kiosks and human bodies. He gathered his courage and went into a broken hut. He found the food supplies almost immediately, but they were all wet and coated with mud.

He managed to salvage a few bottles of water, a little bread wrapped in polythene, biscuits wrapped in foil and a glass bottle of squash. He ate and drank a bit of everything. He walked around the village trying to find his pick-up again. Everything was covered in muck and mud, making the original colour of objects difficult to recognise.

Every now and then he referred to his hill and moved in the direction of the waves. He finally saw a pick-up lying on its side. When he got closer, he saw that the front of the vehicle had been smashed in and the steering wheel was jutting out awkwardly. There was no mistaking it now, it was his pick-up.

Through the open window, he could see the burly but mangled body of Poto stuck in the vehicle. He was still for a moment, "God, how cruel!" he cried. He covered his face with his hands and cried. He looked for the watchman and Huku, but could not find any sign of them. He decided to get back to the tower and get some help.

He heard the copter again and ran towards the tower, dropping everything, except a bottle of water. He splashed muddy water while running on both sides. He discarded his shoes. He could see a helicopter halting probably to photograph the inclined tower. Its tail was pointing towards him. He yelled like mad and ran for his life. He fell down a couple of times, barely reaching the tower, before his only hope flew away. He was panting heavily and cursed his fate.

As he neared the site, he saw something small emerge from the control room. "Huku?" he called out and started walking fast. The animal saw him and came running towards him.

"Huku! Huku!" It was indeed Huky. When the two met, Huku, though weak by now, jumped up to Raj's throat and started licking him all over his body. The loyal dog wagged his entire body with his ears back and barking faintly with delight. Although both of them were very weak and tired, the man and his dog were happy for the first time in ages. Raj was on his knees and hugged Huku. Huku could not be controlled. He ran all around, jumped over Raj, licked him and peed in excitement. Both were dirty with mud, both were injured, both were crying. Poor Huku wanted to tell his story but could not do so.

Thanking God that he was not alone anymore, Raj set about the task of getting help.

It was the third day after the quake. Bonde and his team had reached Mwanza with a few donkeys and two gunmen with food, water, and medicines. Other essentials and a caravan were trucked in.

The donkeys were wondering why they had no load on their back and were being given a ride on the truck instead. They stopped by a broken bridge about thirty kilometres from Mwanza. Many NGOs and government aid agencies had set up camp there. Many vehicles were stranded on the road. Bonde saw Zuly standing there with Raj's parents.

Though not sure about his own son's fate, Bonde tried to comfort Raj's parents, "Mzee, don't worry. Mungu (God) Atubariki (will bless) us. Your son and my son will come back. I promise you, I will bring them."

When Leena saw Bonde, whom she had gotten to know so well during her stay, she felt close to Raj. Raj's father joined Bonde's caravan. Others stayed back. Once they were dropped off the truck, the donkeys were loaded with supplies and led towards the town. Donkeys were back to their normal routine. *Donkeys were donkeys again.*

It was difficult locating the road to the hill. As they moved closer to the site, they kept glancing up at some prominent rocks and trees along the way that were being used as landmarks by locals who knew the site. Both fathers were oblivious to the pain and fatigue of walking barefoot in muddy unpaved terrain. They passed by several people who begged them for medicines and water. A few people tried to grab the rations tied on the donkeys' backs.

They could see the tilted tower on the hill. Both fathers stopped looking down. Their eyes were glued on the tower. They were charged suddenly and so was the group. As they neared the tower, the two men stopped to look at the tiny cabin at the base of the tower. They started running towards it. On his high perch, Raj could see small ants moving towards him. He started waving his t-shirt again. Someone in the group spotted him. "He is Mistaa Raji, I think," said Juma.

Tears blurred Raj's father's eyes. He looked at the sky and prayed to God. As the group climbed the hill, Raj knew it was his family and friends.
He could see Bonde clearly now. This brought him back to earth painfully. He wondered how he would answer what was bound to be Bonde's only question — Poto yuko (is) wapi (where)?
He was surprised to see his father. His fatigue forgotten, Raj got off the tower and ran down the hill. Huku followed.
'Ata (even) Mbwa (Dog) yupo(there).'
Bonde was alarmed to see only Raj and the dog, "Poto wapi?" he asked.
Raj's father said, "He will be there, do not worry."
Raj went to Bonde first. He took the older man's hands in his and started crying. Bonde understood and could not stop his tears as well. Raj's father was elated that his son was well, but he felt the grief that Bonde was going through. He knew that he could have been equally unfortunate.
Raj led the group to the pick-up. Everybody was aghast at the sight. Bonde tried to regain his composure, and whispered Ayahs from the Koran.
"Innalillahi wa inna ilahi rajioon, Allahummag fir lahu war ham hu(God sent us to earth, to him we shall return)."

Juma asked Raj to take Bonde away while they tried to get Poto out. Poto's body was covered in a cloth and put on a donkey's back. The unloaded foodstuff was partially served to the group and transferred on the other donkey. Everybody started walking back silently. Bonde kept whispering religious prayers for the dead.

After a while Raj narrated the whole story. Bonde was tired. The group stopped in their tracks. Raj's father gave him water and a packet of juice and tried to comfort him. They walked till late in the night and rested till sunrise.

When the caravan reached the camp, there were emotional scenes. A large crowd had gathered to observe the rescue operations. Raj's mother ran towards her son. She hugged him and cried. So did Leena and so did Salome. Zuly also hugged Raj and said, "I am so happy you are back, brother!"

They could not express much as Poto's body was alongside. They held Bonde's hands and tried to console him. The big man broke down and told Raj's mother 'Bibi, I promised you both our sons alive. I could bring only your son alive..my son…' He broke down into sobs.

Bonde and his team took Poto's body to his native place for the funeral rites. Raj and the others stayed in Shinyanga town. Salome wanted to be with Raj, but he was constantly surrounded by his parents, Leena and Zuly. Many times she was left alone. She told herself that Raj was safe and taken care of. Her mission was over. She slipped away from the camp and went home with her friends.

Huku would not leave Raj's side for even a second. He would tail Raj even to the toilet. Raj did not mind this attachment at all, as both had seen death together. The bondage grew stronger when they came out of the calamity. Raj would somehow get a feel of Poto when Huku was beside him as the three of them had spent a lot of time together. There was some trouble with the airline while returning to Dar but Zuly managed to make things work out.

Chapter 18: The monkey runs away to the jungle

Zuly understood the apprehension that Raj's parents experienced. He assured them that he would not mind if Raj settled down in India. If Raj wanted to come back again, he would be stationed in Dar, overseeing the entire operation of the company as CEO.

The devastation of Mwanza had received extensive coverage all over the world. When Raj and his family landed in India, news reporters and TV channel crews pounced on him. He stood there with Huku beside him, trying to answer their questions patiently. It was a strange scene. His parents were annoyed and wanted it to get over soon. Even at home, Raj had to relive his experiences for the benefit of curious relatives and friends. He was busy the whole day answering calls. Everybody wanted him to come back.

Although his parents said nothing about his settling down in India for good, Leena seized her chance the next afternoon. She asked him what his plans were now. Raj was quiet; in his mind he still kept seeing the flood and the annihilation of Mwanza. The building wherehe had rented an apartment had been swept away. He lost many of his close friends and had come close to being killed himself.

After two days of seclusion and quiet, he suddenly remembered Salome. He felt bad that he had been unable to thank her for coming out to find him.

He realized how quietly she had left seeing him with his own people. He knew now that she loved him very much. He also knew that she had sacrificed a lot for his sake.

She did not have a telephone connection in her house, but he knew someone who could convey his message. After a lot of requests and failed connections, he got her on the line.

"Salome! I am really sorry. I just… I do not know how, but I forgot…"

"Don't worry Raji. I am happy that you are safe and fine. In fact, you should forget not only me, but the whole country, Tanzania."

"Why?"

"It has given you so many problems. Your parents, Leena, they are all nice people. Stay with them. Make them happy," her voice faltered.

Raj was silent.

"Hello! Raji, are you there?"

"Yeah, Sami. But I feel like meeting you and… and..." Raj stammered, "Having a glass of beer in the Moshi bar."

He could hear her laugh, "That won't be possible now."

"No? Why not."

They kept up the desperate conversation, neither of them wanting to hang up. Raj asked about her family, the children, Moshi town, the weather, till there was nothing left to talk about. They had to stop. But they could not put each other out of their minds.

Raj met his friends and found that they were all well established in their careers. They all treated him as if he was mentally sick and abnormal. They avoided talking about his job in Africa. Instead of the usual witty exchanges, they counselled him about where he could get a job in India. Leena was busy with work again. She would call him up every day and visit him twice a week. When they would go out for dinner, she talked about her boss, her clients, her promotions and then finally asked him if he had applied for a local job. She lost no opportunity to criticise Tanzanian life and his job there. She would also give a piece of advice in the end. Raj found himself even more of a misfit in his own society. He could also sense Binoy taking over Leena's mind.

Meanwhile, Leena's parents were trying desperately to get their daughter to marry Binoy instead. Leena resisted for quite a long time, but her parents did manage to make her at least think about her boss in a new way.

Sure enough, in time, Raj noticed a lack of warmth while talking to her or her parents on the phone. Leena was in a quandary; Raj or Binoy. Her logical mind tried to assign scores to both her suitors on various attributes. Binoy scored on all of them. But she could not move Raj out of her heart. Raj was like an affectionate, innocent puppy in her lap. By dumping him, she was sure she would be putting a razor blade on the puppy's throat.

Nature is wonderful. A boy and a girl apparently may not like each other because of looks or colour or physique or any such feature. If they are put together in isolation on an island for a long time, they will first start noticing each other. They will begin with formal friendly relations. After some time, they will not remember the ugly features in each other and notice small but good physical features like 'She is dark but her smile is beautiful'. Their minds will make a compromise and give free rein to their hearts. Physical passion will take over. They will start missing each other. They will crave for each other. They will long to get close physically.

Raj's prolonged absence and Binoy's constant presence started affecting Leena's heart. She remembered her intimate moments with Raj in Africa and could not forget their friendship. But like sea waves breaking over the rocks on the shore, her infatuation for Binoy broke the old, rock-like memories of Raj into shapeless, diminutive sand.

One afternoon, he was flipping television channels, when the whole world was busy at work. His parents had decided not to talk about it even if Raj stayed without work for a year. They knew their last encounter when Raj had come to convalesce. They thought it could further put him off from India. They wanted him to be happy. They hoped that after some time, Raj himself would like India and opt to work. They could not and they did not want to enforce their wishes after he came back alive from the jaws of the death.

He stopped suddenly at the amazing sight that he had seen so often. It was Mount Kilimanjaro. The show's anchor was praising the mountain for its beauty.

There followed a dance (Ngoma)performed by the local tribe. Huku raised his ears and barked on hearing the familiar sounds. He looked at Raj and whined. Raj smiled at Huku and asked, "Uta rudi, Bwana (you will go back)?"

Raj was confused again. He thought the mountain was mocking him. What had happened to the promise he had made to himself? Had he come to recover, or become mentally sick? Who needed to recover?

He or Bonde who had lost Poto? Was he not being timid in not facing the challenge thrown by his life? If a vehicle has a problem, one can't just discard it. One can't just forget the destination totally because the vehicle had problems. This stirred his ego. He told himself, wewe mayayi tu (you are soft like an egg).

He started going to the beach twice a day to jog. He remembered a slogan written at the back of Bonde's truck.

'Kuteleza sio kuanguka' (you may slip but have still not fallen down). His parents thought he was trying to rebuild himself.

***

After two weeks, he told his parents of his decision. "I am going back." They did not say anything. Everyone else thought he was crazy. For Leena's parents this was the final straw.

"He is destined to die in Africa. Do not spoil your life. He does not care for you otherwise he would have stayed back. Binoy is better educated. Binoy will also help in your career. He is looks better too. What's your problem?" they asked her.

Leena's last encounter with Raj was like breaking a coconut — brief, a sharp crack, followed by tears. She reminded him of their love for each other and the night they had spent together. She reminded him of their promise to find a solution. He apologised and told her he had tried his best. He would still love to take her to Dar and settle in the city with the Tancell job. She could get a good job in a bank, he told her. But Leena did not like the idea. They wished each other a better future and promised to remain friends even later in life.

It is a universal practice at the time of breaking off, to promise each other to remain good friends for the rest of their life. It does not happen that way. Everybody builds a life of their own with their spouse and family; and it is a rare spouse who can tolerate a partner who has a friend of the opposite sex who calls up or visits too often.

228

Chapter 19: Jambaazi!

When Raj returned back to Tanzania, Zuly and Karimji could not hide their pleasure. Karimji said happily, "You are my adopted son. You took a bold step. You will not ever repent it in your life."

The site in Mwanza would take some time to repair. The last major site was in southern Tanzania where the Great Rift Valley lies. It originates from the north of Syria and runs through Israel, Egypt, Ethiopia, Kenya, Tanzania and Mozambique; a stretch of about five thousand kilometres. Fifteen million years ago East Africa started to separate from the African continent, making deep cracks as much as a kilometre long in the earth mantle along this rift valley. It also created the deepest lake in the world, Lake Tanganyika, and the second largest fresh water lake, Lake Victoria. The rift consists of a series of hills and mountains with ranges as wide as a hundred kilometres.

Southern Tanzania is the green rain-forest area—the hills are dotted with tea estates. It is also considered the birthplace of humanity.

Due to movement in upper crust of the earth and severe climatic changes about 8 million years ago, tropical forest and wet lands thrived on western side of the valley. A clan of apes went there and survived as Chimps till today. But other clan went to the drier, eastern side open grasslands, Savannah. Food was difficult to get, prey were running away in open land. The clan had to struggle to survive. They had to move from place to place. They had to run after the prey, devise tools to hurl or hit them. Lack of forest cover and hostile climatic changes forced them to look for shelters and later devise shelters on their own. These apes ultimately turned out to be humans.

Mother Earth had to undergo severe labour pains to deliver current mankind. When it evolved as a molten mass from a solar nebula, it was a ball of boiling lava. It had no oceans, no atmosphere. It was less than half in size. It took about 150 million years to form outer crust. It was constantly bombarded by asteroids and other heavenly bodies exhuming lava from its interior and shaking it in its orbit with large explosions. But asteroids also brought water with them and changed earth's atmosphere.

Earth cooled down. It rained about 750 million years back and it covered herself with oceans. Continents were formed.Bacteria was first to arrive in oxygen less atmosphere. As atmosphere changed, multi-cellular organisms and algae developed and bacterial life disappeared. Nature started its experiments of bringing life on earth. Earth was growing in size and trying to reposition itself. Earth was tilted towards Sun in such a way that North Pole was facing Sun. It would broil under Sun for 6 months while the other end, South Pole would freeze. Continents started colliding with each other to form a super continent Rodinia. Earth cooled too much to plunge into Ice age.

Suddenly Earth became a ball of ice except around its tropics where it gave different forms of life. Multi-celled Marine life thrived for millions of years and then underwent mass extinction due to change in formation of land mass and atmosphere. Fungi, insects arrived on land mass first. Early forests consisted of 1 meter tall ferns, horsetails and other plants. Vertebrates first started in marine life before arriving on land.

Earth again changed its tilt. Climates changed. Ice age started waning. Most of the earth started having temperate climate. Ice plates melted. Life changed. More landmass was submerged under water.

After experimenting with small insects on land and fishes in Oceans, Earth gave birth to large dinosaurs and mammals. They survived for 200 million years. She was hit again by a comet. She was shaken. Climates changed. Dinosaurs became extinct due to climatic changes. Earth's major land mass shifted from Southern hemisphere to equator and Northern hemisphere. It went through mini ice ages too. After all these labour pains, mother earth seems to have settled with Mammals and humans and current stage of climate and land mass.

Though, it may be a transitional period of another 50 million or so in its life..

Serpentine, undulating, roads take you away from the modern world into serene, quiet, natural ancient world. One can feel his ancient hominid forefathers roaming in the valley without clothes! Had they not crossed over, you would also be roaming in these great green heavens.

Raj's agony through the past few days vanished, as he drove through the mountains. Bonde and his team were following him and the smoke was following their trucks. The site was a few kilometres away from Mbeya town. Work had started but not with the usual spirit as Poto's memory haunted everybody. Poto was replaced by his younger brother, Jumainne also known as J4, since he was born on the fourth Friday (Juma) of the month, considered an auspicious day. He was much younger than Poto, but looked much, much bigger than him. He was almost as big as a baby elephant. He was very fond of driving and would find any excuse to go to Mbeya town several times in a day.

One day, while Raj was returning from Mbeya, he saw a white man standing beside a pick-up stuck on the side of the road. Raj stopped to help. When the man turned to see him, Raj exclaimed,

"Jonathan! What a surprise in this jungle. What are you doing here?"

"I have a missionary project nearby. These days my wife, Winnie, and I stay in this area. How about you?"

While Raj and Jonathan chatted, J4 tied a rope to the vehicle and they tried to tow it out of the sand, but the wheel was firmly stuck. Raj and Jonathan wondered how to pull it out. The others gave them some ideas. A group of young boys were passing by, riding their bikes. They were talking loudly, yelling and laughing. When they saw the stranded visitors, they got down immediately. They laid their bikes aside,

Some of them got behind the vehicle and tried to shake it, while the others tried to put stones and twigs under the tyres. After several minutes, the group's leader went in front of the vehicle and ordered them to stop.

He waved away Raj's suggestions and said, "Hii ni mambo ya akili (it requires brains). Wewe kaa pale tuu. (you just stand aside)."

Raj smiled and stood aside. Raj told Jo what the villager told him. Both burst into laughter.

The boys discussed the best strategy and started to remove the mud from around the wheels. They dug a little below the tyres and filled the hole with stones. Everybody was full of enthusiasm. They joked as they worked. They asked the driver to start the vehicle again. Everybody shouted encouraging slogans and pushed the vehicle. Somebody advised the driver how to move the steering wheel. The wheels spun around uselessly, throwing mud on the boys standing at the back. But they were unperturbed. Soon enough, the vehicle moved a bit. They put more stones to prevent it from falling back. This did not work out.

Again, they got into a huddle and discussed the problem. The driver got impatient. He asked if there was tractor around.

The leader interjected, "Wait. Let's go for step number 2 before going to 3. We have so many alternatives. Why a tractor? We have our cattle to pull the vehicle out. You just look after your steering."

A boy slipped under the vehicle and put a big stone as far behind as possible. Then he put the jack and lifted up the rear wheels a few inches. The others removed mud from the surface of the area around the vehicle to ease the movement. Again, some smaller stones were laid out under the tyres. The vehicle was tied to Raj's vehicle with a piece of rope. Everybody pushed the vehicle again. Raj's pick-up pulled it from the front. The wheels came out of the grooves slowly. Two boys constantly placed stones underneath. Others were in ankle-deep mud. They were laughing, shouting and abusing freely. The vehicle revved up and slowly moved on the edge of the pit. It bounced and then it suddenly zoomed ahead. Some boys jumped aside. Two of them fell on the others who were putting stones under the wheel. There was relief and joy all around.

Jonathan thanked the leader and gave him some money. No one was upset about the dirt on their clothes. They got on to their bikes and sped away.

Raj went with Jonathan to his camp. Winnie welcomed Raj and offered coffee. They narrated the entire story to her and got talking about their common interests. It was found that Raj liked playing bridge, as did Winnie and Jonathan.

Raj was happy to have someone to talk to. He told Jo about his problems back home. Jo reassured him that what he had decided was not wrong.

"God gives you a life only once. Try different combinations, if you are not happy with it. But lead and live your own life," he said

Raj stayed close to the site and Huku stayed with him. One night, when everyone was asleep Huku started barking and growling. The workers woke up and saw a group of men trying to steal the cement bags.

"Wezi! wezi!"

They ran after the thieves and caught one. Within seconds that man was surrounded by all the workers and was beaten up. Bonde started it with a resounding slap. J4 kicked the man in the balls. It was a free-for-all.

Raj hurried over, "Hand him over to the police."

Bonde said, "Mistaa Raji, you just go in your room. Let us do our work."

Mama Rose appeared from somewhere with a log from the kitchen. She whacked the man with the wood. The guy stumbled and fell down. The workers cheered and clapped. The thief pleaded that his life be spared.

Bonde shouted, "Get the tyre!"

Raj yelled, "No! Don't do it on my site. It is murder."

Bonde shouted back, "If you leave him, he will come again."

"Let him go. Stop beating him. He will die."

"Let him die."

"No. Tie him and take him to the police station. I don't want any problem. Eti, shimame (stop)," Raj screamed at Bonde.

When the police arrived, the thief was unable to walk and was bleeding profusely.

"Good job, Jamaani. It seems you did not get the tyre."

"Let's rush him to the hospital," said Raj.

"Mistaa Muhindi. Is he your relative?"

"No."

"Then we know where to take him, asante Jamaani, you can go now."

The police left. As usual one by one everybody started narrating the same story with actions, expressions and sounds. When things were quiet a bit, it was time for the Profesaa.

"I am wondering what would have happened if the thief would have died here?"

Everybody chorused, "Ndiyo-o-o."

They laughed then. J4 asked, "Profesaa, you do not know Tanzania? So many times when the thief is caught, they put a tire around his neck and burn him. Have you seen the police arresting anybody?"

Profesaa countered, "But that is done on the road. Everybody runs away when the police come. Here they can say that we have done it. They can arrest Mistaa Raji or Mzee Bonde saying your men did it. I am sure punishment for stealing is not death penalty."

Raj heard it all, he said, "Ndiyo."

Everybody else was silent.

"Now you are talking, Profesaa! At least, you have sense. I genuinely pray for his life, Bwana. Otherwise, there would have been a big problem."

Bonde lost his cool. He told Profesaa in their native tribal language, which Raj could not understand, "After eating Muhindi's food, you have started thinking like him. Keep your mouth shut now."

He turned to Raj and told politely, "Mistaa Raji, you do not worry. We shall handle it. It is my responsibility."

Like a small schoolboy who gets reprimanded by the teacher, in front of his friends, the Profesaa looked away shyly.

***

Zuly briefed Raj about a new project. Jean-Pierre de Limbe Shayo wanted to erect a few towers to have a mobile link on the Zaire side of Lake Tanganyika since trade along the shoreline was booming. Shayo was well-connected with the government and the rebels. He would not have any problems getting permits, and erecting and operating a mobile network on his side of the border. They could charge a thirty-percent-higher rate for airtime in Zaire.

Shayo was expected to visit Kigoma, a port on the Tanzanian side of the lake, where Raj could meet him. Raj knew that this deal was very important for Zuly and decided to reach the port a day early and send a messenger across so that Shayo could come with a delegation to talk technicalities.

The roads there were very bad. Raj and J4 started early in the morning and after travelling about fifty kilometres, they took a break in a small village. Once they got back in the car, it would not move. There was only one car in the village. It was an absolutely rundown vehicle, desperately in need of repairs. The owner asked for an exorbitant fare. Raj decided to go with him while J4 got a mechanic from Mbeya, repaired the vehicle and joined him at the port.

After a few moments of silence, Raj and the owner who was driving him started talking.

"If I knew that I have to travel this far, I should have brought my girlfriend," he said.

"Still not married?" Raj asked.

"No, married. I have three children."

"And still you have a girlfriend?"

"We are allowed up to three."

"Your wife knows about it?"

"Yes."

"But, it is unfair."

"You see, Mzee. There has to be some competition. If she is sick or not behaving properly, I can always go to other one, Mama Ndogo (young)."

"What if your wife also wants competition and goes to another man?"

"Why should she be unhappy? I am doing all this for her and her children only. Life is very difficult these days."

He added, "Let me ask you something. What did you eat for breakfast today?"

"Bread and butter."

"Ahaan. You do not like only bread. You put butter on it because you like its smell or its taste, or maybe just to make the bread soft. But can you eat only butter without bread for breakfast?"

"No," said Raj.

"So you need both. Now if you go on eating bread and butter everyday, you will get fed up. So, sometimes, you apply jam just for a change of taste. But you cannot eat jam alone. Now you understand what I am saying?"

Raj started laughing. He wondered what Leena would say, if he had to tell her this. He put himself in the driver's shoes. What if he was married to Leena and fell in love with a local girl? As if on cue, a remembered face danced in his thoughts. Salome. How silly, he told himself. Again, he had forgotten to get in touch with her. He felt guilty again at the way he had been treating her.

Suddenly, the car stopped.

"What happened?"

"Panchaa."

"Do you have a spare tyre?"

"Yes."

Raj got off the car and went to the bushes to relieve him. He did some stretching, looked around surrounding hills for a while. He listened to sounds of birds and streams and came back to the car. He saw the driver digging the ground with a big butcher's knife he kept for safety.

"What are you doing?" Raj asked.

"Do not worry you just see."

The driver did not have a jack. He dug the ground below the punctured tyre, so that it could be slid out. It took 45 minutes to do this. They got into the car again, but the car seemed to be slowing down.

Clouds of dust rolled into the car, but the windows could not be rolled up as the car did not have an air conditioner. Raj was angry at the driver and at himself for having hired such a lousy vehicle.

But for an occasional lorry or a passenger bus, there was no vehicle on the road. What if the other tyre got punctured? There was no repair shop for miles, Raj thought.

One can't speak ill of midwives, while the childbirth still continues. (Usitukane wakunga na uzazi 'ungalipo.)

The car stopped again. "Nini tabu (what's the problem)?"

"Engine is very hot," the driver replied. ' Engine head gasket has gone. Radiator has dry steam left.' The driver took a piece of cloth and put his hand on the cap to open it.

"Do not open it now," Raj cautioned.

"Aaaaa! You do not worry, Bwana," the driver laughed.

He had hardly turned the cap when it blew up like a hand grenade. The driver fell down backwards; his face and hands were burnt. Raj helped him get up.

After a few seconds, the driver smiled and said, "Eeeh, this car!"

It was clear that they could not go further. Raj blamed his stars. He waited for an hour or so, till a passenger bus rolled by. Raj stopped it and asked the driver for the fare.

The taxi driver asked for exorbitant fare giving some weird logic. Raj was fuming but partly gave in as he would miss the bus otherwise.

Other than him, all the others in the bus were locals. The roads were like frozen sea waves and dusty. There was hardly room to move, and the bouncy roads made the ride all the more uncomfortable. He was shifting his weight from one leg to the other. The stink of sweat and the clouds of dust entering through the open windows suffocated him. The driver seemed to have prior experience running a speedboat. To try to take his mind off the ordeal he was going through, Raj started looking at his fellow-passengers.

The one thing he noticed right away was that African buttocks are distinct compared to those of other races. There seems to be extra protruding flesh. The people seemed to be hardly bothered by the bumpy ride. Sometimes, they would say, "Eeeh (high pitch)..... this road!" and smile.

Suddenly the driver took a sharp turn. Everybody was flung to one side. It seemed that the bus was pelted with stones. The driver stopped the bus. Soon, people realised that the bus was being pelted with gunshots and not stones.

"Jambaazi (bandits)!" screamed the passengers.

The women and children cried, while the men panicked. Raj could see a car parked in the bushes. Four men, wielding guns, surrounded the bus. The driver was pulled out. One man got into the bus and shouted.

"Be quiet! Any one shouts, I will kill him. Sikliza vizuri (listen well) Everyone — men, women and children, remove all your clothes, ata chupi (even underwear), leave them on your seat along with your wallets, purses and ornaments. Get down quietly, one by one, and go stand under that big tree. One mistake and you will have to leave your body also," the man said.

A fellow Jambaazi near the driver's cabin fired two shots in the air. People saw the driver running nude towards the tree, following the instructions verbatim. Maybe he was experienced in this nude warfare, Raj thought. Within seconds, clothes started dropping.
"For half an hour, do not come on to the main road. We are coming back. We will shoot you," the bandit said.

The Great Rift Valley had hominids again. Anthropologists say hominids mean extinct humans. They were followed by Homosapiens, wise humans. Current model of humans is Homo sapiens, sapiens - Very very wise humans.
Their wisdom was manifest in their mobiles, in their clothing, in their walkmans, in their paper money, in their jewellery and so on. But every thing had gone. Very very wise humans knew that if they did not obey bandits they will be extinct soon, much earlier than their less developed ancestors.

Everyone looked tense when they got down on seeing the guns. Although they all feared for their lives, they could not help laughing when they saw their fellow travellers running in the nude. Raj was numb, how could he strip in front of so many people? He had never done it, or even seen it before. He had only heard about the British and Australians stripping and running on the cricket ground during the match. He thought he should argue. Almost immediately, the man sitting next to him warned him, "Do not do it. They will shoot from there. Any one coming in the way will die. Just follow what they are saying; otherwise you will get us killed."

The gunman at the door heard the whispers, "wewe muhindi (you Indian) you do not know Swahili? Just do what others are doing or…" He pointed his gun at Raj, who started removing his clothes. He felt like killing himself.

The gunman drove the bus away, and the other bandits left in the car.

Raj stood out because of his colour and race. People were checking to see if God was fair to all the races. There was plenty of whispering and laughter. It was fun to see a Muhindi running nude.

In Kiswaihli there is a saying 'Uki kutwa Uchi, lazima uchutame'. If you are forced to be nude, cover your front side.

Raj did not stop at the tree. He kept walking. He could see a few huts in the distance. He thought of asking the people there for a piece of cloth and covering himself first, before looking for a way out of this place. The others walked back on to the roads, nude, to stop vehicles.

The children were the first to greet him. When Raj got close to the huts, they ran away yelling names. There was an old man and a few ladies in the huts. They laughed openly.
Some ran into their houses and shut the door. Raj used sign language to ask for clothes. The old man gave him a khanga (a cloth used by women to cover their torso and legs). Raj folded his hands and tried to explain that he had nothing to offer in return. But he gave them his address and promised to pay them back some day or at least bring a new khanga back.

Raj finally made it to Kigoma. Zuly contacted his friends in that town and arranged for money and clothes for Raj. The meeting with Shayo was confirmed, and Shayo boarded a ferry to get to the port.
The ferry carried bananas, hides, stolen vehicles, cassava, weapons in fifty kilo-flour bags and diamonds. The ferry, MV Saratoga (MVS), would start late at night from Bujumbura town in Burundi, and halt at one or two islands along the Congo shore line of the lake to collect people and fish. Nobody asked her age as one does with ladies but it was time for her to undergo cosmetic surgery and look younger. The word sea worthiness was for sea going vehicles, not for ferries that ran on the lake.

Shayo, being well-known, got a cabin next to the captain. The ferry had twenty cabins on board and about fifty in the steerage. There was also space to pack more people on wooden berths. Unofficially one could get anywhere on the ferry, lay out a rug and sleep after the ferry left the last island. The ferry started late at night. After stopping at the two islands, the captain's cabin door opened. A lady in black robes peeped into the room and smiled. The captain told his assistant, "Hebu, one kidogo (take care)." The assistant obliged and took over "Sawa (okay)."

The captain walked away with the lady.

The assistant looked at the sonar device. No major white dots were seen. After some time, he pulled out a bottle of whisky from the captain's cupboard and poured himself a glass.

He wondered when the Captain would hand over the lady in black robes instead of the ship at night. Black-robed ladies were plenty on both sides of the lake, but this one was special.

She was the captain's prized possession, like this bottle of whisky in his hand. Her charm, her body seemed to denote that she was made for the captain only. He hoped that someday he would buy her out.

Usually dreams follow sleep. But the Assistant fell asleep following his dream. It was four in the morning. He did not know that under the black robes, a tiny white speck had appeared on the sonar screen. The tiny speck slowly came towards the centre of the screen. Time passed by.

Everyone was snoring in harmony with the noisy but rhythmic engines of the ferry, including the lady in the black robes.

Suddenly there was a loud bang, as if the sky had fallen. This was quickly followed by human cries. The front of the ship was torn into two halves by a lava rock. Water seeped into the boat and most of the ship dipped into the water. Most of the cabins over the deck were sunk under water. A few people were flung into the water, some tried to struggle against the waves and others drowned. People inside the submerged cabins stared horrified at the water entering through the seams of the door frames. Some prayed to the Almighty and started crying. Death was knocking at the door. Some opened the doors because they hoped to swim out of the boat. They were pushed away by the gushing water. The dead bodies in the passage further sealed their escape. The lake was silent. It was hearing the babies crying inside the womb of MVS and around it.

Disaster seemed to have escaped the engine room, since that end of the ferry tilted towards the sky. The other end of the ship, with engines at its bottom, was raised and floating due to the air trapped inside. It was dark inside. People came out of their cabins and started climbing towards the raised end. About a hundred people were huddled inside the engine room and a common sitting area just before it. A few fishermen had seen the ferry doing the dolphin act and crash into the rock. They intended to loot the cargo, but on seeing the flotilla of the hurt and dead people, they decided to go away. They feared that their tiny boats would sink if too many people tried to get in. There was calm once again. People trapped inside the ferry began to make plans. Luckily, a technician was around. He was used to making minor body repairs to this ship. They decided to cut open a hole and come out

Archimedes died many years ago and his teachings never reached this part of the world. The welder was having a shower of sparks, trying to gas cut and to open a hole as fast as he could. He made a straight slit. As the slit started opening, the boat kept sinking further, millimetre by millimetre. People thought it was because they were crowding at one place. They started shouting not to crowd at one place and to have patience. The shouts of 'Harakka (hurry up)' never stopped.

After struggling for about an hour, a square-shaped opening was created. The welder thanked his stars. He could see the open sky and raised his hand with closed fists as if he was victorious. People ran towards it to get out. But, as soon as the air trapped in the engine room escaped, the water rushed in till the entire ship sank to the bottom of the deepest lake in the world. There are no creatures or plant life at the bottom the lake as there is no oxygen and light.

When Raj got back to the site, he told everyone about his latest misadventures. Everybody laughed at the thought of Raj wearing a khanga.

J4 said, "Last time you ran nude, was when you were toto (child) isn't it? Mistaa Raji, if you give me 5000 Tanzanian shillings, I will remove my clothes."

Raj agreed, "Done!"

To his surprise, J4 started removing his clothes. The workers gathered around him and cheered him on raucously. Within seconds, just the underpants were left and he asked Raj for permission to remove them. Raj laughed and shook his head and gave him a 5000 shillings note, and shook his hand too. J4 bowed and accepted the prize. Juma got up, took out a 500 shilliing note, circled it around J4's head and gave that to him as well. J4 bowed and accepted it again. Many did the same. J4 did not seem to be in a hurry to dress up. Mama Rose came forward. She raised her hands, asking for silence. People obliged.

"'Semaje..(tell us)'

'Mistaa Raji, if you give him another 5000, he will dance too."

J4 nodded his head several times. Raj agreed again. Someone got an empty paint can and utensils to set up improvised Ngoma beats. J4 started dancing, wearing nothing but his underwear. A worker removed his shirt and joined him. He ran towards Mama Rose inviting her to dance with him. She ran behind Bonde for help. Bonde got up and pulled out a 1000 shilling note, circled it around J4's head and waved him to go away. Raj got up, took J4's pants and with folded hands, asked him to wear it. Everyone clapped for a long time. Smiles had returned to their faces for the first time after Poto's death.

Jonathan came to meet Raj at the site. He had a technical problem. They had built a water tank. After using it for a few days, it started tilting. He wanted to know what had caused the problem. Raj went to the site.

He got down from the car. He looked at the tank from a distance and said, "Mr. Jo, can you see the landscape? You have put this tank on a dried up riverbed. It still has moisture in the sub-strata. See the green grass all along the bed surrounded by dry patches on uneven ground," he explained.

"Change the location of this tank and get it on to dry land, and your problem will be solved. Do not mess around with reinforcements or supports," he suggested.

They sat down to have a beer.

"Looks simple now, the way you said it. I have been asking my architect in Dar and he sends me drawing after drawing for reinforcement here and there."

Raj smiled and said, "He must come to the site first, and then suggest solutions. Otherwise you have problems in the kidney and Doc gives medicine for headaches."

Jo laughed, "It reminds me of something I heard recently. In a big government hospital, a man with a leg problem was admitted. There was another who had a tumour in his brain. Both had identical names. The neuro opened the brain of the guy with the leg problem. When he found nothing, he closed the cut he had made and the guy died in three days."

"Are you serious?" Raj asked.

Jo continued, "Yes, I am. The guy with the tumour was operated in the leg. When they tried to remove the tumour later, he slipped into a coma. He has been rushed to India."

They shook their heads.

Winnie joined the conversation, "But they must have prepared for the operation, like shaving the head or the leg. Why did the patient not ask anything? The doctor or nurse must have asked them questions regarding their pain before filling out the reports."

"It seems the report did not go with the patient and one of them did object to the nurse, but she was stubborn. Both were under anaesthesia and their stretchers were interchanged at the time of the operation."

Raj said, "But what about the relatives? They must be asking questions too."

Jo said, "Well, I do not know any more, but it was a classic mess, and I quote it frequently to people when they do not analyse the problem correctly and jump to conclusions."

The conversation turned to other matters with Winnie wanting to play bridge.

"Mr. Jo, what is your profession?" Raj asked.

"Well, social service now. Otherwise, I am a vet."

"You left your practice in UK?"

"Yes, I would have gone on for another ten years, but then I liked the idea of coming down here and working for a good cause. Winnie is a pharmacy graduate. She was a sales executive in a good pharma company."

"I guess she was visiting you as a sales rep and then the two of you took up a common prescription," Raj said mischievously.

The couple laughed. "Not a bad guess!" Winnie said, "I was his neighbour. One day he helped me prepare a technical presentation. The rest is what you guessed."

"It must be a difficult decision to leave an advanced country like the UK, a good career and life and settling down in this jungle," Raj said.

"Fortunately, both of us are impulsive. We love nature. We love Africa. We love our social work. It is something; both of us enjoy doing it together." Winnie said.

"The clock does not set our day. Bosses do not write our future. People respect us, not as professionals, but as human beings. In the modern world, work and personal life are separate. Here, they are not separate."

Raj was silent. He wondered if Leena could think the same way. He felt alone. He finally said, "I envy you folks."

"Find a girl who likes Africa, and you will also enjoy Africa with her," smiled Winnie.

"I did find a girl, but, unfortunately, she does not like Africa."

"Oh! Why don't you call her here? She might change her mind after she stays here for a few days."

"We tried that, but it did not work out."

"Pole saana. Hope things work out some how," said Winnie

Jo tried to ease Raj's worried mind. "Why don't you marry an African girl? You have a problem with colour?"

Winnie glared at her husband, "Come on Jo, don't joke about this. The poor boy is passing through a bad patch."

Raj smiled, "Not a bad idea. Let me seriously look out for one."

Before he could complete his sentence, an African face appeared in his mind; gentle smile, sharp nose, charming face and innocent eyes. He was mesmerized.

He told himself " No, it is not possible."

"Raj, how long will you be around?"

"Maybe a week or so, and then I may have to go to the site in Mwanza for a few days."

"I am planning to climb Kili again. You want to join me?" asked Jo.

"Yes! when?"

"My friend can arrange it around March."

"Done. I will be there."

"On the roof of Africa?"

"Yes. This monkey will be right there on the top."

Jo and Winnie laughed. "Cheers!" Their beer session was followed by dinner. The best part of Africa is that clock stops ticking when you live there.

Chapter 20: Voodoo thunder

One day J4 went to the town to buy food and building materials. The entire town seemed to be excited. A popular Congo artist and his troupe were going to have a concert sponsored by a multinational soft drink company. J4 decided to watch the show. He was about to order groceries at the shop when he heard a band and saw a colourful, lively procession coming down the street. There were hardly any vehicles in the street.

First came the young boys, dancing and running along the streets. They were clumsy-looking street boys. They were yelling to the music and dancing with athletic movements. They were also snatching away bags from curious onlookers, if given a chance. They were ecstatic and waving to shopkeepers and onlookers.

Then came an open-bodied truck decorated with soft drink posters. There was a wooden stage on the back. Eight ladies wearing bright yellow frilly, short skirts and competing 'broad band' bras, yellow scarves and black shorts were dancing vigorously. They were inviting people to climb on the stage and dance with them with erotic gestures.

From the ground below, they looked like inverted sunflowers swinging in the breeze.
Standing in front of the dancers was the singer for whom the people were waiting. He was also dressed in yellow robes and dancing with the girls. Since the roads were uneven, they would frequently lose their balance and almost fall. The people cheered,

clapped and laughed. Even the shopkeepers clapped and shook themselves to the tune.

J4 followed the procession in his car. The crowds converged at an old football stadium. The singer and his troupe climbed the stage there. Within an hour, the Congo music had taken hold of the crowd. Everybody was dancing, so was J4. There were three men standing behind him. One of them had long slimy hair and sunken eyes He was wearing some threads around his neck. He pointed out J4 to the other two.

"That fat pig is good," he said.

They came closer to J4. They had soft drink bottles in their hand.

After a couple of songs, they started talking and dancing with J4. One of them offered a soft drink to J4. He hesitated.

"It is free from the company; you will get more from that stall there. Have it man!" one of them said. J4 thanked him and drank.

After a few sips, he felt giddy and collapsed into the waiting hands of the men. They told the people around them that their friend had fainted

Since J4 was heavy, they had to ask others to help. J4 was put at the back of their pick-up. One man sat next to the prone J4, and the other ahead. The vehicle left the town and disappeared into evening shadows of the roadside trees. It stopped near a hill. There were a few huts in the distance. They tied J4's hand and legs to a metal pole. The men lifted J4 by lifting the pipe and walked to the huts. He was dumped on a country-made, fragile wooden bed with a very fragile frame and sisal ropes tied like a net. His hands and legs were re-tied to the wooden frame of the bed. It had become dark and it started to rain. Lightning flared across the sky, from one end to the other, almost blinding those who saw it.

The man who had first spotted J4 was a voodoo priest. He changed into his traditional garb and looked scary

"Mungu likes us today, that is why there is thunder," he said.

The other two men were his customers, and were very worried. The thunder made a loud, cracking sound over their heads.

Lightening was running all over the sky from one end to the other giving an eye-blinding glow. In the southern regions, particularly, it was customary to offer human skin to a deity to solve health and fertility problems. The victim is either killed or made unconscious. Skin is removed with a razor from the face and the torso.

The priest was chanting while lighting a fire. He placed small wooden human figurines on the threshold and dried up pumpkins just outside the door.

J4 woke up and was really scared when he realised that he was tied up and the man had voodoo dolls with him. He started yelling and crying. The two men looked at the priest.

The priest said "Do not worry. Nobody can hear his cries."

J4 started pleading desperately to the men.

Bonde was worried and started making inquiries about his son's whereabouts.

Somebody thought that since J4 had gone to the city, he might have stayed behind to watch a popular music show. Juma felt that J4 could have had a problem with the vehicle. They sent Profesaa with two workers in Raj's pick-up. They came back after an hour. They had seen the vehicle outside the stadium, but not J4. He could not be seen in the crowd.

Bonde was relieved and said, "I know my boy, he is crazy. He will be in the stadium. He will come back when the show gets over."

The rains had wreaked havoc on the singer's party. The transformer short-circuited and blew up. The grounds became dark and the crowd that had been excited by the music and the dance decided to seek its pleasures in other ways. Some people lost their valuables to pickpockets; the police, armed with torches, could do nothing to control the wild crowd in the dark.

Even the singer was not spared; his gold chain and wrist watch was stolen. His golden robe was torn off him as well. Some people seized the opportunity to satiate their sexual appetite in the dark. The men thrilled at the prospect of jumping on the scantily-clad ladies who had been inviting them all evening with their suggestive gestures while dancing. Under the cover of darkness, their invitations were accepted and they were squeezed and squashed like a Tetra pack filled with juice.

The rains also delayed the priest. J4's voice had turned hoarse and feeble. He cried and trembled, begging for his life. The men had to carry him out of the hut, still tied to the bed, and take him up the hill. The heavy rains made the long climb difficult, but the priest wanted the offering to be made at midnight.

Bonde and his men came to the town. All they could see were shoes and slippers strewn around the stadium. They asked the policemen there what had happened. Bonde and his team knew now what had happened. They searched the stadium and came to the pick-up J4 had parked outside. They went to the police station. There was no one on the street to enquire. Shops and petrol pumps would close by 5 PM even on a normal day for safety. But even the police had no idea how J4 could have disappeared.

***

The men and the priest lifted J4, who had been knocked out with chloroform. The men walked for a few meters and stopped for breath. The rains had stopped for a while, but the thunder and lightning scared the two customers. The priest kept on his chant and urged the men to not bother about the noise. They were scared by the priest's chanting also.

After about an hour, the party reached the hill and started climbing. They had to stop every few steps as it was very difficult to climb with J4. They could not see what was on the top of the hill and kept struggling to reach the peak.

Nor could they guess how steep the climb was. Black granite rocks small and big, were scattered all over, covering the ground. They gave the appearance of a black army waiting to pounce on them. The priest was in a frenzy, dancing and screaming, looking at the sky with his arms open wide.

They were just a few steps away from the peak, balancing themselves carefully on the rocks, when there was a sudden bright flash. Lightning had struck a rock close to them and the ensuing thunder rang in their ears. For a second, they forgot the weight on their shoulders. They could feel as if they were standing on the ground. They lost control. One of the customers slipped and let go of the weight he was carrying. The other man could hardly keep holding on, either. J4, still tied to the bed, slowly tilted to one side and then went hurtling down a few feet, rotating from one side to the other like a skilled diver and crashed on a rock. He was lucky that he was tied to the bed since the wooden frame absorbed most of the impact. The frame broke into pieces and J4 fell to the ground. He woke up, it took him a few seconds to realise that he was free, though his hands and legs were still tied with rope to small pieces of wood. He jumped a few steps like a rabbit, fell down and rolled further, crawled a few metres behind the bushes and was swallowed by the night.

The priest shouted at the men and asked them to find the bulky offering. J4 circled the hill, trying to find a way down, while the men started the hunt. Probably the deity was dieting.

J4 freed himself and started running down the hill; sometimes dodging the rocks, sometimes tumbling wildly. The thorny bushes grabbed at his shirt. He didn't bother stopping. His pants were torn and his feet had several bruises and cuts. His thick skin and fat protected him from the sharp pain. He got off the hill and walked into a paddy field. He was almost breathless.

It started raining again and J4 had no idea where he was. He could see the lights of vehicles, far away. As he walked through the fields, he waded through knee-deep muck, but he kept his eyes on what little he could see ahead and behind him. He was too scared to go to a hut at the edge of the field. Finally, he reached a road. He hid behind a tree trunk.

When the rains stopped, he walked on the road and reached a small town. He could see a woman and her children sitting inside a half open door, in candlelight. He knocked at the door softly, but the woman was too scared at J4's appearance and shut the door. He just wanted to know if he was walking in the right direction to reach the town.

He continued walking for a long time. He could see a vehicle coming towards him and hid behind a tree. The vehicle was moving very slowly. It stopped a few feet away from him. People got down. J4 started praying to God. He could see the people go behind the bushes to relieve themselves.

He caught a few words of conversation, but could not see their faces. With great relief, he realised that he recognised the voices. He ran towards the vehicle.

"Baba! Baba! Juma!"

He got the response. 'Juma (inne) uko wapi?' (Where are you?).

It was Bonde and his team. They were happy and horrified to see him. They could hardly recognize him. He was bleeding and covered in muck and crying like a small baby. Everybody comforted him and the Profesaa offered him water. The party returned to the camp listening to J4's ghastly story.

Chapter 21: Passion flowers bloom

The morning brought much cheer. The workers were up early after last night's events and were laughing about J4's plight while relishing black tea with sweet bun 'Mandaazi'. J4's story was told repeatedly by many with actions and funny gestures. People were laughing. There were many 'I thought' editions to the main story.
Raj was still asleep, when a knock on his door woke him. He stumbled to the door and opened it. Sunlight fell on his face making it difficult for him to see his visitor. He narrowed his eyes and looked at the silhouetted face smiling at him. It was Salome.

Her hair was lit up by the sunrays, and it seemed as if she had a halo around her curly hair. She smiled and watched Raj. Her eyes were full of affection. Raj was elated. He felt as if he had been reunited with a close relative after a long time of solitude.

"Jambo."

"Mama, mama! What a surprise, I can't believe this."

They shook hands and hugged each other.

"I came last night to Mbeya and stayed with my relative."

"Oh, Salome! You made my day. I did not know, but now I realise that I need someone like you for a break in this jungle life."

Rose had prepared breakfast; she laid it out on the table under a tall mahogany. Raj and Salome sat down to eat.

"I am sorry, I never realised when you left me the last time."

"I just wanted you to be alive and safe. You were happy with your family so..."

They talked for a long time, catching up once again on each other's lives. The tall green trees, the bright sunshine, the scantily seen azure sky, the cool breeze, the mild flutter of leaves and quiet countryside put them in a landscape of their own. They enjoyed each other's presence and warmth.

"After this assignment, I will be posted at Dar as CEO and may live the city life."

"And then?"

"Not then, before that I want to climb on to the roof of Africa and shout out loud that I made it. I am happy."

"I will also climb Kili with you."

"No, no! You are in charge of getting a band to play when I return and get a big party ready."

Raj did not feel like getting back to work. He thought, for the first time, that he needed a break. So did Bonde and Mama Rose.

They suggested a change of plans for Raj.

"Mistaa Raji, there is a good hotel on river Ruuha. There are many animals around there. Why do you not take Salome there, enjoy the holiday and come back? Work will be over then," Bonde said.

Raj accepted the suggestion wholeheartedly. He took Salome to the game park hotel. On the way, they talked like long-lost friends. Raj remembered the time when he had travelled with Leena. He became quiet when he pondered over the subsequent ebb in their relations.

"Raji, you are very quiet."

"No, no, just enjoying the day."

The thick rain forests gave way to the grassy plains and baobab and acacia trees. They arrived at the hotel in the afternoon and found that there were very few visitors there. Their room was not very far from a water hole where animals could be spotted easily. The river had many crocodiles and hippos. Raj and Salome chatted in the restaurant facing the river over drinks and some food.

They walked around the fenced and safe area around the water hole. They were able to get a good view of the animals that came to the water hole. After dinner, they went into their separate rooms. They decided to go for a safari next morning.

Salome was content with the time she got to spend with Raj. She thought this was all she could expect from him in her life. She had stayed away from Raj for so long, but it was worth waiting for such brief moments together. She wondered how she would feel if she had to marry another man. Contemplating an unhappy future, she fell asleep.

But, Raj could not sleep. He could not explain why, but he knew that he wanted to be with Salome. He found her very presence soothing. Her thoughts, the way she spoke and her ideals led him away from the harsh realities of life. There was no pressure of

time or other worldly commitments. Life had its motions. It had come to a standstill.
He could feel the warmth of her unflinching dedication in her eyes.

He pondered his future again and again. Could he go on with his current life or would he get fed up after a few years of isolation from his own people and country?

The generator was switched off. He opened the curtains of his window and watched the moonlight embrace the river. The water glowed between the black silhouetted trees on the bank. He watched the calm scene for a while and fell asleep too.

It was drizzling in the morning and Raj was not sure if they should drive out. They had a leisurely breakfast. The hotel staff said that the roads might be slippery and the culverts might overflow if the rains did not let up. Unable to decide, they sauntered in the passage and veranda.

"The weather is really nice, isn't it?" Raj asked.

"Yes."

"Let's wait for an hour or two; if the rains stop we shall go for a drive."

"Yes."

They walked till the end of the passage. He took her to a small round hut (Banda) open on all sides with a roof of dried grass and waist high wooden railings. It was a viewing point from where they could see the river. Several hippos could be seen, blobbing up and down in the river.

Every now and then, a hippo would partly emerge from the water, squirt water from his nostrils like a fountain or raise his head, open his mouth wide and yawn. A few amorous couples indulged in underwater performances. The crocodiles slowly moved from one place to the other. They would submerge their head, only to resurface at a place further away.

Their peaceful co-existence was possible because their food preferences were different. Hippos would graze on the ground, while the crocodile would wait for an animal to lower its head and drink water.

While Raj and Salome were engrossed in the sounds of flowing river water and the wild ambience, there was a sudden commotion on the other side of the hut. A cloud of dust ran through the bushes, the loud sound of animals stomping the ground and cracking dry leaves caught Raj and Salome's attention. A herd of antelopes emerged near the river. Some of them ran across the shallower parts of the river and ran away.
"There must be something chasing this herd," Salome said.

A lone antelope had lost its herd and came near the water, hesitating to plunge into it. A pack of hyenas were now visible. They stopped a few feet away from the antelope and moved towards it slowly. The antelope weighed its chances. It jumped on a stone jutting out of the river and jumped on another one, but its third leap landed it into the wide open mouth of a crocodile. Raj closed his eyes.

"Oh, no!" Raj moaned.

"What a fate! Poor thing," Salome said.

Other crocodiles started cruising towards the prey. The hyenas looked at the river for a while. They were panting because of the chase. They looked at each other and returned to the bushes.

After a while, Raj and Salome put their forearms on the wooden railing and stood next to each other. They watched the river that had turned calm again.

"Raji, you would not have seen such a rare scene, if you had gone for a drive."

"Yeah. Isn't it wonderful to just stay here and spend time like this, Sami?"

"Very," she replied and blushed. Raj caught her expression and felt shy.

They realised that they were standing very close to each other. Their bodies were touching and neither minded that the other one knew what was happening.
They could smell each other's body, they could feel the warmth. They were silent like a good old computer that goes numb after 'start' command is given. What ever it thinks it silently displays like a confused soul. One can only see a Green LED of processor flickering for a long time. Screen saver clouds the writing on the screen. Here the processing was done in 'Pantiums'.

Love is like a drink. It always has a libidinous effervescence. For some, it is like beer. It does not lose fizz. For some it is like an antacid powder. The effervescence is high but short-lived. Lust took them over.

Whenever they were looking diagonally across, their noses would be just a nose apart. Salome felt like resting her head on his shoulder. Minds need to communicate through a language or expression. Hearts, once they turn to each other, do not need a language.

Raj took Salome's hand and put his elbow across so that their hands crossed each other, their chests touching each other's hands slightly. He took her palm in his hands.

"Salome, you are a very nice person."

Salome finally gave in to her desires and rested her head on Raj's shoulder. She could not say anything.

"I have been looking for such delicate moments all my life. You are a very soothing companion. I like you."

She turned her head slowly, brought her face very close to Raj's cheek and whispered in his ear, "I love you, Raji."

Raj was now assured that they both felt the same way. They looked into each other's eyes and their pulse quickened as Raj pulled her closer. They could feel their warm breath. He held her by her shoulders and looked at her face. She was looking very pretty. The rains had dampened her hair. A few strands of hair hung like a creeper from a tree on her cheeks. Her sharp nose, gleaming ebony face and affectionate eyes made her a perfect natural beauty.

It started raining heavily. Hippos, crocodiles, the hotel, everything disappeared. A heavy curtain of water falling from the roof's edge protected them from the rest of the world. Salome closed her eyes. Raj took her in his arms and hugged her. Raj gently tucked a lock of her hair behind her ear and whispered into her ear.

"Mimi na ku penda (I love you)."

He planted a soft, gentle kiss on her cheek. They remained in that posture for a long time. There was no one to disturb them.

Mother Nature had put a curtain of rains over them. Raj started stroking her hair and she gently kissed him on his chest.

Raj embraced her again and kissed her cheek. He nudged her nose gently with his; again they looked at each other and smiled.

All inhibitions disappeared. They knew that they felt the same way about each other. There was nothing wrong with their feelings. If it was love, let it be. If it was lust, let it be.

Nature gave a wonderful forest to graze for antelopes. It never announced. Nature offered an antelope into open mouth of a crocodile. It never repented. Nature does not justify. Nature does not plead. Nature united two humans from different continents. Nature provided a perfect cover to pour their hearts over each other.

'Raji, asante (thank you)," Salome whispered.

They stayed there till the rains stopped, hugging, gently kissing each other.

"Shall we go to the room?"

"Okay."

They went to Raj's room. They wanted to hide from the world now. Raj placed the 'Do not Disturb' sign on the doorknob and locked the door.

They stared at each other for a while.

Raj said, "Are we sure we want to… do it? No repentance later?"

Salome came running into his arms. Raj held her tightly and moved his hands all over her back, neck and hair.

Then he held her face in his palms and brought her lips close to his. Salome closed her eyes and parted her lips. Raj moved his hands to hold the back of her head and pressed his lips to hers. They took a deep breath as if taking a long plunge into a deep sea and locked themselves mouth to mouth, body to body.

Salome put her hands around Raj's back and stuck to him. It was the first intimate kiss of their lives. Once was not enough. They became more and more intense. They moved hurriedly, strongly.

.Lava spewed from the mouth of the crater and spilled over the mountain. As they drew their bodies together, they could feel each other's contours. It was like the big bang. Those contours incited further passion. They started breathing heavily. Raj moved his lips from her lips to her chin, to her throat and then below it. She opened her shirt. Raj held her lower back and started kissing further down till her navel. He kissed her stomach and slowly came back up. She shrugged her shirt off her shoulders. Her skin was smooth like butter. Her breasts were ensconced in lacy lingerie. Raj was in flames now. He moved his mouth to one breast; he kissed the skin just above the hem of the bra and then to the other. He bit her gently. He tried to open her bra, but Salome did it for him. Raj removed his shirt; both were half naked and extremely aroused. Salome's protruding breasts were erect with excitement. They looked at each other and hugged again. They sucked each other's tongues and Raj held both her arms up as if she was tied with ropes and moved his mouth all over her breasts, her stomach and her armpits.

He then kissed her back, stroked her breast from behind and pressed, while kissing every inch of her sexy back.

She murmured, "Raji, take me to the bed. I can't stand anymore."

Entangled, they walked like a walking tree. When they reached the edge of the bed, they dropped their pants.

The more they revealed, the more they craved each other. They both sat on the bed and engaged in a long kiss. He lowered her body gently on the pillows and pulled her under him. As their bodies rubbed against each other, they got more and more aroused, enjoying the blissful feeling. But they could not stop now.

"Salome you are so sexy, I love you."

"Oh, Raji! Kiss me! Bite me, squeeze me, tear me!" Salome whispered.

Raj kissed her all over her body. The smell of her body turned him on even more. He squeezed her shapely thighs and entered her. She cried out in joy.

A sexual tsunami swept all over their bodies and bed. Clothes, bed sheets and pillows went tumbling all over the place. Once it left, they were panting, kissing, smiling and thanking each other.

But the sexual fire was far from doused. Salome had a perfectly carved figure. Her sexy cleavage and narrow waist were in perfect symmetry with her curvaceous figure. Her shapely legs would be a tailor's delight. Raj had to enter her again. She found Raj a passionate mate. They were more composed and controlled during their second encounter. It was more like a celebration.

They prolonged the climax this time by breaking the rhythm deliberately. They were relishing Nature's wonderful gift, sex.

After a few hours, they ordered coffee and huddled together under the blankets and sipped the hot beverage. Raj was silent. Like a lorry driver who leaves his truck on the way side, eases himself in the bushes and comes back on the wheels, slamming the door and turns on the ignition switch, his mind turned on. He did not repent what had just happened. He was just preparing to face the world. He was trying to imagine the reactions from his family and friends in India if they knew about what he did. Salome sensed what was on his mind.

"Raji, are you worried?"

"No."

"You know, Raji. You gave me some thing that I could only dream about. It was my wish. I could not believe that it would come true."

Raj listened silently.

"I won't bind you further, or ask for any commitment, even if you leave me and go away, or get married to somebody in India. If I have a child, I will look after it happily. I will never call you or involve you, if you so desire. You are free. I want you to be happy. You made me so happy for ever."

Raj was moved by her selfless love.

"No Sami, I promise that I am going to marry you. We shall live our life together. I am just preparing to face the world. Don't worry. Don't ever doubt my commitment."

"Ours is a very open society, you know. In Africa, every sexual relation may not end in marriage. An unmarried lady with kids or a divorcee can get another companion easily. It is not a bad thing to have sexual relations without the intention of marriage."

"But we Indians, though you may find us conservative, usually get married first, have sex and then stick to the same partner. It is a matter of commitment. How will you feel, when I say that I am committed to you and will not leave you for ever?" said Raj.

"Too sweet to believe, Raji!"

Raj did as he had promised. He first declared his love for Salome to those he felt closest to, his team. Bonde and his army celebrated over beer, meat, rice and music. All through the impromptu party, the workers kept harassing Professa. People were sitting or lying down on the floor and having food. Some workers were hurling pebbles and fish bones at him. He was trying his best to ignore them. The seniors were watching the fun with amusement. Raj asked them, "Why are we harassing him?"

J4 told, "He has taken off his shoes, but not his socks. He is stinking, Bwana."

Suddenly, Profesaa got up.

"Jamaani! I want to say something to Mistaa Raji."

Like monkeys hooting in a tropical forest, all the workers said,

"Ndiyo-o-o."

"Mistaa Raji, we are seeing an Indian marrying a Tanzanian girl in our close circle. Similarly, when will Indian girls marry Tanzanians?"

There were multiple Ndiyo-s and 'Hapo, saafi (Now correct).'

Raj waited for a while and said, "When you wash your socks everyday and throw away these shoes."

People burst into laughter and the Profesaa sat down like a shy schoolboy.

Raj wrote a long letter to his parents, explaining his decision and requesting them to accept Salome. He also enclosed a photograph of him and Salome standing together with Huku between them.

On receiving the letter, Raj's parents were livid. They blamed each other for being responsible for this.

Both wrote angry letters to Raj, highlighting the dangers involved in such a cultural mismatch and the future problems. They asked him to reconsider his decision. His father put the photographs in a frame on his writing desk.

The next day, the mother went to Raj's father to remind him to take the letters to the post office. The father was putting the letters in the envelope. He glanced at the photos again. He personally thought that his son's choice was not bad. Together, Raj and Salome looked nice. He smiled at his son's happy face. When Raj was worried about his career, he had advised him, "When the situation defies logic, do what your heart says. Do not think too much."

He whispered to the photograph of his son, "I never knew you would stretch my advice so far, bugger!"

He put the photo down, put the envelope in his briefcase and turned around only to see his fuming wife.

"I do not find anything funny in all this," she said and stomped out of the room banging the door shut behind her. His father started laughing aloud.

Some of his elderly relatives, who visited his house, advised Raj to reconsider. Vicky tried to get Raj to forget Salome and get back with Leena again.

Zuly chose the middle path "Get to know her for some time and then decide, maybe after one or two years. You never know, Bwana, this is Africa. You may get fed up."

Leena could not write what she felt. She felt guilty about her obsession with her career and the way she had paid more attention to Binoy. She cried about her lost relationship. But Raj's other friends were ecstatic. This was a sensational story for them. They knew what had happened between Raj and Leena. His friends called him up only to say, "Get one for me too", "Well done Raj", "Bravo" and "We are with you".

Raj decided that he would finish the Mwanza and Mbeya assignments, climb Mount Kilimanjaro and then join the Dar-es-Salaam office as CEO. He would then get married with lots of fanfare. It would take about three to four months according to his estimates. Salome was patient as ever. She wanted her dream to last as long as possible.

Every day for her was long and the nights longer; waiting for Raj's letter or call, dreaming about him and the time spent in the hotel, and her future life. She would go to church every Sunday with a big smile and shower her gratitude on Jesus.

One day Raj called her up from Mwanza. She told him, "You are running behind schedule in your work Mr. Raji."

"You are sounding like my boss: why?"

"Its been three months, and then you want to climb mountains, and join Dar as the big boss and then… You may have to go to the maternity home first, before getting married."

"Why? You mean… What!"

"Yes, I mean it. Decide you want to be a husband first or a father."

"You must be joking!"

"I am not."

"But I do not think I did anything to be a father!"

"So you doubt me now!"

"No…no! I was joking. Your parents won't mind, but my parents will not attend the marriage with their grandchild next to them. You made my day, Sami. I feel great. If it's a boy we will call him K2, if it's a girl, Kili!"

"What is Ketu?"

"The Everest is in Nepal. K2 is the second highest peak in the world and the highest in India. It is 'K' followed by the number two, not the sound 'tu'."

"You are joking. How can we number our child?"

"If we can number our car with alpha numerals, we can put part numbers on items in a store with alpha numerals, companies and government people can mark their assets with alpha numerals…"

"Sawa, Bwana. I agree. When are you coming here?"

"Humans are being treated like machines and parts already. It does not matter what you are, people know you by what you do or what you have…"

"Okay, Raji! When."

"My son will be the first human being in the world to have an alpha numeric name."

"Raji, listen to me," Salome started laughing as Raj was unstoppable in his plans. "My children need not be the best in the world, but they will be great in their own way."

Salome finally screamed, "Wewe Raji! You better wind up your work fast before daydreaming, and yes, Huku is missing you."

Salome had conceived. It is very common in Africa to get pregnant and then get married.

It took about four months for Raj to wind up his projects. Tancell was now the only cellular company in the country to cover most of the mainland. Zanzibar and the Pemba islands were on his agenda when he would take over the office in Dar. Despite the mishaps, they had finished seventy percent of the project several months ahead of the schedule.

Raj had become a family member for Zuly. He could even walk into Zuly's kitchen and speak to anyone there. Karimji treated Raj like his son, asking him to do small chores, such as fetching a shawl from his bedroom, and so on.

The opening ceremony for Tancell's operations was well-attended. Raj had taken care of all the preparations. Zuly had used his contacts and invited senior bureaucrats and ministers to the grand function. Karimji introduced Raj to all of his relatives and friends and called him his adopted son. He was so busy telling everyone about Raj's feats in the past year that he forgot to mention anything about his own son, Zuly.

The president cut the ribbon and the state-owned television channel covered the event through the day. There were press conferences, billboards and a lot of publicity country wide. Raj's reputation soared in the corporate world.

Chapter 22: Up above the world so high......

In Marangu, a localilty in Moshi where Salome stayed, there was excitement in air. Not only her parents, but Salome's friends and acquaintances were also excited about the Indo – African wedding. It was a sensational for the small town. Raj stayed with Salome for three days and then set out for the climb.

"Don't worry Raji, if you can't make it, please come back fast. I want to get married."
"I will make it and invite him to our marriage," said Raj, touching Salome's stomach. They laughed and bid goodbye. She went straight to church.
"God, please help Raji. He is such a nice man. If he can't make it this time, he will be disappointed. He will hate himself. Please do not be harsh with him."

Jo had made arrangements for a guide and porters at a reputed hotel at the base of Mount Kilimanjaro. Raj spent another three days getting acclimatize to the thin air on Mount Kilimanjaro's high altitudes. Raj had a group of six people including Jo for the climb. A Chinese couple and three men from Europe were also making the attempt. They had an eleven-member team including a head guide, an assistant guide, cooks and porters.

"All the best Raj, all the best folks," Jo said. The group responded by wishing each other good luck as well and the ascent began. While Raj and Jo were talking, others looked at the lush green, rain forest with tall pine and cypress trees. Lichens, ferns and mosses hung on trees and blocked sunrays from falling on the ground. The vegetation en route was so thick that the entire way ahead was dark.

There were hardly any birds or animals to be seen, but the sound of gushing streams drove away the silence. The best part was that the water was clean and cold.

The wet, slippery path and the humid climate slowed them down.

All the mountaineers were feeling very tired. Their faces were red and their legs felt stiff. Boredom replaced the ecstasy they had felt when they first saw the calm green forest around them.

Conversation kept them going. After four hours the groups reached Mandara, a camp site. The tents were pitched for the night.

They set out early in the morning for another marathon climb to Horombo at an altitude of 3720 metres. By now, Raj had become friendly with everyone. He was also trying to learn a few Chinese words and joking with the couple.

They took a sharp turn and suddenly, the thick green forest was replaced by a plain with gorgeous flowering shrubs. The open view elated the group's spirits. The guides continued to give them hope by saying "Only two hours now", although, they had been saying this earnestly for about four hours.

Raj asked the Chinese, "So, Mr. Wuu, where are we going to camp tonight?"
"Horohoro."
"No! It's Horombo."

"Haromho."

"Horombo."

"Ho-ro-mbo."

Raj shouted, "Like Bruce Lee, Hooo-rooo-mbooo."

Wuu repeated it and laughed.

"Mama Shanghai, your turn now."

The Chinese lady did a fairly good imitation of the Bruce Lee cry. Everybody laughed.

'Jo, hujambo'

'Sijambo'

'Horombo'

'Horombo'

Raj made everybody shout. This became a ritual every few metres. Suddenly one of them would shout 'Horombo' and the others would respond with an even louder 'Horombo'.

The light was fading. Slanted rays falling on the land gave a golden sheen to the ground.

One of the Europeans, Alex, got a little wild with the guide, "Your two hours are over yet, or not?"

"Very little now, do not worry," said the guide.

Alex was impatient, "I am going to complain to the hotel. A guide is supposed to guide us, not fool us."

People tried to lighten the mood by laughing and changing the topic. One of the other Europeans narrated his experience in the Alps. After half an hour, the group had fallen silent again and were lost in their thoughts, when the guide shouted 'Horombo!'

It took them a while to realise that they had reached their destination. The guide was pointing at huts, and behind it, touching the sky was one of the peaks, Mawenzi (5149m).

The cooks who had gone ahead had already prepared warm water, tea and food. The group relaxed, chatted and forgot their worries. The people had come together because of the hardships that they had experienced together. Kili had brought them together.

Alex asked Raj, "So now, what are you going to shout? Kibo?"

"Yes, Kibo," Raj shouted out, to the delight of everyone. Raj wanted to eat a lot and drink a lot of alcohol, but he had lost his appetite. He thought he would crash after dinner, but could not sleep.

The next was a day of rest. The water had frozen and the attendants were serving hot coffee. Raj was coughing a bit. While his guide forced everybody to consume as much liquids as possible, Raj could not eat much.

To acclimatise themselves to the high altitude and thin air, they walked till Mawenzi peak base (4320m) for about four hours. Everyone was very tired. The guide would frequently say, "pole pole (slowly)".

While they were resting for a short while, Wu looked at Raj and mocked Raj.

"India" he showed his thumb down and then he said.

"China" he put his thumb up.

Raj responded "India" and pointed to his head meaning intelligent.

He continued "China", and acted as if he was carrying luggage on his shoulders.

Everybody laughed.

After a while, Raj called out, "Wuu!"

He pointed to a colourful rock lizard and asked him to eat it.

"Raj!" Wuu replied and plucked a twig from a shrub and told Raj to eat that.

Everybody was enjoying the India versus China game. The guide called out to both of them and said, "Africa" and pointed to one of his attendants who had a beetle-like insect in his hand. He plucked its legs, wings and head and put the body in his mouth. The Chinese couple laughed and clapped, while the rest tried to forget the sight. They were panting even while laughing.

The area was an Alpine desert. The temperature during the day would be very hot, but the nights would be freezing cold. The thin air and strong winds made flying difficult for most birds. Only a few frost-resistant shrubs and plants could survive such a hostile climate. But even in these harsh conditions, small yellow and purple flowers would bloom everywhere.

In the evening they gathered around a campfire. It was getting cold. Hot drinks with crumbs of bread were served. One of the white men was coughing and had a body ache. He was talking about it to Jo, who said, "It is understandable. Your body is subject to so much fatigue. You hardly walk in your normal day, and here we are climbing from morning to evening for the past three days. And, what is more, the climate is extreme. It was so hot during the day and the night will see sub-zero temperatures.'"

Everybody was listening to Jo as this was the second time that he was climbing Mount Kilimanjaro.

Raj added, "Yes, yes, anything extreme is bad. Always follow the middle path. Isn't it, Wuu? You are a Buddhist, right?"

"No I am not a Buddhist. I follow Confucius."

"Well, I do not know what Confucius said, but Buddha preached about the middle path. No extremes."

"What do you mean by extremes?"

Raj was in his element, he started, "You see airhostesses. Have you seen their stockings?"

The men grinned.

"In most airlines, air hostesses have semi-transparent stockings. The stockings are special ones, made from very fine mosquito net. So you see, you can only partially see the legs. If they wear pyjamas or pants, there is no charm. If the legs are totally exposed then there are two possibilities. Ask me what they are."

"What?" the men asked.

"One, if the air hostess is a little careless about looking her best, you feel you are sitting in a bullock cart and watching the bullock's legs. This is one extreme.

"Now ask me, what is the second possibility?"

This time the guide and his assistants also joined the chorus.

"If the lady is beautiful, then passengers will be distracted. One of them may extend his hand and like Maradona... you know Maradona, the football star of Argentina? He pushed the ball in the net in the famous world cup final and said that it was the hand of God. So the passenger will say it was the hand of God."

Everybody laughed.

'I say! This is another extreme.'

Wuu added, 'Socks should be like fishnet not mosquito net.'

Raj went after him 'These Chinese people, Bwana, always think of eating things. An air hostess's legs, they imagine like fish, dogs, mouse and cats!'

'No, no no..I am saying...fishnet...you can see more!'

Alex interrupted 'We were talking about Air hostess's stockings.'

Raj said, "Aaaahen. So, these very fine stockings continue to excite you, tantalise you. They make you curious. No extreme. It is in-between. Not obscene. Not unseen. Just about seen."

Raj continued "To cover is dead. To uncover is an act. Any thing in-between is a play. An air hostess's stockings incite your passion for play. We Indians call it *leela*. To cover is a farce. To uncover is crass. To reveal partially is class."

It was over the heads of many who were not very conversant with English. They were faintly smiling as if looking through the stockings of an air hostess.

Jo interrupted, "Mr. Guide, please check him. He has mental edema."

"Mr. Jo, clean your mind. Look at Kili. He is always partially revealed. Neither fully covered with clouds, nor totally bare. He is a class act like the stockings of an air hostess."

The guide brought the discussion to an end, "Excuse me, sir! We must sleep if we want to reach the top."

Everybody agreed and went off to sleep.

The night was freezing.

Next day, they started very early for the Kibo Hut.

The group could not shout 'Kibo' due to the extreme weather. The rocky terrain known as a saddle between the two peaks--Kibo and Mawenzi--was deceptive, according to the guide. It was a relatively flat climb tempting some to speed up, but the thin air would induce mountain sickness in no time.

Everybody was walking silently and slowly. Every now and then, they would stop for rest. Raj's mood had changed. He had stopped smiling. He was thinking about his father. He wondered how he must have felt when he had declared his intention to marry an African girl, without even consulting him. He felt homesick. He felt like going back to Mumbai and seeing his parents.

He was frequently coughing now. The attendants immediately caught on to Raj's changed mood and physical condition.

"Mistaa Raj, are you okay?"

"Yes, I am."

"Can't hear you."

"Why can't Mr. Kili come to me?"

The guide took it as a joke, "Oh, he is a very big man."

"That's the problem."

The groups managed to reach the Kibo hut. Everybody was exhausted. It was a tough struggle to climb to the top, testing their endurance and patience. Some of them wondered if they should turn back tomorrow. Raj tried to sleep, but could not. He remembered Salome. She must be waiting. She was so nice. She supported him in his stupid adventure and had agreed to postpone their marriage. He could not breathe properly and tried to hide this fact from the group.

Raj was not used to such extreme cold and thin air. At midnight, the full moon shone down on them. It was the biggest and cleanest moon he had ever seen. He could see the shadows of the slopes of the craters.

The next morning's climb was slippery. People would stop every few steps and ask for rest. They would fall off to sleep in seconds if they rested long on their ski sticks. The guides were advising everyone to climb slowly and breathe enough. Everyone was taking this seriously. The dark sky turned to light blue. Dawn broke and the mountaineers thought that the peak was nearby.

They reached Gilman's point (5685m) and stopped for a while. The guide cautioned everyone to stop from straining themselves and to decide if they were up to it. He also cautioned that they were running a real risk of cerebral edema, commonly known as mountain sickness.

Cerebral edema causes swelling of the brain. Because the cranium doesn't expand, it pushes the brain downwards through the small opening of the spinal chord. This compresses the centres that regulate breathing and the heartbeat, and can kill a person.

Jo, Wuu and Raj decided to go on. The guide spoke to Raj.

"Mzee, I find that you are not well. You should not take risks. You can always come back again."

Raj shouted, "Let's go."

They would walk three to four steps and rest. In the faint morning light, he could see the glaciers shine.

"There you are Kili. Bwana, I am coming," Raj started shouting. The others thought he was joking. Jo wondered how he could joke at such a time. But Raj was slowly slipping into delirium.

The high altitude pushes down the oxygen levels, causing cerebral blood vessels to dilate. Blood flow to the brain increases and causes fluid to leak into the brain tissue. He started having hallucinations. He thought his mother was climbing next to him and was very tired. He stopped and took some breaths.

"I am sorry to have brought you here," he said.

Jo looked at Raj. He realised Raj was not normal.

"Shut up, Raj. Take a deep breath. Go slow."

Raj could see the sun rise over a sparkling glacier. He smiled. The roof of Africa is so beautiful and he was right on it. He felt Salome was looking at him from below. He could not figure out where Marangu valley was, but whatever part of the valley he could see, he felt Salome must be looking at the peak from down below. She was cheering for him. He could see for miles and miles below. The clouds were below their feet. As a child, he had always dreamt of standing above the clouds. Today, the clouds were under him.

Raj remembered all the failed interviews he had gone for. "'You did not work on any hi-tech project in Africa, Mr. Raj…Have you worked on a big multinational project? Only a few months?…We have a financial crisis, so just take some advance instead of this month's salary.

…we have very big orders…." He started recollecting the difficult times he had had. The more he remembered his past, the more agitated he got.

He shouted aloud, "You rascals, I am not mediocre. Don't you…"

He started panting heavily. The guide tried to help him stand. Jo and Wuu looked at each other. Jo waved at him to ignore Raj and keep moving.

The men were resting more and walking less. Inside the crater scree, they could see, very sharply and clearly the 350 ft diameter crater as if about to spew lava.

They would rest their head and upper body on the ski stick, take a few breaths and walk again. Jo and Wu were ahead of Raj. The guide and a porter stayed with Raj. Icy winds slowed them down.

"Mzee, can you see that? UhuruPeak! (5895m)..Our final point…ile kule (there)'" the guide told Raj. Raj tried to see. His vision was very blurred. He narrowed his eyes, "Wapi (where)?"

The men looked at each other. They knew Raj was not well now. They tried to take his hands over their shoulders and support him.

Raj shouted, "No. I am alright."

They were walking on the edge of the two and a half kilometre wide crater. He was quiet for a while. Raj wondered if he was seriously having a problem. Was it edema? If it was, then he was on the point of no return. It meant his end. Was this how death would come? He did not want to die so early. He had promised Salome and his child.

He tried to look at Uhuru peak. He could see it gleaming. He looked at the sky. It was dark blue. It had no life. He looked down. The earth was covered by a grey-brown smoke.

"The-e-e-rrre is life," he slurred, pointing down, "and my wife, Salome." He felt nauseated, he coughed and felt giddy, but he trudged on. He could see his friends celebrating. They were cheering him on, "Come on Raj! You can make it."

He replied in a hoarse whisper, "I will."

And he did. He reached the peak, but did not have the strength to dance and celebrate. Slowly, he looked around him. He smiled at Wuu and Jo. He was half-bent, resting on his ski stick. He looked at the valley.

He remembered his father again and turned to face the northwest. He said in a feeble voice, "Dad, I made it! I am on the top of this world. Can you see me? Thanks for sending me to Africa. Sorry, Dad. I wanted to take you on a world tour. I wanted you to relax on Dar's beaches with Mom. So much you did for me, and I… "

He felt giddy again. He could see all the snow around him turning into a white shining blur. His eyes were moist, but the tears were frozen in his eyeballs. For the first time, he felt lonely.

He felt Salome, Leena, his parents, his sister, watching him from a distance, helplessly. He was caught in a whirlpool, while they were shouting from the bank of the river, extending their arms.

He was too far and alone. He wanted to shout and tell the world that he made it. He mustered his strength, but no sound came out. He slowly collapsed like a blob of melting ice cream on his ski stick.

Jo shook him, "Raj! Get up."

Wuu slapped his chin to wake him up. The guide radioed for an emergency vehicle at Horombo hut. Raj was carried on the shoulders of three men and was rushed to Kibo hut. Wuu and Jo were assigned to an assistant guide and two porters. When the mountaineers who had stayed behind first saw three men carrying someone, they could not make out who it was. The Chinese lady closed her eyes and prayed it was not her husband. Others could guess from the color of his blazer. When Raj was brought into the tent, people were stunned.

"My God, this young man did not deserve this."

Alex tried to rub some warmth into Raj's body. Raj was put on a stretcher. He had a faint smile on his face. His breathing was very slow. Everyone prayed for his life. Two men lifted the stretcher, while the other two joined them to take over. They started walking briskly towards Horombo hut.

The news spread like wild fire, "A Muhindi is seriously ill."

The hotel manager was ready with an ambulance at Marangu base camp. Raj was rushed to the same hospital in Moshi where he was admitted for typhoid. The doctor checked Raj's pulse.

He opened the eyelids and checked the pupil. While the guide was narrating the story, the doctor interrupted.

"You have brought him dead. Samahani (sorry) uli cheleva (you are late)."

When Salome heard that a Muhindi was serious, she panicked. She got to the base camp at Marangu, but the ambulance had left.

When she reached the hospital, she saw many people outside the casualty ward. Since Moshi was a small town, the casualty department was rarely busy. She pushed aside everyone and went into the room.

She could see policemen, hospital staff and a body covered in a white sheet lying on a stretcher. She was panting. The doctor looked at her.

She asked, "Muhindi?"

He gently uncovered the face. Her lips started trembling. Tears started rolling down. Her voice was choked. "Raji! Come back! Raji!"

She shook his body. He was dead, but the faint smile on his lips had not gone. She broke down. Not many knew the story and thought it strange that an African girl was crying for an Indian, like his wife.

Zuly and his family were too shocked to speak. Karimji cried as if he had lost his own son. Zuly did not know how to break the news to Raj's parents.

***

Raj's father picked up the phone.

"Uncle, I am very sorry."

"Mr. Zuly? How are you?"

Zuly took a deep breath and said it in one breath.

"Very bad news. Raj is no more."

"What?" His father's hand started trembling. His throat was choked. He did not know what to say.

"Please tell me again. Mr. Zuly."

"Yes, uncle, he died after climbing Mount Kilimanjaro, due to mountain sickness, immediately."

His father almost collapsed on the chair. He dropped the phone and started crying.

Raj's mother came running, "What happened?" she asked, fearing the worst.

"Why don't you tell me?"

He could only say, "Ra-a-a-a-j."

She found it difficult to stand on her feet. She sat down on the ground next to him and started crying.

"You killed your son. I told you, don't allow him to go."

"Yes, I killed my son. God, kill me now."

Indian society, unlike the West, is a very closely knit society. A person takes care of not only his parents but his Grandparents also. There are many joint families separated by rooms or floors but they stay under the same roof. Parents expect their son to take care of them in their old age. Parents look forward to rearing their grandchildren.

Fathers work while grandparents tell stories, give cookies and refuge when a child is being scolded by the parents. They feel that this is a fitting finale to their fading lives. They look forward to such days of retirement. They suffer many hardships during their active years in earning for and building up a family. They undergo a lot of stress, make compromises to impart a better life to their offspring and look forward to the good times in their old age.

The sole purpose of life, for Raj's parents, was suddenly lost. They had nothing to look forward to. Only those who undergo such moments can imagine their pain.

They recovered after a few hours. They called up Zuly again. They heard the entire story. They knew that their son wanted to prove himself. He had deserved a better professional life in his own city.

The mother lamented, "it was my fault. We should have accepted him as he was, rather then forcing him to leave Africa. We should have stayed there for a few days. We should have reassured him in whatever he was doing, rather than being disapproving all the time."

The father said, "He was at war with himself. Africa gave him solace. This was his destiny, but he should have lived life merrily."

They called up their daughter, relatives, friends and all those who mattered.

Zuly told them, "Uncle, I know you lost your son. You must hate this place that snatched away your son. I am also a party to it. But Raj was a local hero. The community here has organised a function to pay him tributes. You will see who your son was, if you come here. We cannot bring him back, but we can live with his memories. We can remember his achievements and the good work he did. He was like my brother. He is still a son for my father. We want to have stronger relations with you, though you may be angry with us. Please do come. We want to help share your grief."

They decided to fly to Dar and Zuly took them to Moshi. Milie came there from London with her husband. Raj's body was in the morgue. They went to Salome's house. They could see Raj's pictures everywhere. People offered their condolences to Kiswahili, while Zuly translated their messages.

They met Salome. They felt Raj's presence, when she came towards them. They just looked at each other, through a curtain of tears. She told them all she knew about Raj's last few days, his cheerful plans for their wedding, his reason for climbing Mount Kilimanjaro, his memories of life in India, his love for his parents. Her voice was feeble and her eyes were swollen because of her tears. Huku got up from a corner of the veranda and came to sit beside them. Milie was touched by Salome's feelings and innocence.

Raj's body was brought in a coffin before it was taken to the community hall. The parents gathered all their strength to see their dead son. They tried to comfort each other. They could see their son nicely dressed in a suit, lying in the half-open casket, as if he was just asleep. They had placed his guitar on his body. They turned their faces away from the sight and they broke down. Milie took her mother's hand in her hand and escorted her to the van. Milie's husband took care of her father and led him to the van.. Before going away from him, his mother hugged her son. Father stroked his head. Both could experience now that he was dead. Milie led her parents to the prayer service.

The mother cried, "I am very sorry, my son, I will miss you so much. Come back again in our next birth. I promise I will never deny anything you need."
Milie and Salome sat beside each other. Salome tried to comfort her, but ended up sobbing herself. Raj's sister rested her head on Salome's shoulders and cried.

Raj's body was brought to the community church. People Stood up.
The priest started the prayers. "Receive Lord, in tranquillity and peace, the souls of your servants who have departed out of this present life to be with you. Give them life that knows no age, the good things do not pass away; through Yesu, our Lord. Amen."
People sang hymns in Kiswahili and the church bells reverberated in the valley. Everyone paid rich tributes to Raj and beseeched God to bless the kind young man's soul. Bonde, J4 and Mama Rose spoke as well. Rose told the congregation that she had become so used to staying with Raj that she would have never imagined that it would be a temporary phase in her life. She had looked after him as a mother would have and now she did not know what she would do.

After some more prayers, the body was handed over to the parents.

Bonde and his team once again expressed their sorrow. "My son, Poto, and Mistaa Raji were good friends, always together. I lost my son, you know. I know how you feel now. Hope Mungu does not give such a day to anybody. Mistaa Raji was my bossi and my son too."

Raj's parents had arranged to take the body to India the next morning. Zuly took them to a hotel and urged them to eat some food. Just then, they were told that some people were waiting to meet them. Raj's parents and sister came out and called Zuly too. It was Bonde and his entire team again.

"Sorry to distaab you again, Baba, but we want to tell you more about your son." As Bonde, prompted by his team, described Raj's feats, his parents forgot their grief momentarily. There were smile on every body's face only to plunge into sighs. The parents realised why Raj loved Africa so much. It was worth leaving their jobs and watching their son leading such an eventful life here. But now, it was too late.

Finally, Bonde dropped the bombshell unintentionally "But Mistaa Raji has not gone kabisa-a (completely). He has left a gift for us. We pray Mama Salome delivers a son, so that we can see Mistaa Raji again. Even if it is a girl, it is a zawadi (gift) we will be happy to receive. Thank you for spending time with us. May Allah help you recover fast from this shock. Mistaa Raji has not gone. He will be with you. Don't worry.

Whenever you need any help please remember us. We are not bad people. Asante, Mama na Baba."

They left, but now the parents and Zuly were dumbstruck. Raj's father said, "We never realised that he… his girlfriend is expecting their child."

"We must talk to her… I do not know," the mother said hurriedly.

Zuly told them not to worry, "In Africa, an unmarried mother is not a stigma. I shall pay for her delivery and other expenses. As they said, they will be happy to carry on Raj's legacy."

Milie pointed out, "Salome never told us. She did not want to bother us with the responsibility. Neither did she ask for help or money."

The father said, "If people can carry Raj's legacy, we as grandparents can't? What if Raj was alive? Would we not have accepted them?"

The mother said, "Think of the grandchild. I am sure there will be a little Raj in him or her. And this poor girl, how can we just leave her? No! We must take her with us."

Zuly was surprised. "All I can say is that Raj was very lucky to have such parents. You are great."

Salome was sitting on the veranda. Her friends had left and her parents had gone into the house. She was alone looking at the starry sky. She could still not believe that Raj was no more. She kept thinking that Raj would be back from Mount Kilimanjaro.

Tears would slowly trickle down every now and then. Sometimes she would go into a trance, remembering her moments with Raj.

She remembered her first encounter with Raj in the restaurant. He looked so cute. She loved the way he had played the guitar and sang Kiswahili song. She remembered his performance during the local function and how he had helped to collect a lot of money for the local dispensary. She remembered how he had revealed his inner conflicts, when he had explained to her his reason for climbing Mount Kilimanjaro. She remembered their honeymoon before marriage. She could still smell him. She gently put her hand on her stomach as though she were trying to reassure her child.

"Almighty God, author of life, I thank you for the gift of new life. Bless our child in my womb. Protect him or her from all harm. Grant that he or she will be a healthy child," she prayed softly, "I make my prayer through Yesu our Lord, Amen."

She opened her eyes on hearing the sound of a car pulling up in front of the house. She saw Raj's parents, sister and Zuly come in. She called her parents and got more chairs. Salome and her mother sat on the veranda's floor. Milie sat next to Salome. There was a moment's silence.

Raj's mother looked at Salome and smiled gently, "You did not tell us that you are going to be a mother. You do not want us to be grand parents?"
Salome started sobbing; she could not say anything.

"You are like my daughter. You are coming with us. We are not bad people. We can live together and remember Raj together," Raj's mother said through her tears.

Raj's father spoke to Salome's father, "If she does not like India and she wants to come back, even to get married to someone, she is free. We will take care of the child. If my own daughter loses her husband and if she likes someone else later, I would let her do whatever she wants. We want Salome to be happy."

"She is your daughter too, take her with you," said Salome's father.

But Salome was firm. She would deliver the child in front of Kili. As Raj had said, if it was a boy, it would be K2 and if a girl, her name would be Kili.

She would bring up her child in the same place that Raj had loved; a place where they had spent the most memorable moments of their life together. She wanted her child to love Mount Kilimanjaro and stay in its lap. She would go to India with the child and spend time with Raj's parents so that the child would know and inherit Indian culture and values.

Raj's parents also promised that they would come to Moshi often. They went back to the hotel. When they were lying down in bed, Raj's father said.

"I wonder why we are taking Raj to Mumbai."

His mother replied, "So that our relatives, and his friends, can have a last look at him..."

Father interrupted, "Only to forget in a few days time. If I asked Raj now, he would prefer to be buried here, like the locals, and stay here even after his death."

The mother was silent for some time.

"You mean we leave him here?"

"Yes, he will remind us to visit our grandchild and take care of it."

They could not decide. They could hardly sleep. They remembered Raj's childhood, his nature, his schooling, his low moments, his joys, his nasty habits….every thing.

All the treasure that was lost in the archives of day to day life, was found and reopened and the life lost was resurrected. They were silently crying and smiling. After a while reality would hit their minds like a hammer again that Raj was no more.

***

Early next morning, everybody was ready. Salome and her parents decided to go to the morgue and accompany Raj's body to the airport for the final farewell.

When Raj's parents reached Salome's house, everybody got down from the vehicles. There were many vehicles filled with people to travel with them to the airport.

Raj's father looked around him and at the clear sky. He saw the valley that was lit by the sun.

Zuly said, "That's the mountain."

Raj's father saw the magnificent Mount Kilimanjaro. He called his wife and Milie and pointed out the mountain. Mother and sister stood there for a while. Their eyes were glued to the peak. They thought, "Our Raj was there." Cool breeze and morning sunrays tried to sooth their minds. They watched the mount, the valley, the houses and the large number of people nicely dressed in black robs watching them intently. His mother and father looked at each other. They had found the answer. They approached Salome's father.

"Our son liked this mountain, this place, and all of you, very much. If he were alive, he would have stayed here. Will you accept him here in your soil?"
"No problem, Saa! Our privilege. Thank you. See all these people. They love him. They will thank you." He turned to tell this to Salome. Zuly could not believe his ears.
"They will not cremate…" he started to say.
Raj's father interrupted, "*Yes Mr. Zuly. But, my son had no religion, no country, no ideology. He was like a butterfly, which enjoyed nature and the people around him, wherever he was. Let him be in the midst of these people.*"
Milie said, "I am so lucky to have parents like you two. I love you both."
Both parents looked at each other. They silently reassured each other. They looked at Mount Kilimanjaro again. He was quiet with his head above the clouds. They felt as if Raj was waving from the peak and smiling

His father whispered, "You made it Raj! I am very proud of you. We will miss you."
He broke down. So did his wife. Raj's soul really rested in peace.

The monkey goes to the mountain. The monkey never comes back again.

Akhilesh Joshipura 'Joshie' was born in India. He graduated in Bachelore of Mechanical Engineering and post graduated in Management from India 1984. After working for more than a decade in Indian manufacturing industries, he went to Tanzania as an expatriate to set up manufacturing projects. He was fascinated by Tanzania. He traveled extensively and enjoyed working with Tanzanians. While traveling upcountry, he was cutoff from family, friends and usual means of entertainment like TV, Internet, cinema etc. Being a teetotaler, he could not kill his evening time in bars. He decided to use his spare time in writing this book on Tanzanian theme.

Happy to receive your feed back at monkeycalling@mail.com

Made in the USA
Charleston, SC
13 March 2013